THE KEEPERS OF THE LIGHT

LOGAN LEVEC
BOOK 1

TREVOR A. DUTCHER

The Keepers of the Light

Copyright © 2024 by Trevor A. Dutcher

ISBN 978-1-7330990-3-5 (print)
ISBN 978-1-7330990-4-2 (ebook)
ASIN B0DHFPH9LG

First Edition: October 2024
Cover Design by Trevor A. Dutcher
Printed in the United States of America

For Chase.

All the darkness in the world cannot extinguish the light of a single candle.

-St. Francis of Assisi.

1

September 10th. Many years ago.
Suburbs of Newhaven, Connecticut.

❧

"Finish up, so we can open gifts," Mom said.

"He gets gifts?" Bryce snorted. "Whatever. Dweeb."

"Of course he does, Bryce, don't be ridiculous."

"Bryce," I said. "You crack the same stupid joke every year, maybe try out a new one."

"I sense a noogie in your future, little bro. A really good one. So you better just watch it."

"That's enough, Bryce. Go see if they need any help in there."

We moved to a new house in a quiet neighborhood at the edge of Newhaven a while back, but it still felt new to me, even after more than a year. It's a great place to live, with mild summers, tons of trees, and plenty of shade. In the winter, we even got some snow. Fall was definitely definitely my favorite, though.

I know what you're thinking—that's when school starts, but that's not the reason. Good things happen in the fall, some of my favorite things of the whole year. The trees turn the most amazing shades of yellow, red and gold. And when the sun shines through, they glow like stained glass. On weekends, we'd take long drives as a family, just to get outdoors. It was magical.

Occasionally, we'd stop to have a picnic or build a pile of leaves in the park. Some days Bryce and I would belly-flop into the pile; other days, we would run straight through it as fast as we could. Mom usually watched and cheered us on, while Dad spent much of the time on the phone, reading a medical journal or doing something important for work. I treasured those moments, and it was always fun. That is, of course, until Bryce found a way to ruin it for me. He had a unique talent for that.

Bryce is my older brother. He's fifteen, and at this point, I think his favorite hobbies are popping zits, flexing his chubby arms in the mirror and, most importantly, making my life an absolute living hell. These days, his favorite method of tormenting me is with a sinister five-star right across the belly. He slaps me so hard, a swollen red imprint of all five fingers shows on my stomach, hence the name.

As much as I hate it, I'm sure this phase will pass like so many others did before. I prefer it to the ear-lobe-flicking phase of last spring. Or the crop dusting phase before that, which felt like it lasted forever. Crop dusting is what Bryce calls it when he farts and walks by to waft it in my face. Then he shouts, "Crop dust!" as he runs out of the room cackling like a complete goon. He did it when I watched TV, read a book, or just daydreamed. He'd just stroll on by and let one rip.

Yeah, crop dusting. That was a special kind of horrible.

Anyway, before we moved here, we used to live in Stamford, and my dad still works there. He's a doctor, and my mom used to be a second-grade teacher before we moved. We moved here last year to be closer to my grandpa Gideon. Mom says he's getting up in years, and he needs someone to keep an eye on him. He hates it when she says that, so she doesn't say it in front of him anymore.

Changing schools was challenging, too, but Mom says Brixton Private Academy is one of the best. It's going pretty well so far. I've been on high honor roll for perfect grades, and I've received the citizenship award, volunteer award and the perfect attendance award every quarter so far. I do miss my old school, though. I had some pretty good friends there, and it hasn't been easy to make new ones here. I shouldn't complain, though; my grandpa Gideon and I get along great, and we spend a lot of time together, now that we live so close. He's one of the coolest, most imaginative people I've ever met. He retired from regular work a long time ago, and now he works at Smerconish's hardware store. He says it helps to keep him busy.

He also says that Smerconish's is where he found his true calling and that no matter how old you get to be, it's never too late to find it. Working there also helps him *keep the rust off*, as he likes to put it. The store is just a few blocks away from his house, toward downtown.

He is amazing. He knows pretty much everything. But most important, my grandpa Gideon tells the absolute best stories. Of course, not everyone agrees. My parents certainly don't, especially my mom. But he and I have a pretty special bond. He and I are *tuned to the same wavelength*, as he likes to say. I don't totally know what that means, but I'm pretty sure he's right. We get along great, and we always have.

We often go to Grandpa's house, especially for holidays and special events. The house we moved to is just a few blocks away. That was on purpose, since Mom wanted to be close. His house is pretty incredible though, and he has a huge lawn in the backyard. It's just off the back porch and really good for parties. Tonight is one such occasion—we came here tonight to celebrate my twelfth birthday. It's a small affair. Just me, my parents, Bryce and Grandpa. But that's fine, I guess.

The lawn out back runs from the porch to the woods, and since there's no back fence, Grandpa and I can go explore whenever we want. Sometimes he goes out there by himself, and says he has to *go check on things*. There's even a fort right at the edge of the woods. It's like a treehouse, but down on the ground, so it's easier to get to.

Aside from it being my birthday, it was an otherwise predictable evening at Grandpa's house. Dad tried to barbecue and got annoyed because my mom kept telling him what to do. In her defense, he really is terrible at barbecuing. She once asked why he even bothers lighting a fire - and why we don't just cut to the chase and eat the charcoal. He didn't think it was very funny, but she did. He tries, though. He really does.

Mom is still working on transitioning out of teaching grade school. Ever since she stopped teaching, she's become more involved in the normal stuff, including telling people what to do all the time. It's like she misses bossing her second graders around and needs someone else to boss now. Grandpa gets it the worst, but sometimes it spills over onto the rest of us. On top of that, with me being the youngest, I also get smothered with motherly love, whether I like it or not. I know she means well, but jeez. I was twelve, after all, and I could use a little space.

So yeah, my family is a pretty interesting bunch, and gatherings like this can turn into quite a spectacle. Dinner was largely a success this time around; Dad managed not to burn the meat into hardened lumps of coal and after dinner and cake, I got to open a few presents. I got some clothes, a Fortnite battle pass for gaming, and I even got the newest iPhone as my big gift.

I also got a present from my brother, Bryce. That was highly unusual. And I was highly suspect.

"Go on, open it," he said.

"What is it?" Mom asked.

"Just a little something for my dear brother, Logan," he said, snickering. "You'll see."

It was a gift bag lined with tissue paper. I reached in and pulled out an old watch case. Bryce looked pretty proud of himself. Experience had taught me to proceed with caution when he had that look. Maybe this year, he actually decided to do something nice. One could only hope.

But when I opened the watch case, Bryce almost peed himself laughing.

"It's a dried-up dog turd," I said. "Thanks, Bryce."

I flung the turd back out to the lawn, where it belonged.

"Logan, your brother loves you," my mom said. "I hope you know that, honey. He just has a strange way of showing it."

"Yeah. I'll say."

"I have one more for you here," Grandpa said, chuckling to himself. "And I promise it's not a dog turd. Don't you worry about Bryce, young man. Karma has a funny way of sorting things out. She always does. Bryce really should be more careful."

He looked up crosswise, still addressing me but looking Bryce right in the eye.

"But you know Bryce, I can't tell him anything, and trust me; I've tried. He just doesn't listen."

I nodded, knowing exactly what he meant. I tore the wrapping paper and wasn't sure what to say.

"It's a coffee can," I said curiously.

To be fair, it was no ordinary coffee can. It was the fanciest coffee can I had ever seen. Not that coffee cans are ever that fancy to begin with. But if you take the fanciest coffee can that you could ever imagine, this one was even fancier, with shiny gold foil paint and exquisite detail; and it was big, like a restaurant-sized can of tomatoes.

"It feels empty," I said.

"It is empty," he said. "For now, anyway. But we can work on that together. You've got it upside-down though."

He grabbed the can and flipped it over, revealing a slit punched in the top.

"It's a piggy bank?"

"It is, indeed."

"Thanks, Grandpa."

"Don't thank me now, Logan. Thank me later when you see what it can do. This right here, you see, this is no ordinary piggy bank," he said, his voice rising with excitement. That's how I knew it was going to be a good story.

"Oh, good grief," my mom said, rolling her eyes. "Here we go again. Dad, please don't."

Grandpa's voice became more mysterious, like it always does when he tells a good story.

"This bank here is special, unlike any other you've ever seen. Most piggy banks just hold your money for later. But this one pays you interest. What you have here, Logan, is an interest-bearing piggy bank, and it pays much better than your parents' bank account. I guarantee it."

"Really?" I said. "That's amazing!"

"Absolutely. Put in a penny, and it becomes a dollar. A nickel becomes five dollars, and a dime becomes ten. Put in a five-dollar bill, and I think you'll be pretty happy with what happens."

"Whoa," I said. "Where did you get it?"

"At the store, of course. Smerconish's has all kinds of great things. Stuff you could never, ever imagine on your own, no matter how hard you try. You just have to know where to look for things, and *bang*, there they are."

"Dad, please stop," Mom interrupted.

"Stop what?"

"Stop with the stories, you're going to confuse him. Or worse, you'll disappoint him. Believe me, I should know."

"There's nothing to be confused about, Sissy."

He spoke sadly, without making eye contact. Her actual name is Barbara, but Grandpa always called her Sissy. He has ever since she was a little girl. I think it's because she was the youngest child. The baby sister. *Sissy*.

"Don't mind her," he said with a wave of his hand, turning his focus back to the bank. "Here, I'll even get you started."

He pulled out five nickels from his pocket and plunked them in, one right after the other. They sounded heavy as they hit the bottom of the empty can.

"These nickels here, these are extra special," he said. "These are going to become—"

My mom interrupted him again. She used her big voice this time —the one where you know she means business.

"Logan, you have school tomorrow, and your oral report. Let's get you home to print your paper and practice your presentation."

"Oh, come on, Sissy," he pleaded.

"It's late. We should get Logan home."

And just like that, sadly, my birthday party was over. Mom collected our things and rushed us to the car. She always does that when Grandpa gets going telling some of his best stories, just at the part where it starts getting good. And all too often, I don't get to hear the end of it.

He hung his head and moped as we collected our things. He gave me a comforting nod, as if to say everything was ok, even if it didn't seem like it was. On the drive home, Mom gave me another one of her lectures about understanding the difference between real things and silly stories that people make up. She tried to be subtle about it, speaking in general terms. But I knew she was talking about Grandpa.

～

7:30 a.m. September 11. The next day.

"MOM, have you seen my report?

"It's on the table by the door, sweetheart."

"It's not there. I'm going to miss the bus. Can you drive me?"

"I have to take Bryce to the orthodontist, Logan. There's no time."

"Nevermind, I found it. It was in the freezer again. Thanks, Bryce, that's awesome."

I could hear Bryce in the bathroom, cackling as I ran out the front door.

"Stay cool, little brother," he said.

So clever.

I slung my backpack over my shoulder and ran across the lawn, but the bus had already pulled away. With nothing less than my perfect attendance at stake, I pulled my bike from the backyard and pedaled to school as fast as I could. With a touch of luck, and no small amount of effort, I could still make it. When I got to the bike rack, I jammed my wheel between two bars and ran down the hall to my classroom. I was two tiny steps from my desk when the bell rang.

Brrrrinnggggggg.

Two. Tiny. Steps.

"Tardy, Mr. LeVec."

Mr. Sloan knew no mercy. He wielded his pen like an executioner's axe and spoke in the harshest possible tone as he marked me late. Had he been declaring a death sentence, his voice would have been no different. As I dropped my backpack to the floor and slumped into my chair, something hit me in the back of the neck. I reached back, only to find a nice, soggy spit wad stuck to my skin, courtesy of Chet Masterson. It was one of Chet's signature moves.

"You're late, douchebag."

Thanks for the news flash.

Let me just cut to the chase here. Chet Masterson is probably the most horrible person I've ever met in my entire life. He makes Bryce look like an angel. I drew the short straw this year. I was the poor soul assigned to sit at the desk right in front of him. Tensions on the first day of school ran high, and for that very reason. Nobody, and I mean *nobody*, wanted to sit in front of Chet Masterson. At recess on the first day, my classmates offered their polite condolences for my unfortunate luck, but I could tell they were mostly just relieved it wasn't them.

It's only been a few weeks now, and it's every bit as awful as you might imagine. Chet's dad is super-wealthy and he donated a lot of money to the school. So, Chet never got in trouble the way the rest of us did. And it didn't help that he was tall, muscular and good at every sport he tried. He's everything I'm not.

I turned slightly back considering my retort, but was simply left wondering - why was his voice so deep? And was that a mustache? How could someone have a mustache in the sixth grade? I was still a little boy compared to him. Anyway, all the girls swooned at his nice clothes and wavy blond hair and freakishly large muscles. Most of them, anyway.

"You're *disgusting*," Ginny said.

As the words gracefully flowed from her shining lips, she turned away and flipped her hair in disgust. That flowing auburn hair that smelled like fresh cut flowers and nirvana. Ginny Mason was the girl who sat next to me in class. I hadn't quite figured her out yet. She didn't say much, and we never actually spoke to each other. She was new here, and it was her first year at Brixton. She glanced back at me to see if I was alright.

In that fleeting second, I missed yet another chance. We made actual eye contact this time, so that was progress. I should have said 'hi' or 'good morning' or something. Anything at all. But I froze. I just stared back awkwardly, not sure what else to do. Mercifully, Mr. Sloan cleared his throat to get our attention.

If my morning hadn't been bad enough already, it got worse in a hurry.

"Mr. LeVec, why don't you start us off with the oral reports."

He'd already declared a death sentence for my attendance award by marking me tardy. Now I was being summoned to the chopping block. In front of the whole class, no less. I got good grades on tests, did my homework, researched my topics thoroughly, and practiced my reports. I had known it cold since last Friday, and I practiced three more times last night with Mom after we got home from Grandpa's, just to be sure.

But despite my best preparations, I was nervous. Oral reports were my kryptonite. I walked as slowly as I could to buy myself some time. My mouth went dry and my pulse raced. Between the narrow rows of desks, I walked to the front. I turned, looking back out at my classmates and swallowed dryly. I could feel them staring, ready to mock me no matter what I said. Mom always says to find a friendly face when I get nervous. So, I found Ginny, the friendliest face the room. She sat there looking calm with her milky skin and emerald green eyes, flicking her hair in slow motion. I swear it moved in slow motion.

Before long, I found myself staring awkwardly, distracted by my own paralyzing crush on her.

Look away. Look away! She's going to see you staring at her. Look away!

I shifted my gaze and searched for the next friendly face I could find that wasn't hers. Any face would do—just not that one. Too late.

My eyes locked on Chet Masterson. I froze. My cheeks burned. I panicked. Chet had caught me staring at Ginny for a little too long. I could tell from the look on his face; he'd figured it out. He knew I had a secret crush on Ginny Mason. He would tell everybody now. From this day forward, my life would get so much worse.

"Mr. LeVec. Please proceed with your oral report," Mr. Sloan said.

"I—"

Everyone stared blankly. I was sure they all knew by now, every single one of them. It would be all anyone would talk about at lunch. Logan has a crush on Ginny. I felt like I had a cheeseburger stuck in my throat, like I'd tried to swallow it whole, and wash it down with a mouthful of dry cotton balls.

"I—"

"Mr. LeVec?"

I couldn't get a word out.

"I'm sorry, Mr. Sloan," I said with a heavy sigh.

"Not prepared. Very disappointing, Mr. LeVec. I've come to expect much better of you."

I scurried back to my desk and slumped into my seat as he marked his grade book with a swirl. His pencil nearly tore through the paper as he scrawled in the zero. My face burned with embarrassment, and I could hear Chet whisper behind me as he gave a high-five to the kid next to him.

"Genius-boy totally choked again. That was friggin' awesome."

IT TOOK an eternity for the burning sensation to come out of my cheeks, but not much else happened after that. As it turned out, it was just a pretty average day at school, much to my surprise. I had expected the worst, but lunch went smoothly, and nobody even mentioned Ginny, or my oral report. I was sure they would, so it was a relief that they didn't. I'm not sure what I was so stressed out about.

After the bell rang, I ran to the bike racks, where I met up with Teddy and James. I guess you could say we were friends. If not actual friends, they were the closest thing I had here. They grew up next door to each other, so they were close. They both lived right around the corner from me, so sometimes we hung out at lunch or after school. But I wasn't as close with them as they were with each other.

"Hey Logan," Teddy said, as we rode our bikes down the street. "James is spending the night this weekend. Do you want to come? We're going out TP'ing. We might even do Chet's house. You should totally come."

"Thanks guys, but you go ahead. I'll pass this time."

"C'mon," James said. "It'll be fun. Don't be a chicken."

"I'm not chicken," I said.

They looked at each other, nodded, and said it together in unison. "Chicken."

"I'm not chicken. I just don't want to deal with getting in trouble over something so stupid if we get caught. That's all."

"It's not stupid," Teddy said. "It's fun."

I shrugged, unconvinced.

"Maybe Chet's right about you," James said. "You never do anything fun. Live a little, why don't you. Take a risk once in a while."

Never do anything fun? Have they not seen me play chess with Grandpa? That was serious fun.

His words cut me deep. As we got to my house, I turned up my driveway, and they rode off toward the corner.

"I'll see you guys later," I said. "Have fun."

"Let us know if you change your mind," James said as they rode away.

When I got inside, Mom had already set out a snack for me. Just like she always does. Today, it was sliced apple and a glass of milk at the counter. It was probably my favorite spot in the house, other than my bedroom. It felt like a safe place. It felt like home.

"How was your day, Logan? How was school?"

"Fine," I said dismissively.

It was the standard sixth-grader's response to most questions. In fact, as you might recall, my day wasn't very good at all, but I didn't want to revisit it. I thought my tone conveyed that clearly enough, but apparently not.

"How did your oral report go?"

Man... She was all business. I hadn't even bitten into my apple.

"Terrible," I said. "I froze up again. And Chet Masterson was a jerk to me."

"Oh, honey," she said.

She came around the counter and put her arms around me from behind. It was one of those Mom hugs that make you feel better, but also kind of awkward at the same time. It feels good at first, like you're six years old again. But then you realize you're not six years old anymore, and it gets a little weird.

"You prepared so well, Logan. It sounded so great last night. You were perfect."

"I know," I said.

"We both know how great you are. Let other people see it. Don't be shy. You have so much greatness inside of you, you need to let it out for the world to see. Let your star shine bright."

"Ok," I said. "I will. But I still don't understand why Chet has to be that way. Why can't people just do what's right, or kind?"

"I don't know, honey, but never lose those ideals. You have to do what's right for you. But just remember, not everyone will agree with you."

She smiled and stroked my cheek, looking at me with her big Mom eyes.

I felt better in the moment. The stroke of her hand and the softness of her words were like a warm blanket straight out of the dryer.

"You just be you. Ok?"

"Ok," I said. "I have to go do my homework. Tomorrow's a new day, I guess."

2

Lunchtime. Brixton Private Academy cafeteria.
September 25.

∽

The cafeteria is a weird place, if you think about it. It has rows and rows of tables, and you sit with people you might not know, eating food prepared by someone you've never seen, spooned out by a lady nobody ever thanks and rarely makes eye contact with. Don't get me wrong. I liked our lunch lady. But I have to admit I never actually knew her name. She always smiled at me though, and she made a point to pick out one of the bigger brownies for me on brownie day. I'm not sure why she did it, but I liked it, so I always made it a point to thank her.

I strutted out of the serving area with my extra-large brownie on my tray, and a little extra swagger in my step, to go sit down at a table with some people I didn't know. They were different, however, from the people I didn't know yesterday. James and Teddy were probably around somewhere, but I couldn't find them. So I sat, quietly minding my own business and eating my lunch. As I finished my ham sandwich, Chet Masterson walked by and grabbed that extra-large brownie right off my tray.

"Hey," I shouted with my teenage-boy-who-still-sounds-like-a-girl voice.

It was my most powerful retort, the fiercest in my arsenal. But Chet was undeterred.

"Looks delicious," he said. "Thanks, douchebag."

He walked off with his friends, and my extra-large brownie, to sit at a table with some girls who would no doubt be cheerleaders one day. I was never sure why he had to be that way, or why I always had to be the victim. It was just the way the sixth-grade social system worked.

In my view, here's how it works. There are two primary classes. There are "haves", and there are "have-nots." The haves, of course, were the popular kids. Fancy clothes, good looks, attitude, privilege, all the latest gear. You name it, they have it. And then there are the have-nots, playing foil to the haves as their unwilling victims. These two groups sit at opposite ends of the social spectrum, where the haves somehow feel entitled to make the have-nots' lives miserable.

In addition to the haves and the have-nots, there is also a large group of *invisibles* who make up the vast middle in between. Invisibles are the kids who come and go quietly, taking up space in the hallways and filling up seats in the classrooms without any incident. Drama never finds them, and bullies never bother them. Just once, I would have liked to be one of the *haves*. And most days I would have settled for being one of the *invisibles*. Today, however, I was just a *have-not*. That's usually the case, after all.

Anyway, since Chet took my brownie, and I'd already eaten everything else, there was little point in sitting around with today's strangers who were only slightly different from yesterday's strangers. So, I headed to the garbage can to dump my tray, keeping a close eye on Chet as I passed. The last thing I needed was for him to trip me or to flip my tray in front of everyone. That would be embarrassing.

Not today, Chet Masterson; I've got my eye on you.

I was proud of my awareness. There would be no stealth attack this time. I'd already learned my lesson. But as I walked by, with my head turned and my eyes fixed on Chet, I ran right into Principal Fogarty. Despite my best efforts, I tripped and fell anyway. My metal tray sailed through the air and hit the ground with a clang. When my chocolate milk hit the ground, it sprayed all over, even onto someone's nice white pants. As I lay on the floor trying to pull myself together, laughter spread through the cafeteria. I glanced up from the milk-speckled pant legs right into the emerald-green eyes of Ginny Mason.

I had ruined her pants. If she hadn't hated me before, she certainly would now. As the janitor wheeled his mop bucket over, I picked up my tray, tossed it in a stack by the door and spent the rest of the lunch period walking alone outside, trying not to be seen.

One of these days I would be a have. Just not today.

~

After School. My House.

IT WAS A ROUGH DAY, and the bus ride home was painfully long. After I got home, I ate my after-school snack.

"Oreos and milk, one of my favorites," I said.

"I know it's not the most nutritious," Mom said, "but I thought it would be a nice treat. Enjoy."

"You know I will!" I said with a chuckle.

When I was done, I went out to sit on the porch. It was warm out, and there was a nice breeze. It was nice and quiet. No Chet Masterson. No Bryce. Nobody in the cafeteria laughing. It was just me and the creak of the chains on the porch swing, drifting back and forth in calming rhythm, and a soft breeze rustling leaves in the background. It was absolutely perfect. The leaves had started to turn orange, but they weren't quite falling yet. It would still be another week or two, and we'd be taking drives and building leaf piles in no time. I had only been sitting on the swing for a few minutes when a car pulled up in the driveway next door. Ginny's mom got out of the car and took some grocery bags in.

Yeah. So, about that—Maybe I neglected to mention this before, but Ginny doesn't just sit next to me in class. She also lives next door. She moved in before school started, and it's just her, her mom, and her dad. The family that lived there before had rented for a while, but the dad got relocated for work. All things considered, I would call Ginny's family an upgrade.

The prior family had a little boy named Ponce who was as obnoxious as his name might suggest. He was two years old, and he never stopped crying. Ever. His dad used to sing a made-up song about Ponce de Leon for reasons that I'll never understand, but the song never worked. That kid just kept on crying.

I would have chosen Ginny Mason over Ponce any day. No question. Even though we'd never actually spoken to each other, and we probably never would. Especially not now, not after what happened in the cafeteria. It's a real shame, too. She might have been the cutest, sweetest, most amazing girl I had ever seen. I liked looking at her. Sometimes I would accidentally stare. But every time I tried to think of something to say, my tongue swelled up and I forgot how to talk. Like when I have to do an oral report in class, but so much worse. So, I just stared at her like a big creepy goofball, not knowing what to say.

After her mom went inside, Ginny got out of the car to follow. But as she walked up the driveway, she glanced over my way and caught me looking at her again. Or staring, as the case may be.

Be cool. Just look away.

I tried to play it off. I shifted my eyes across the street and started whistling a song. I wasn't sure what song it was. It might have been that horrible Ponce de Leon song, but I hoped it wasn't. I prayed she didn't notice, but she probably did.

She immediately changed direction and walked across her lawn, right toward my porch. Right toward *me*. Her flowing locks of hair bounced and swayed with every step, as the sun glistened off her curls. It was a big lawn, and she was picking up speed, probably coming to scream at me about ruining her pants.

What had I been thinking? As if I could actually escape the issue by simply running out of the cafeteria. She lived next door for crying out loud, and I only delayed the inevitable. As she marched closer, I noticed she was actually pretty tall. Her limbs were long and trim, like a swimmer. I wondered if she was a swimmer, and for some reason concluded that she must be. Definitely a swimmer with arms like that.

Anyway, my pulse raced as she got closer. I was afraid of what she would say. She walked right up onto my porch. She stood right in front of me, fearless and confident. I braced myself for what would come next. Would she call me names? Scream at me about her pants? Just shriek right into my ear as loud as she could to hurt my ears? But it was none of that.

"Are you ok?" she asked.

Her voice was so sweet, and so kind.

"What?" I said.

"You had quite a fall today, in the cafeteria. I just wanted to see if you were ok."

"Oh. That. I'm fine," I said, blushing anew.

I glanced down at her chocolate-speckled pant legs.

"I'm really sorry about your pants," I said. "Do you totally hate me?"

"Of course not. Why would I hate you?"

"I don't know. Because I ruined your pants."

"Forget about it," she said. "They're just pants. I have others."

I nodded knowingly.

"Yeah, me too."

Why did I just say that? That doesn't even make any sense.

"Besides," she said. "It might just come out in the wash. Then there'd be nothing to be upset about, right?"

"Yeah. I guess that's right," I said.

I smiled, and all of a sudden I felt calm and free. It was a strange feeling. Rarely did I ever feel so at ease talking to another person that wasn't in my family. I wasnt' sure what to call it. But whatever that feeling was, I really liked it.

"I have to be honest," I said. "I thought you were coming over here to yell at me; I thought you'd be mean. Or rude. Or make fun of me or something. But you're actually really nice."

She wasn't even offended.

"Thanks," she said. "That's really funny, because I thought the same thing about you. I was really nervous about coming over here."

"Why?"

"Well, I've been sitting next to you in class, and living next door to you, for over a month now, and you never even say hello. You just stare at me with that blank stare. I couldn't tell for sure, but I thought maybe you were scowling at me."

"Really?"

"Yeah. When we moved here, my parent's said this town had a lot of rich and snooty families, particularly the kids at Brixton. They said some of the kids here might seem entitled, or act like they're better than everyone else. So, I just figured you were one of those kids."

"No way," I said. "That's not my style."

"Good," she said. "Because, me neither."

I laughed in relief and snorted a little in the process.

"Did you just snort?" she asked.

"Yeah, sorry," I said sheepishly. "That happens sometimes. I hate it."

"Don't be sorry," she said. "It's cute. I wish I snorted when I laughed."

"That's a weird thing to wish for, but ok."

"Is it, though?" she said with a giggle.

And just like that, Ginny and I were tuned to the same wavelength. We really got to chatting, and before long a most wonderful conversation developed. I walked her through my theory on Brixton's haves, its have-nots and, of course, the invisibles. I also explained my permanent placement among the have-nots. From there everything just got easier. My mom brought some lemonade out, and Ginny and I sat under the weeping willow tree, sharing stories about our old homes, old schools, old friends and old problems. We laughed more than I ever remember laughing before, and we ended up talking right until dinner time when her mom called her in to eat.

"Gotta go," she said.

"Ok," I said.

"This was fun," she added, looking back over her shoulder. "We should do it more often."

"Yeah," I said. "We definitely should."

That day changed everything. With Teddy and James, we got along well enough to pass the time. But they'd also probably be fine enough if I wasn't there.

But within a minute of Ginny stepping onto my porch, I felt like I was talking to my best friend. Someone special. Someone I'd known my whole life, even though we had just met. When we talked, it was like there was no other place she'd rather be. I felt as if she was really listening to me. And when she laughed, my god. She was so relaxed and so free.

Even if I didn't realize it back then, I certainly realize it now. Ginny made me feel like a *have* from the moment she entered my life. It made me wish I could feel as comfortable around other people. That comfortable kind of happy, where everything was fine. That easy kind of happy. That *Ginny* kind of happy.

That would be nice.

Saturday morning, October 12.

THE WEEKEND STARTED off with a savage five-star from Bryce, right after Mom asked him to wake me up for breakfast. I really wish she'd be more specific about how to wake me up, though. Or at least provide some guidelines. I guess he got it out of his system early, though, because he wasn't completely horrible to me for the rest of the day. After breakfast, our parents took us on a long drive to look at the foliage, and Bryce and I actually got along for the most part. There was a park about an hour away from the house that we liked to go to that had a big pond in the middle, surrounded by grass and trees. The leaves were orange and golden amber, just approaching the height of their brightness. The leaves reflected off the pond like a mirror, and Mom insisted on taking a picture of us in front of it. Just like the one she took last year, and the year before.

As tradition requires, Bryce and I made piles from the fallen leaves and ran through them a few times.

"Did you boys have a good time?" Mom asked as she got in an shut the car door.

"I guess," Bryce said dismissively.

"Absolutely," I said with contrasting enthusiasm. "It's one of those things we have to do! I don't think that will ever get old."

She stared back at me smiling, and taking in the moment.

"Oh good," she said. "I'm glad to hear it. I need to stop by Grandpa's house on the way home to see how he's doing, just so you know. Maybe we'll stay for dinner."

"Sounds good," I said.

~

"How's your burger, Gideon?" Dad asked.

"My hockey puck?" Grandpa replied. "Just dandy, thanks for asking."

Dad just grinned and shook his head.

"You know, Robert," Grandpa continued, waving his burger. "The thing about hamburgers is that they aren't supposed to crunch when you bite into them."

"Thanks for the tip."

"Dad!" Mom exclaimed.

"Well, it's true," he said. "They're not. This is barely recognizable as beef. Or food, even."

My dad nodded and laughed it off. But Grandpa had a point. They were pretty burnt.

My dad and my grandpa actually got along pretty well, but Grandpa liked to give him a hard time now and then. From what I hear, it's been that way ever since Mom and Dad started dating. Some things never change. After we finished eating, Mom collected the plates and took them into the kitchen while Grandpa chewed on a toothpick.

"Why don't you boys go play in the fort," Grandpa said. "I built it just for you, after all. It would be a shame not to enjoy it."

Bryce looked up from his phone. He had been using the front camera to zoom in on a pimple on the side of his nose, but he had since dispensed with it.

Nasty.

"I'm good," Bryce said, turning back to stare at his phone.

"How about you, Logan? You've barely spent any time in there. You should go check it out."

"Did you really build it yourself?" I asked.

"Of course, I did, with my own two hands."

He paused.

"I guess I had a little help from Muggins. He deserves some credit, too."

"Muggins? Who's Muggins?" I asked.

Bryce snorted and shook his head like he already knew.

"Who's Muggins?" Grandpa repeated back at me, as if offended.

"Muggins is my friend, a magical toolbox troll, of course. He's a very helpful chap, he does all sorts of things. Muggins and I have had many great adventures together. I'll tell you all about them one day when, you know, it's just you and me; when we have some extra time to talk about those sorts of things without getting interrupted."

He peered toward the door where Mom had gone inside. And just as the words left his mouth, she came back out to the porch.

"Dad, seriously. Just stop with this. You're going to give them nightmares or something."

"I had a nightmare last night," Bryce said. "It was terrible. I had a stupid little brother named Logan."

"Bryce, that's not very kind, dear," Mom said. "How would you like it if someone talked about you like that?"

Grandpa leaned in toward me and whispered, motioning his thumb toward my mom.

"She never believes me. She never has," he said. "But you do. I can see it in your eyes. You and I, we're tuned to the same wavelength. We understand each other, am I right?"

I didn't know what to say. It was really uncomfortable for me. Mom was standing right there, and she could totally hear him.

"Don't do this, Dad. Ok? Just let him be. Logan, go play in the fort, honey. Have a good time."

She took my plate and nudged me off the bench to go play.

Grandpa sighed.

"I'm going for a walk," he said.

I could tell his feelings were hurt. I could hear it in his voice.

"I need to go check on things."

Then he walked off into the woods.

I spent a little time in the fort waiting for him to come back. It was better than I had remembered, but I mostly just wished he was there with me. I wanted to hear more about Muggins.

WE GOT HOME LATER than usual from Grandpa's house. I was brushing my teeth and getting ready for bed while my parents were in their bedroom talking. Their door was open, so their voices carried right across the hall. I could hear every word.

"Hey Barb," Dad said. "I'm worried about Gideon. The stories he's been telling. His detachment from reality. It's not just his imagination running off. I feel like he really believes some of the things he's saying. It's troubling."

"He's been like this ever since he retired," Mom said.

"I've been around him since he retired, Barb. It used to be some funny quips, something clever, creative, slightly strange here and there. It's different now. I'm starting to wonder how much longer he'll be able to stay in that house by himself. There might be, you know, issues."

"What are you saying," she asked.

"I'm just worried about him taking care of himself. You hear stories all the time. I'd hate for him, you know, to become one of those stories. I'll be back at the hospital on Monday. I can talk to some colleagues in Psych if you want. Just ask for suggestions or thoughts they have. Nothing drastic. Just think about it, ok, and let me know."

There was quite a pause.

"I have to be honest, Robert. I hate the idea," she said. "But I've been wondering the same thing. Maybe you could just ask if there's anything we should be worried about. No commitments, but just ask around."

I didn't like the sound of that, or what it might mean for Grandpa. I thought some more about his stories as I walked back to my room. I had to admit, some of them were pretty far-fetched. I looked over at my desk, where my coffee can bank sat. When I picked it up, it weighed about the same as it ever did. I gave it a shake and it sounded the same too. Just the five coins he put in when he gave it to me, nothing more. I added some loose change from my desk, since I figured why not; it couldn't hurt.

3

Evening of December 25.

~

I couldn't believe how quickly Christmas had arrived that year. The school year was going by so fast. My aunts and uncles had come into town to celebrate, and they brought my cousins with them. It's always nice to see them, but only in short spurts, really. As was tradition, Aunt Lucy burst through the front door and ran around hugging everyone, spreading her uniquely screechy brand of joy, whether we wanted it or not. And if you didn't hug and kiss her as much and as often as she wanted you to, she'd lay on the guilt trip.

"You're breaking my heart, Bryce," I heard from the other room. "What did I do to make you stop loving me?"

Classic Aunt Lucy. Uncle Bob wore his awful Christmas sweater again. The ill-fitting one with the snowman stretched across his big belly. The cousins were loud and ran all over. And, of course, there was eggnog—plenty of it. Grandpa had a fire going in the fireplace and Christmas music on the radio. It was all standard fare, and I wouldn't have had it any other way except for maybe Aunt Lucy. My mom was the youngest in her family, and I happen to be the youngest in ours, so that basically makes me the youngest person in the whole house. Even my closest cousins were a couple years older than me, so other than a catchup conversation when they first showed up, or a game of cards after dinner, we didn't talk much. And when I say a game of cards, I mostly mean an argument over what game to play, with very little actual play. I never got to know them very well, but they were family, and this is what we did.

We had opened gifts earlier in the morning and I got some great stuff: A fully-automatic Nerf machine gun with fifty-round clips. I'd be confined to target practice, though, until I could find someone to have a war with. Maybe James and Teddy, if they got nerf guns too. There were clothes, of course, socks and underwear were required each year. Bryce and I both got remote control race cars, and they were really fast! I got a Lamborghini and Bryce got a Bugatti.

"Bugatti's are way better than Lambo's," he said.

"Says who?" I asked.

"Says everybody, you little dweeb. It's common knowledge, little bro. Better luck next year, though."

It wasn't a battle I needed to fight. I'd probably end up with a bruise on my arm anyway. And for what?

I had just finished setting up my car up in the kitchen to charge and came back out with a couple of Aunt Lucy's fudge cubes in hand, dusted with powdered sugar. Grandpa was standing by the tree, checking the time. He snapped his watch shut, put it back in his pocket and came over to talk.

"Hey there, Sport. How's your Christmas going so far?"

"Really good," I said. "Except for Bryce."

"Oh, pay him no mind," he told me. "He's just acting out. It makes him feel better about himself."

"I guess."

"You know what, Logan? That movie you wanted to see is coming out in a few days. And since you're on a break from school anyway, I thought we could go see it together. We can catch an early show, and grab lunch at IncrediBurger. What do you think?"

"Oh. My. God. YES! That sounds great. Thanks, Grandpa!"

"Good, I'm looking forward to it. And I hear you're having another strong quarter at school, Logan. I'm very proud of you."

I beamed.

"So far, so good," I said.

"Your grandmother would be proud, too, rest her soul."

"Yeah. I miss her," I said. "A lot."

"I do, too," he said. "She was the love of my life. I don't know if I ever told you this, but I caught lightning in a bottle the day I met your grandmother."

"Lighting? In a bottle?"

"You bet," he said. "I really did. It was March 3, if I remember correctly. What a day that was. She was such a lovely woman, bless her heart. Such a shame she couldn't be here to see all this. She would have enjoyed having all the family together."

"Yeah."

"It's also a shame about that one little tardy messing up your perfect attendance," he said.

I shrugged.

"Yeah, that kind of sucked. Bryce strikes again."

"It's not the end of the world, you know. Not by any stretch. You just keep up the good work, Ok? Mind your Ps and Qs."

"Ok," I said.

I wasn't sure what Ps or Qs were, but I just went along with it. Then something hit me.

"Wait, how did you know about my tardy?"

"My friend Grimes told me."

"Grimes?"

Why had I never heard of this Grimes fellow?

"Yes. Of course. Good old Grimesey, we go way back. He's a very close friend. A very good friend, indeed. Guys like you and me, we can use a good friend now and then to show us the way, can't we? I don't know how he does it, but Grimes seems to know pretty much everything there is to know. Well, maybe not everything, but pretty close to everything. He's almost always right, no matter what the topic is. Very confident in his own knowledge and rarely steers me wrong on anything. Maybe once in a while, but not too often."

This Grimes dude sounded pretty legit.

"Where do you know him from?" I asked.

"We met at Smerconish's, the hardware store, a long time ago. He and I—"

But he stopped talking as my mom got closer.

"What are you boys talking about over here," she said.

She walked over with a big smile and an even bigger glass of eggnog in her hand. She looked much happier than usual. Christmas always put her in an extra-good mood.

"Grandpa was just telling me about a friend of his."

"Oh yeah? Which one?" she asked.

"Grimesey," I said, as Grandpa looked the other direction.

"Is that so?"

"Yeah. He sounds really smart."

"I'm sure he does," she said with a weird tone.

I was all out of fudge, and things had suddenly gotten awkward for reasons I didn't understand. So, I took a step to the side as I talked, and expertly steered the conversation into the kitchen so that I could get more fudge. Mom and Grandpa followed perfectly.

"Grimesey?" she said with a sharpening edge to her voice. "Is that so?"

"Yep."

She was holding something back. There was a weird pause as she stared back at Grandpa, but he avoided her gaze.

I popped a piece of fudge into my mouth as Bryce walked in to charge his car, but I was already using the last outlet to charge mine. I'd finally won one over Bryce. Or so I'd thought. He just unplugged my car and plugged his in instead. While I was standing right there watching him.

"Hey," I yelled.

"Suck it," he said.

"Bryce, honey, what's on your face?" my mom asked.

"Nothing," he said.

She grabbed her purse from the counter and pulled out her makeup mirror.

"It's not nothing, Bryce. It's definitely something. Here, have a look," she said.

He opened the compact and looked in the mirror. He smiled, took an extra moment to admire himself and ran his fingers through his hair.

"Whatever. It's just a little fudge," he said.

He rubbed it from the corner of his mouth and sucked the flavor off his thumb. As he pulled his thumb from his mouth, there was a loud pop. Sparks shot out of his Bugatti, and it started to smoke. Grandpa ran over to unplug it, and he turned to Bryce.

"What have I been telling you, Bryce? Karma's a bitch. But you don't listen."

"Dad!" my mom shouted. "Language! Unacceptable!"

Bryce and I were shocked, but in the most awesome possible way. I'd never heard Grandpa talk like that before. Ever.

"I keep trying to tell him to straighten up," Grandpa said. "Or Karma's gonna have her way with him. Maybe now he'll start to listen. You see what I'm talking about now, don't you? I'm not just some crazy old man telling crazy stories anymore. This is real."

He turned to Bryce.

"You should have just left Logan's car alone. Logan knows; he listens to me. He always makes good choices, and that's important. A life lived true, the truest of the true, that is the best way. Keep your heart true, Bryce. If you don't, you'll have consequences to pay."

Mom pulled Grandpa aside.

"Dad, once again. Can you stop, please? It's Christmas."

"There's nothing wrong with what I just said, Sissy. And I've never told him anything that wasn't absolutely true."

"Really? Like your stories about Muggins? And Grimes? Or lightning that hit a tree and opened a magic door? Please, Dad. Just stop."

"It's all true, Sissy. Every last word."

"Dad I'm really worried about you. I don't want to make a scene right now. But you need to stop. Ok?"

"I'm just fine, Sissy. Don't you worry about a thing. And Logan is fine, too. He believes me. He likes my stories. Not like you. You were never ready to believe. You always thought I was just a kooky old man telling crazy tales."

"Can you blame me?"

"I tried to teach you, but you wouldn't have it. I can see it in his eyes, though. He believes me. He gets it."

Mom sighed.

"He gets picked on enough at school as it is. I don't need him repeating things like this. It'll only make things harder. When he was younger, we could write it off as him being a first-grader with an over-active imagination. But he's older now. He's expected to know the difference, and you're making it so much harder."

"Oh, come on, Sissy. I just wanted to share some stories with my grandson. Is that really so bad?"

He sounded sadder than anyone should ever be on Christmas Day. Or any other day, really.

"Now you've got me all upset again. I'm going out for a walk. I need to go check on things, anyway."

He walked out the back door without another word.

"It's best if we let him go walk it off," she said. "Get it out of his system."

"Is he ok?" I asked.

"He'll be fine," she said.

Out in the front room, the adults sat comfortably, gathered by the fire, sipping from glasses, telling the same old stories they always tell. I made a quiet exit and walked around the other rooms of the house. I went looking for a cousin or someone to hang out with, but I had no luck. I wished Grandpa hadn't left. It's times like these when we usually hung out.

I poked my head into one of the bedrooms, where Bryce was talking with Bob Jr. They were talking about girls.

"What are you guys up to?" I asked.

Bryce looked up at me standing in the doorway.

"What do you want, booger-face?"

"Good one," I said. "Never mind, Bryce. I don't want to interrupt whatever this is."

Feeling adrift among my own family now, I wandered outside to Grandpa's garage. Sometimes it's nice to just get away from all the racket. And his garage was a good place to do that. He had a lot of stuff out there.

I found myself standing in front of his big tool chest, the stacking kind, with wheels underneath. It was tall, with lots of drawers. Almost as tall as me. *Muggins the magical toolbox troll*, I thought to myself. I had to admit it sounded pretty ridiculous, even for one of Grandpa's stories. And he told some good ones.

It was cold out in the garage, as it turned out, and pretty lonely. So, I went back inside where it was warm, hoping Grandpa would be back soon. He must have been freezing out there, he didn't take a jacket with him.

Back inside, the fire felt nice. I sat on the floor in front of it, staring into it, and halfway listening to another one of Uncle Bob's recycled stories. Everyone laughed, like it was the first time they had ever heard it, which made me wonder if Bryce and I would get this way when we got older. I glanced over at the clock and realized Grandpa had been gone for over an hour, far longer than usual. He must have been pretty upset to be gone so long. Bored with Uncle Bob's stories, I went to the kitchen to play solitaire. I'd been playing for about fifteen minutes when Grandpa came back in.

"Hey Grandpa, how about a game of rummy?" I said.

But he didn't look very good. He was pale and exhausted, and was having trouble walking.

"Are you ok?"

"I'm fine, he said, I'm just feeling a little under the weather. I think I need to go lie down."

"You'll be lucky if you don't have pneumonia," Mom said,

appearing out of nowhere. "It's freezing cold out there. Let me make you some honey-lemon tea."

"Don't worry about me, Sissy. Logan, remember, it's up to you to keep the light now."

I nodded.

"Ok, sure," I said.

Once again, I wasn't really sure what he meant; but I figured he did, and that was probably good enough.

"That's a good boy."

"I hope you feel better, Grandpa," I said. "Build up some energy for IncrediBurger and the movie. Just a couple more days!"

Christmas was great and all, but I was really looking forward to our big day out. Just me and him. It was going to be great.

WE WENT HOME SHORTLY after that. The day had run its course, and the adults were tired. Some of them even fell asleep in their chairs, glasses of eggnog in hand. I helped Dad load the gifts in the car and we said our goodnights.

This year's break had been good so far. Ginny and I had spent a lot of time together, and it was always so much fun when we did. It was way too cold for lemonade, so we had been drinking hot chocolate under the willow. My mom made a mean cup of hot chocolate. We even rode our bikes over to grandpa's house and wandered around in the woods behind his house one day. As it turns out she's not a swimmer. I mean, I'm pretty sure she knows how to swim, but she's not on a swim team or anything like that. She's really good at basketball though. And although I hate to admit it, she can ride her bike way faster than me.

She's still one of the funniest people I know. I laugh more with Ginny than pretty much anybody. And that feeling I used to get, where I'd forget how to talk whenever she was around me; that feeling had completely gone away.

I still wasn't sure if she knew about my crush, but I could never say anything to her myself. She probably knew. But I didn't know if she actually knew. And I'm not sure how to tell her if she doesn't.

Being twelve is hard. But my parents always talked about how easy it was, and how they wish they could go back to being twelve again. They liked to talk about how much harder things are when you get older. I just smiled and nodded when they did that. I figured they had probably forgotten how hard it really is. It had been a long time since they were twelve, after all.

~

December 28. 8:00 a.m.

I WOKE up that day to the sound of the phone ringing. Grandpa was probably on his way to pick me up for our big day out. Lunch and the movie weren't until later, so I figured he must have really big plans to pick me up so early. I sprung out of bed to get dressed so I'd be ready to go when he arrived. Not even Bryce could spoil this for me. I was finishing tying my shoe when my bedroom door opened.

"Is Grandpa on his way?" I asked.

There was no response.

I looked up. Mom's eyes were welled up with tears, and wet streaks ran from her eyes down to her chin. Dad looked so serious.

"Logan," he said. "Have a seat on your bed, Sport. We need to talk to you about something."

He sat down next to me and took a deep breath. Mom sat on the other side, put her arm around me and pulled me in tight.

"That was Uncle Bob," Dad said. "There's no easy way to say this, but Grandpa passed away last night. Peacefully, and in his sleep."

"What do you mean?" I asked.

I could feel the tears welling. I knew exactly what he meant, but I couldn't think of anything else to say.

"Grandpa hasn't been feeling well since Christmas. Yesterday, it got really bad, just all of a sudden. Nobody expected this. He passed last night. He's with Grandma now, and I'm sure they're both delighted to be back together again. It's been a while since they've seen each other, you know."

"No," I said. "I don't understand. He was fine just a couple of days ago. How can this be happening?"

Mom squeezed me, my face pressed into her warm, soft bathrobe.

Then I totally lost it. I was too young to really remember my grandma dying, so this was the first time anyone close to me had ever passed away. I cried into her shoulder until my muscles were too weak to cry anymore. I cried until I ran out of tears. I have never cried so hard in my life as I did that day.

December 30. Grandpa's House.

IT WAS a rough couple of days that followed. I never missed someone or something so much in my life. My parents were doing a much better job dealing with it than I was, at least as far as I could tell. After a quick breakfast, we went to Grandpa's house to sort through his things. Mom needed *get his affairs in order*—that's what she called it. Most of the relatives who had come into town for Christmas had gone home by now. Mom packed up a few boxes with some of Grandpa's stuff.

After we'd been there for a while, I wandered off to look around. I reflected on the countless times I stubbed my pinky toe walking past his old buffet, or hid and played under the dining room table, concealed by the long draping tablecloth. As I wandered, I found myself looking through the drawer in the kitchen with all the odds and ends that don't have a proper place to go. He called it his *what the hell* drawer. Lots of memories in that drawer - the tweezers that he used to get that enormous splinter out of my hand. The old folding cribbage board he taught me to play on, and his worn-out deck of cards, tied up with a crusty rubber band that was way past its useful life. So many memories in this drawer, and in this house. Eventually, I found myself in his bedroom, standing in front of his old wooden dresser.

His pocket watch sat up top, next to a picture of him and my grandma, taken on their wedding day. They looked so happy. I could tell from his face that he really loved her. There was another frame on his dresser, with a picture of me and him sitting on his back porch from a few years earlier. I can't remember when it was taken or what we were talking about, but we sure looked like we were having fun. And he loved that old watch, too. It felt heavy in my hand when I picked it up, heavier than I thought it should have been. I glanced down at the pocket watch and ran my thumb over the cover. I was just about to flick it open when Mom walked in.

"Oh, there you are," she said. "I was wondering where you had gotten off to."

"Yeah, I'm right here," I said with a sigh. "I was just looking at some of Grandpa's stuff."

"That's fine, Logan, but why don't you come out of here for now and be with the family? It's probably good for us to all be together."

She walked over and picked up the picture of me and Grandpa from the top of the dresser. Then she glanced at the pocket watch in my hand.

"Do you want to take these home with you, sweetheart?"

I nodded quietly. I swear, she really could read minds sometimes.

"Yes, please," I mumbled.

"I've got a box of things on the kitchen table," she said. "Go put the frame in there."

I nodded again and I put the pocket watch in my pocket.

"Honey," she said, wiping a tear from my eye with her thumb. "Everything will be ok. We'll get through this, just like everything else. I'm sure you don't believe me. You probably feel like your whole world has collapsed right now."

"That's exactly how I feel," I said. "How is this ever going to be ok?"

"I don't know, sweetheart, maybe with time. We'll just have to see.

But for now it's going to be pretty hard, and that's totally normal, and it's totally ok for you to feel that way."

She was right. It was awful. Even Bryce cried at one point. I didn't expect that.

Mom forced a smile.

"We'll get through it together, ok? Now go on."

When we got home, I went to my room and set the picture of me and Grandpa on my desk, right next to the coffee can bank so I could always see it. So many stories. And now, just like that, it was over.

I picked up the bank and rattled it again, just to check. Of course I had my doubts. And of course it still sounded the same as it ever did. I sat pondering and remembering some of his best stories. As I thought about his stories, one really stuck in my head. An urge came over me that I couldn't fight off. I had to get back to his house immediately. I ran outside, hopped on my bike and pedaled back over there as fast as I could. When I arrived, I stood alone in the walkway leading up the porch.

It was eerily quiet, apart from the wind blowing through bare trees, crisp leaves rolling across the ground, and the sound of my own breath. I walked my bike around to the garage and found the side door was still unlocked. My parents hadn't packed anything up yet and Grandpa's toolbox was still there—the tall one with all the drawers. The biggest, deepest drawer was at the bottom. That's where he kept his power saws, and other bulky tools. Once in a while he'd let me use them, but usually I was just in charge of getting them out or putting them back.

I started looking through the drawers. Just some screwdrivers and crescent wrenches in the smaller drawers up top. Same as always. Box cutters and socket wrenches in the next one. Hammers and chisels in the next. Something about that bottom drawer just felt different, though. It was calling me.

I knelt on one knee and slowly slid it open. Then I jumped back in fright, hardly able to believe what I saw. Something, some creature, was lying inside, on the bottom of the drawer. The inside of the drawer was made up like a tiny bed, and whatever that thing was, it appeared to be sleeping. A really old man maybe, but small —small enough to sleep in the bottom drawer of a toolbox. His head was balding on top. He had a hooked nose and sparse stragly hair. His clothes were old-fashioned, even older than the stuff Grandpa used to wear. He wore a drab brown suit with sleeves rolled to his elbow. His skin was the texture of dried apple, and he wore goggles, even while he slept. As I stood there staring, he opened his eyes, sat up, and stretched. He looked up at me, slowly awakening.

"Aw, Logan," he said. "It's so good see you. I'm glad you finally came."

"Hey," I said. "How do you know my name? Who are you? Or what are you?"

"Well, I'm Muggins of course. Gideon never told you about me? I'm sure he must have. He must have mentioned me at some point."

This is Muggins?

As he talked, his really bad teeth showed. They were even worse than Bryce's were before he got his braces.

"Well, yeah," I said with my voice trembling. "He mentioned you, alright. But we all thought he was, you know, making it up or something."

"So, you didn't totally believe him when he told you," Muggins said. "Is that what you're saying? You heard of me, but you didn't believe in me? Maybe you changed your mind later? Maybe just today, even? That's pretty remarkable now, isn't it? You decided to change your mind, and now here I am. Ponder that for a second. What do you think about that?"

"I'm not exactly sure yet."

I could feel myself scooting backward, away from Muggins until my back hit the wall behind me.

"Relax," he said. "I'm a friend, not a foe. Things are about to change for you, Logan. And in a very big way, if I'm being honest. A very big way, indeed. Enormous."

He chuckled to himself.

"But I'm here to help you with that, you see? I'm on your side."

"Help me with what?" I said with panic. "What side? What's my side? Why do I have a side? Who is on the other side?"

He hopped out of the drawer and stepped toward me. Standing upright, he was only about as tall as my knee. He waved a friendly hand.

"Come on outside with me. I need to show you something."

There was something very soothing and familiar about his voice. I found myself trusting him immediately, even if I didn't want to. We ventured deeper into those old woods than I had ever gone with Grandpa, and stopped in front of a giant white oak. The tree was bigger than most of the others around. It was probably the biggest tree in sight. I'd never seen it before.

The gnarly, twisted tree stood tall and strong like an ancient landmark. There was a giant burn mark on it, a big black groove down the trunk that came all the way down to the ground, like trees get when they've been struck by lightning. The lightning had blown the bark clean off and charred the exposed wood underneath. Muggins looked up at me and pointed to the mark.

"Here we are. This is it," he said. "The entrance to Cameria. They're in a lot of trouble, Logan, and they need our help. They need *your* help, in fact, so let's get going, shall we?"

I stared at the tree.

"Cameria? This is a burnt tree."

"Come down here," he said, motioning for me to come closer.

I knelt on one knee and leaned in, face to face with him.

"The mind is a tricky thing, Logan. It sees what it wants to see. Do you follow?"

"Sort of," I said.

"You see a burnt piece of wood, because that's what you've been trained to see. That's what you *want* to see. It's what you expect. That's what's comfortable for you to believe. So, that's what you see. Are you with me?"

"Well, yeah," I said. "Because that's pretty much what it is."

"Exactly!" he said, pointing a finger up at my nose. "Now we're making progress."

"You're confusing me," I said. "I still can't believe I'm here talking to you."

"I know! And how many times have you moved tools in and out of your Grandpa Gideon's toolbox?"

"I don't know. A lot."

"More than ten times, would you say?"

"Probably more than fifty."

"And all you ever saw was tools, right?

"Yes."

"Until today, right? Today, you changed your mind. Today, you decided to see something else in that tool chest. Today you decided to believe that I might actually be in there. It's crazy. It makes no sense, whatsoever. There's absolutely no reason I should have been there."

"Right. This part I understand."

"But now, here I am. Right here. And in much the same way, the entrance to Cameria is right here, too. All you need to do is believe that it could be there."

"But."

He leaned in closer to me. His voice was wise and confident.

"Listen to my voice, Logan. I'm standing right here, even though I shouldn't be. I'm standing right here, talking to you, and I'm telling you that this is the entrance. Do you believe me?"

"I guess so."

"Oh good," he said. "I'm so glad you said that. Now, please have another look."

I turned and looked at the tree. But I didn't see burnt wood anymore. I could see right through it. Like a window looking deep into another place. A huge and beautiful place, something from a fairy tale. It was utterly magnificent.

"Holy moly, I can see it," I said. "What is even happening right now?"

4

"**O**f course you can see it," Muggins said.

I stood speechless. I stared through the opening, into the vast expanse overlooking this whole new world that, up until three seconds ago, I didn't even know existed. Grandpa had told plenty of stories about things like this, but I'd never seen any of it. Yet here it was.

I leaned in closer to the tree, peering through the new-found opening. Glistening streams coursed through sprawling green meadows across a lush valley floor. Mountains rose up from the horizon as waterfalls cascaded down them and rainbows formed in their mist.

The giant forest in the east really stood out. I'd seen some big trees before when our family went on drives. But I'd never anything like this. They were literally the size of skyscrapers, and I'm not one to exaggerate.

"I just can't believe it," I said. "The way the entrance just appeared like that."

"Yeah, well," he said. "It didn't just appear, Logan. It's been there. The Council elders decided to open it long ago, and to summon the Keepers back to Cameria. You just needed to believe in it to be able to see it for yourself. Now that you've seen it, you always will. Unless, of course, you stop believing for some reason. But until then, you'll find yourself shocked that others can't see it."

"Hold on. Keepers? Council? What are you talking about? What is this place?"

Muggins ran his hand down from his forehead to his chin, and he grumbled in frustration.

"It's Cameria, Logan, just like I said. Gideon always talked about what a smart boy you are. And I'm pretty sure I told you that this was the entrance to Cameria. Just a few seconds ago in fact. I did say that, right? Were you not listening when I said that? Or did I somehow confuse you? You seem confused. I must have confused you."

"I heard you just fine," I said. "Jeez, you don't have to be so rude."

I turned and looked back in to Cameria, and my hurt feelings were soon overtaken by amazement.

"But what exactly is Cameria?"

"It's a very important place. Cameria is the land of the Light, and the Light is the source of all things that are good and right in the world as you know it. It's all very straightforward."

"Oh, ok," I said, pretending to understand.

"The forest to the right," I said. "I've never seen trees that big. Is it some kind of optical illusion, or are they really that big? They seem bigger than the buildings in New York City."

"That is the Qud Palmon Forest," he said pointing to the horizon in the east. "It's the home of the Qud Palmon, a race of mighty warrior-folk. And yes, those trees really are as big as they look. So big, in fact, that the Qud Palmon are able to make their homes between the crevices in the bark. That's now big those trees are."

"They can?"

"Not just can, Logan. They do. It's hard to tell from here, but the crevices are deep and wide. And a single tree can house hundreds of Qud Palmon."

"That is completely amazing," I said. "I thought the fort in Grandpa's back yard was cool, but this is way cooler."

"Would you like to go inside and have a look?"

"Inside Cameria?" I asked. "Like actually go in there? Try and stop me."

Just a second ago, I stood in the woods behind Grandpa's back yard. But with one step forward, I was in a completely different world, in every possible sense. As I stood on a ledge overlooking Cameria, I could see for miles in every direction. It was a bright and happy place, with beautiful dazzling light washing over everything. The air was warm on my face, and a gentle breeze tickled the hair on the back of my neck. The air smelled natural and pure, and the colors seemed more colorful. In the distance, water rushed and birds called out from every direction. I'd never seen anything so spectacular in my entire life.

But for all its brightness and beauty, I couldn't help but notice the dark spot in the distance—a big, black, dark spot at the top of one of the mountains across the valley. The Light didn't seem to touch there for some reason.

"What is that?" I asked.

Muggins grumbled.

"You have a good eye, Logan. Maybe Gideon was right about you. That spot is exactly what we need your help with."

"My help?"

"That's right. That dark spot represents a very dire circumstance. The Light is being taken, and it has to be stopped before it's too late. Otherwise, all of this beauty and grandeur before you will be destroyed."

"Being taken? By who?" I asked. "Or what?"

"There is a dark and powerful force at play, a force that will do anything to seize the power provided by the Light. A force driven by a desire to use it for selfish purposes and to deprive others of its goodness. A strong desire to wield the Light as a weapon against anyone who refuses to pledge unwavering loyalty to a grossly immoral cause."

"Whoa," I said. "That sounds pretty heavy, Muggins."

Muggins nodded as he stared into the distance.

"It is. Very much so. There is so much at stake now. Everything, in fact. Whether you realize it or not, Logan, everything you have, everything you know, everything you love is at risk of disappearing for all of eternity. Unless we can stop the Light from being taken."

"But what am I supposed to do about it? I mean, I'm just a twelve-year-old with a ton of homework to do. I can barely make it through the day without one bully or another wrecking something for me. My own brother doesn't even respect me for crying out loud. So, honestly Muggins, how in the world am I supposed to fix whatever that is? Come on, now. If this is a joke, you're taking it way too far."

"You have something deep within you, Logan. Something special. A gift. A gift that others don't have. And that puts you in a unique position to help. Gideon had it, and you have it, too."

My mood dropped. It was a grim reminder of his passing. He's the one I would turn to with questions at a time like this. But I couldn't.

"You just said Gideon *had* it. You didn't say he *has* it. So, you know he died?"

"Yes, of course I know."

"But how?"

"We have a lot to talk about, Logan. But now is not the time. We'll get there soon enough, ok? But before we do, I need to make sure you understand some of the basics. You'll need to learn and understand a few things. Let's get you back home now and we'll talk more later."

I wasn't sure when we would actually talk, but it was pretty clear that it was time for us to leave Cameria. We chatted on the way back to Grandpa's garage, about Cameria and Grandpa their many adventures together. They were much closer than I had first realized.

"I'm not sure how much Gideon told you," Muggins said, "but your grandfather was actually quite important. You do understand that, right? It should be coming clear by now."

"Important?"

"Yes. Most definitely. There is a certain balance, a very important one that we rely on; not just in Cameria, but here as well. Gideon helped keep that balance. He was a Keeper of the Light, and therefore tasked with being a keeper of the balance. One of three. We just call them Keepers for short."

"Wait, what did you just call him?"

"A Keeper?"

"No. The whole thing."

"Keeper of the Light?"

My mind was blown.

"But what does that mean exactly? When he got sick on Christmas, before he went to bed, he told me I had to keep the light."

"It means he knew," Muggins said with a sly smile.

"Knew what?"

Muggins didn't answer.

When we arrived at the garage, it felt like we had only walked a few seconds.

"You should probably get home," Muggins said. "Take care of your homework and such. We'll talk more soon."

He said it the same way Mom says things, in her serious voice. I had so many questions, but they would have to wait.

"Yeah, ok," I said, disappointed. "I'll see you soon, Muggins."

"Yes. You'll see me very soon, Logan. Very soon indeed."

And with that, we parted ways. On the bike ride home from Grandpa's house, I could barely think straight. I couldn't wait to tell James and Teddy what I saw. Ginny, too. As I arrived home, I rode up the walk and laid my bike on the lawn. I ran up the stairs to go inside when I saw Ginny coming out of her front door to go somewhere with her mom. I gave her a big, excited wave and a smile. She smiled and waved back as they got in the car. I would have to wait tell her, and it was killing me not to be able to share this with her. I heard Mom's keys jingling toward me as I stepped inside.

"Oh, Logan sweetie, you're home. Good. I'm running out for a little pick-me-up. Come to the coffee shop with me. You can get a hot chocolate."

It was always a nice treat to run out for coffee with her. No Bryce, no drama, no nothing. Just me and Mom hanging out together. I always appreciated the one-on-one time with her.

"Busier than usual," she said as we pulled up. "Looks like everyone had the same idea we did. Great minds."

"That's ok," I said. "We get more Mom-and-Logan time that way."

While we waited for our orders to come up, I spied a strange man sitting in the corner. He was wearing oversized dark glasses, like the ones Mom wears when she gets back from the eye doctor. He stood out somehow, like a movie villain, with an unsettling smile, taking great satisfaction in something nobody else knew. I wondered what he was thinking, what he was looking at from behind those big, dark glasses. He just sat there oddly, nodding at nothing with his creepy grin. He just stared out the window, like he was trying to listen to everything at once, and could somehow make sense of it all. All that noise, all those voices mushed together, crystal clear in his head. Or at least that's what I imagined he was doing. My imagination got the better of me, though, and I came up with an idea to test him. I turned my back to him and whispered to myself.

"Can you hear me?" I asked in the faintest possible whisper. I knew there was no way in the world that he could, not over all the noise. I barely made a sound at all.

After I'd whispered the words, I looked back at him. His face changed, and I swear to God he chuckled to himself. Like maybe he was amused that I had discovered his hidden talent. He didn't look at me, he just nodded his head slowly, bigger nods this time, as if to acknowledge he could.

"Barbara," the clerk called out. "You're order is ready. Tall latte and a tall chocolate milk, not too hot."

"Oh, thank god!" I said, feeling completely creeped out. "Let's go."

"Well," Mom said with surprise. "Someone is thirsty."

I snatched both our drinks from the counter and darted toward the door.

"Mom, can we go now? I just whispered to myself, and that man in the corner heard me. How could he hear me?"

"Logan, you know that's not possible," she said. "I know you enjoyed these silly types of games with Grandpa, honey, and I'm sure you miss him dearly. But that's just not possible. You know it's not, and so do I. Let's get home and enjoy our cocoa without the silly stories, what do you say?"

I nodded in unwilling agreement. I checked back over my shoulder as we walked out the door. He watched us leave. He had heard me. I was sure of it.

~

THE NEXT DAY I met up with Teddy and James, at the bike racks after school.

"Hey James," Teddy said. "You want to stay over tonight? Your mom is usually cool with it, right?"

"Yeah, should be good," James said. "I'll text you when I get home and probably head over."

"Cool. Hey Logan, you should come, too," Teddy added.

"Really?" I said.

"Yeah, come along. It'll be good."

I really felt like I was making inroads. I wasn't just the new kid anymore. It seemed like they were actually starting to like me as a real friend now, not just a classmate, which was nice. When they invited me to toilet paper Chet's house, it seemed like more of a courtesy than anything. This was different. In order to return the favor, and treat them the same way, I opened up and told them all about the tree behind Grandpa's house, and what I'd seen.

"It really was amazing," I said. "I've never seen anything like it. I've never even dreamed anything quite like it. I can't even tell you how amazing it was. You really should come check it out."

But my excitement fell on deaf ears.

"That sounds like a load of garbage," Teddy said.

"I'm telling you, it's real," I said. "I was there. I saw it. All the amazing places my grandpa went to, and all things he talked about. They really are for real."

James piled on.

"I don't know. You're starting to sound about as crazy as he was. And that's pretty crazy, you know?"

Teddy nodded.

"James is right. It sounds pretty nuts. Can you hear yourself? A secret portal to an unknown world in a tree? Come on, Logan, quit the B.S. You cant' just walk through a tree."

"Hey!" I shouted in my sternest tone. "Take it back! He wasn't crazy. It's all true. Everything he said was true. I went there yesterday. Muggins, the cliffs, the giant trees. It's all real. I saw it with my own two eyes."

"Yeah, ok Logan," James said as he started to pedal away. "See you at my house. Maybe. Text me if you start to feel better. You know, less crazy."

There was nothing I could do to convince them. Downtrodden, I turned toward the curb where Mom picks me up. But with my first step, I ran into Chet Masterson. And not in a figurative way. I literally ran into him. It was like bumping into a door frame when you're not paying attention.

Why is he so solid? And seriously, how does he have a mustache already?

"Hey, watch where you're going, douchebag," he said.

Perfect.

All I needed now was a soggy spit wad on the back of my neck and an atomic wedgie to complete the Masterson Trifecta. He poked me in the chest with a thick finger.

"Are you the one that toilet papered my house?" he asked.

He sounded pretty angry. It was a simple question though, and it had a simple answer.

"Nope," I said. "I definitely did not toilet paper your house."

He didn't say anything. He just glared at me, then snorted and gave me a good, stiff shoulder bump on the way by. It wasn't the worst I've ever had, but it was pretty jarring. I don't think he believed me, though. Nobody seems to believe anything I say today.

"Don't mess with me, Logan," he said, walking away without

looking back. "Crazy or not, I'll find that precious little tree of yours. When I do, I'll burn it straight to the ground and piss on the ashes."

Oh no, the tree! How long had he been there listening? He must have heard everything I was telling James and Teddy.

"You wouldn't dare," I shouted.

"You want to make a bet on that? Just try me."

Mom arrived at the curb with a honk, just in the nick of time. I slid into the car and sank into the comfort of her company.

"How was your day, honey?

"I don't really want to talk about it," I said.

It was a disaster, after all. That made for a pretty quiet ride home.

5

Another week sailed by. I cruised through my classes and got my homework done with ease. Mom and Dad were working hard, taking care of Grandpa's affairs, as they like to say, and Bryce went to the library a lot. He said he was studying and doing homework. But I think he was meeting a girl there and not really studying at all. I heard them talking on a video chat a couple of days ago. They were so gross with their smoochy talk, it made me want to barf. But apart from having to put up with that, I actually had a pretty good week.

It was freezing cold outside, so Mom picked me up at the curb from school. When we got home there was a steaming bowl on the counter.

"I made you some cream of chicken soup."

"Just like Grandpa and I used to have on cold days."

"I remember."

"Sometimes, we'd dip a grilled cheese sandwich in. And if we were feeling extra fancy, we'd even add some ham between the two slices of cheese."

"That was a classic. I hope you're not disappointed that there's no sandwich."

"Nope. This is perfect."

While I ate my soup, Mom fumbled through her purse to find something. She looked distracted.

"Dad and I need to go see Aunt Agnes tonight," she said. "Do you remember Aunt Agnes? She's Grandpa's oldest sister."

Although I hadn't seen her in a couple years, I remembered her just fine. Given her old age, she didn't really come for the family gatherings anymore, and thank goodness for that. Aunt Agnes hadn't updated her wardrobe since I can't even tell you when. She had big hair that reeked of bargain hairspray, and she wore scratchy polyester pantsuits that looked like something from fifty years ago. Some were bright orange, others were sky blue, and none of them fit right. Her hugs were always rougher than necessary, and she had a musty closet aroma to her. So, yeah, you might say I remembered Aunt Agnes just fine.

The one thing I remember most about Aunt Agnes, however, was the stubbly whiskers poking out from the mole on her chin. Not many - just two or three. But those poky stubs were all I could see when I looked at her. It was like they were shouting my name.

I considered mentioning all of this, to let Mom know exactly how well I remembered Aunt Agnes. But I decided to keep it simple.

"Yep. I remember."

"Oh good," she said. "Well, she needs to sign some paperwork to help us wrap up Grandpa's affairs, so we're going to drive up to her place. We're leaving in just a little bit, and we'll probably stay overnight. Can I trust you and Bryce to follow all the rules, and get along properly?"

Trust me? Right. Like I'm the one you have to worry about.

"Teddy invited me and James to spend the night at his house," I said. "Can I go over there instead? Please?"

"Will Teddy's parents be home?"

"Yes."

"Then it's fine with me. I'll leave it up to you, ok? Just make sure you let Bryce know if you're going to stay over. And make good choices."

"Sounds good," I said. "Thanks for the soup. It was delicious."

I slurped the last half-spoonful into my mouth, went to my room, kicked off my shoes and fell back into my bed. Hallelujah, the weekend was finally here. I was about to text Teddy and James in our group chat, to see if they wanted to meet up early. But something caught my eye.

As I glanced toward the door, Muggins was standing there. I hadn't even heard him come in.

Yeah. Muggins. The magical toolbox troll, standing in my bedroom, wearing his crumpled brown suit with something slung across his chest.

"Um. What are you doing here?" I asked.

"It's nice to see you, too," he said.

"I wasn't trying to be rude, but you startled me. And when I'm not expecting you, you can be pretty startling, just so you know."

"I said I would see you very soon, didn't I?" he said.

"Yeah, but I figured—"

"Figured what?"

"I don't know. I just figured I would be the one who decided how soon it would be."

Muggins chuckled.

"There's a lot in life you won't be able to control, Logan. You know that, right?"

"Yeah, I know."

"Good. So, get used to it now."

"Right. You didn't answer me, though," I said. "What are you doing here?"

"Why don't you put your shoes back on. Let's go for a litle ride. I have more to show you. I'll meet you out by your bike."

I looked at the bag strapped across his chest.

"Is that a purse?" I asked.

He glanced down at it.

"Purse? Heavens no, this is no *purse*. This is my bottomless bag."

He stuck his hand up through the bottom, and it poked right out the top. He wiggled his fingers like a magician.

"See? Bottomless."

"Right," I said slowly. "That sounds super useful."

"It works just fine for me. Now get your shoes on, and I'll meet you out there."

I leaned over and grabbed one of my shoes. When I looked up to say something, he was already gone. With my shoes finally on, I ran out back to where my bike was. Sure enough, Muggins was already standing there, waiting for me.

"Where are we going?" I asked.

"Back to Gideon's house, of course. Back to the tree."

I looked down as I straddled my bike, and then I looked at Muggins.

"How are you going to get there?"

"Backpack-style," he said with a chuckle.

He hopped up on the back tire, then sprung further up onto my back, and grabbed a hold of my shoulders. Muggins didn't look like much, but he was quite nimble for such an old little—whatever he was.

I pedaled us over to my grandpa's house, sure to ride straight through any leaf piles I saw on the way. I dropped my bike in the front yard, and we walked around back to find the tree.

"I can still see inside," I said upon our arrival. "Muggins, do you have any idea how amazing this thing is?"

"Well yes," he said. "I actually have a very good idea. Take a moment to consider that it might be *you* who doesn't fully appreciate it."

"What do you mean?"

"What I mean is that you still have a lot to learn. I understand your fascination, but I'm not sure you understand what it means, that this portal is even here at all."

I shrugged. He was right.

"It hasn't always been here. But it is now, and I can say with a fair amount of certainty that it's not the only one. The powers that be, the wise elders of the Grand Council, made a decision that it had to be opened and that the Keepers of the Light should be summoned to

help restore a very necessary balance. You might remember an especially powerful lightning storm from last year."

"I remember," I said. "There was more lighting and more wind
than any storm before it. It was all over the news and people still talk
about it."

I studied the charred wood and the twisting burn marks that ran
down its hulking trunk.

"Is that when this tree was hit by lightning? Is that where those
burn marks came from?"

"Yes," he said. "This tree was hit by lightning that night, but not
just once. And the burn marks you see are not the only consequence
of that storm. This tree was actually struck by the Five Bolt. Five
distinct lightning strikes, all coming together at this very spot, all at
precisely the same time. You know how they say lightning never
strikes the same place twice? It was the Five Bolt that opened this
gateway, and I assure you, that was no accident. You, me, and of
course Gideon, we see it, or saw it as the case may be, for what it
really is. For pretty much everyone else, though, it's just a burnt tree."

"So why could Grandpa see it? What made him different?"

"The same thing that sets you apart, of course. He had a special
understanding, unique abilities that the Council needed. They
thought he could help in their fight."

"What fight?"

"The fight for what's right, of course. The fight for balance. The
fight to keep the Light itself. There's no greater struggle right now, in
my estimation. And there's none more important happening
anywhere in the universe."

"So, what does this all have to do with me?"

"That will become clear at the proper time. For now, let's go for a
walk inside."

I stepped through the gateway that had once been a burn mark,
and I found myself standing on the rocky ledge overlooking Cameria
again. From where we stood, in the distance, it all looked peaceful
and quiet. It was hard to imagine some great fight that Muggins was
referring to.

"The dark spot," I said, pointing toward the horizon. "It's so much bigger than I remember."

"Let's go," Muggins said.

We made our way along the cliff's edge, down a rocky, windy path that eventually led us down to the floor of the Camerian valley. We came to a stand of trees in a nice, cool wooded area; normal-sized trees, like in a normal-sized forest. Not like the Qud Palmon Forest.

Muggins stopped in the middle of the path and held his hand up. Rustling noises came from behind some brush, moving toward us, but I couldn't see anything. Just a strange darkness within. Then the darkness emerged, and gradually took the form of a wolf. It was bigger than I was, with ratty charcoal hair. Its lips pulled back to bare its razor-sharp teeth.

"Logan, stay behind me," Muggins said as it growled a throaty growl.

I obeyed, of course. At the time, though, it felt ironic. I was more than twice Muggins' size, after all, but I was hiding behind him for protection. Nonetheless, I stood motionless, eyes locked on the wolf. Then another one stepped into the light, and another. They circled us. The first one seemed to be the leader of the pack. It only had one good eye. Its other eye was milky white and scarred over.

"You should all know better," Muggins said, with a scolding tone as they continued to circle.

"You're far from the safety of your home, and you'd be wise to go back there if you know what's good."

One of the wolves snapped its teeth, as if in response, biting the air just inches from his face. Muggins reached into his bottomless bag and, much to my surprise, pulled something out. It was a small ball, or a marble of some sort. He threw it down on the ground and it popped with a bright flash of light, like a camera flash. The wolves returned to their shadowy form and scampered back into the bushes, whimpering with their tails tucked. I'd never seen anything quite like it. They were such strange creatures when they went all shadowy like that, their shape being defined by its own absence. Not invisible, just black emptiness. It was like they were nothing, but they were nothingness in the shape of a wolf. Branches and leaves crunched under foot they ran into the distance.

"What were those?" I asked.

"Shadow wolves. Members of the Shadow Pack, a terrible scourge on all of Cameria. Shadow wolves are fierce and stealthy. In their shadowy form, they can approach you and attack without warning. We would do well to stay alert, Logan. They won't go far. Just far enough to stay out of harm's way, but close enough to keep a watch on us from a safe distance."

Out of harm's way, he says. At a safe distance from us...

I loved his confidence, but I didn't share it. Those things were terrifying.

"But I couldn't see them at first, and then somehow I could. Is it like the tree? Where you can only see it if you believe it?"

"No, not exactly. The Shadow Pack take on that shadowy form, that nothingness you saw, by choice. It's their camouflage. It's part of what makes them so dangerous. They are very hard to detect until it's too late. By then, usually, they're already chewing on the back of your neck."

"Ew," I said.

"Well, it's true. They hate bright light, though, which is why they scattered the way they did. I'm a little surprised they didn't pounce more quickly. They must have already hunted. That would be good for us, but bad for whatever else they found before we got here."

Muggins marched right into the bush—into the bush where the Shadow Pack had just emerged and ran back in. I didn't want to get left behind, so I pushed my way through to catch up when I heard his voice.

"Aw, damn it," he said.

When I reached him, he was standing in front of what looked like a nest. It was on the ground, tucked into the nearby brush, but not hidden well enough. Only a single creature was left, about the length of my forearm.

"The Pack got nearly everything in the nest," Muggins said.

"There were probably a dozen or more before they came. At least we got here in time to spare one of them."

I looked down at the tiny creature, lizard-like in shape. It was curled up in the nest, looking up at me with glassy eyes, terrified and shivering.

"What is it?" I asked.

"That, my dear boy, is a real-life, authentic, genuine Teaspoon Dragon. Just a pup right now, not quite fully grown, but pretty close. He doesn't look like much right now, and he wouldn't have stood a chance against the pack at this tender age. But he'll grow far more powerful as he matures.

"That's a dragon?" I asked. "It's so little."

Muggins grumbled.

"Yes, of course it's a dragon. I thought I just said that. What else would it be?"

In my mind's eye, I had never imagined a dragon to look like this. It was so small, with its slender body like the baby iguanas at the pet store. Its skin was a dull greenish-grey, and smooth. Not rough or scaly at all.

"He looks so scared," I said.

He just stared up at me with those big, doey black eyes. His ears swept back, like a frightened cat, and little wing buds were just starting to grow out of his back, far too small to carry him in flight.

"He's an orphan now," Muggins said. "The pack made sure of that."

"I feel so bad for him. His whole family is gone?"

"It is. We should take him with us if he's going to have any chance of survival," Muggins said. "Leave him here, and the pack will be back for him."

I reached down to pick him up out of the nest, but Muggins swatted my arm.

"He may seem small and adorable to you, but that doesn't mean you can just do whatever you want. You're a smart boy, Logan. So, I'm told anyway. But you still have a lot to learn."

Muggins searched through his bottomless bag and pulled out a small tuft of white flowers.

"Here, use this," he said.

Then he handed me the tuft.

"For what?"

"It's white snakeroot. Be careful with it. The flowers are poison to you and me if we eat them, but it's like catnip for him. It will help you tame him. Just wave it under his nose and let him smell it. They're wily creatures, and he'll take some time to tame, so be patient with him."

I offered the tuft of flowers. He looked back at me, unsure. His jaw quivered as he made a throaty, chittering noise at me, like my old cat Socks used to do when he saw a bird out the window. He sounded really upset and that just made me want to hold him even more.

"Look how adorable he is. He's like a little kitten, trying to roar like a lion. But the roar won't come out. It's just a tiny little *mew* from his tiny little face."

I pushed my hand closer, and he took in the smell of the flowers. His posture relaxed, and his ears turned forward.

"It's working," I said.

"Just wait."

He sniffed at the tuft of flowers again and didn't waste any time crawling right up my arm and onto my shoulder. He nuzzled his face into my neck. Socks used to do the same thing when he wanted me to pet him. I pulled the little dragon down off my shoulder and held him gently. His whole body fit in my cupped hands as he sat with his tail hanging down.

"So, we can take him with us?" I asked.

"We can," Muggins said. "In fact, I think we must."

"Can I name him?"

"Teaspoon Dragons don't have much use for names," he said.

I thought about it for a moment and shrugged.

"That's ok. I'm going to name him Smidge anyway."

"Smidge?" Muggins said. "Smidge, the Teaspoon Dragon?"

I nodded.

"Yeah. I like that. I like that a lot. Smidge the Teaspoon Dragon."

I smiled as I looked down at my newfound treasure.

"So, he's mine now? Just like that?"

Muggins shook his head. I expected him to be crankier, but an adoring smile formed, and he looked oddly proud.

"He's yours, Logan. Just like that. Forever and ever. I must say, I've never seen one tamed so easily. I suspect you two will enjoy a very strong bond. Teaspoon dragons have a tendency to be much more fickle, and far more difficult to tame. Some are just downright mean, so don't let your guard down. You never know."

"Maybe he just needed some family."

"Maybe he did," Muggins said. "Maybe he did. But tuck that snakeroot into your pocket anyway, and keep it close just in case he gets feisty. He'll need to be trained, and we don't have much time for that. We have a lot of other important things to do, so let's get moving, shall we?"

SMIDGE QUICKLY DECIDED he likes to ride up on my shoulder when he's interested in seeing where we're going. Otherwise, he ducks down into the pocket on the inside of my jacket. It's warm and quiet in there, and I think it makes him feel safe.

"Where are we going?" I asked.

"We're going to the Grand Council, for a very important meeting."

"Really? Wow. I've never had an important meeting before."

"Well, today you do."

"What are we going to do there?"

"*We* are not going to do anything. *I* am going to present you to the Grand Council, and *they* are going to evaluate you."

"Evaluate me? For what?"

"Whether to anoint you to be a Keeper of the Light. Like Gideon. The Council will need to approve, of course, and they will need some convincing. But they also don't have much choice in the matter. So, there's that."

I hadn't prepared for this. And how could I? On the one hand, I didn't want them to reject me. Nobody likes rejection. But on the other hand, why should I care? I still had no idea what it even meant to be Keeper in the first place. But I did care; a lot. It was the curse of the overachiever. I didn't want to be rejected for anything.

"What is the Council?" I asked. "What do they do?"

"They govern. All of Cameria's territories are divided into five major factions. Each faction mostly cooperates with the others. But they all exist independently, like states. Take California and Nevada, for example. Connecticut and New York. But here, each faction has its own race, its own culture. They each have their own laws, values, religions, their own everything. While they do tend to cooperate with each other on many things, they don't always agree on everything. That's where the Council comes in. The Grand Council is made up of the leaders of each faction, and each leader is there to represent his or her own people. They meet to address common threats to Cameria and decide the best way to handle them together—most of the time, anyway. Sometimes they end up arguing with each other."

"What kind of threats?"

"Well, that depends. Do you remember the darkness you saw in the distance? The dark spot, as you called it?"

"Yes."

"Well, that. That is the single biggest threat right now," Muggins said. "And it's getting bigger as we talk. Karma is behind it all."

Up to this point, Smidge had been nestled in my jacket pocket, napping quietly. But as soon as Muggins said the word Karma, Smidge sprang to life. He popped up from inside my jacket with his ears swept back. His jaw trembled again, and he made that throaty, chittering noise.

"Easy, Smidge," I said, petting his head gently. "There's nobody here but us. Just relax, pal."

I held the white snakeroot flowers close to his nose to help put him at ease.

"He's got good instincts," Muggins said. "Good instincts, to be sure. But there's no real fight in him yet. That will come later."

Smidge looked around nervously. I could feel him tense up through my jacket, but eventually, he softened and slunk back down into the comfort of my warm pocket.

"Are we there yet?" I asked. "My feet are sore."

"We're making progress, Logan. Just have some patience, please," Muggins replied.

He sounded just like my mom. I could have been more patient and just enjoyed the scenery. It was beautiful, after all. The trees were full and healthy, and the light danced on the surface of a gently flowing stream. Water sloshed against the winding banks, and there was a vivid rainbow in the distance. After walking longer than anybody should ever have to endure in a single stretch, we came to a four-way fork in the road.

"I always forget this part," Muggins said.

"I've got it," I said. "Where are we headed?"

"To the Council building, of course. Have you not been listening?"

"I know, but what's the address?"

I pulled my phone out of my back pocket and opened the navigation app. But there was no signal. I had zero bars.

"That's not going to be any help to you in here," Muggins said.

"Why not?"

"You're in Cameria, young man. There's no cell service in Cameria. Things are different here."

"Oh," I said, sliding the phone back into my pocket. "Sorry. Wait. Do you hear rustling again?"

But he was distracted.

"I can never remember what to do here," Muggins said. "I wish Gideon was here, he always knew what to do. And if Gideon didn't know, then Grimesey certainly would."

"You know Grimes?" I asked.

"Of course I do."

"I never met Grimes," I said. "But I kind of wish he was here, too. Grandpa made him sound pretty great."

As I finished my sentence, I felt a strange sensation. Something in my pocket was moving. Vibrating, or maybe humming. Smidge was still in my jacket pocket, up against my chest, but this was coming from my pants pocket. I reached in and I pulled out my grandpa's pocket watch. It was making a weird noise. Not ticking. Not an alarm ringing. Not a clock noise at all. My pocket watch was mumbling at me. I pressed the button on top and flipped the lid open.

"I'm right here!" it screamed up at me.

The voice was coming from the watch.

"Ahhh! It has a face!" I screamed.

"Of course it has a face," Muggins said, with a chuckle. "All clocks have faces. How else would you tell the time?"

"It's not a clock face," I yelled. "It's a face-face. My watch has a face-face! And It's looking right at me. And it's talking to me!"

"An' who might you be?" the watch asked of me with a fancy English accent.

That's right. I know it sounds crazy. But the watch was actually talking to me, and with an English accent, no less.

"I'm—I'm Logan," I said, confused. "Who are you? And what is happening right now?"

"Ah, Logan, of course, I've heard so much about you. Delightful to meet you in person, young man. 'Ow-do-ya-do?"

"What do you mean?" I said. "How did you hear about me? You're, you know—a watch."

"From Gideon, of course."

"My Grandpa?"

"Yeah, that's right. Gideon used to talk about you all the time. All good things, in fact. He was very proud of you."

"What are you?"

"Well, I'm Grimes, of course. Funny, I thought I already said that. Maybe not, though, I don't know. I might need to get my springs checked. In any event, it's all water under the bridge now, young Logan. So good to meet you after all this time, it really, truly is. I've waited a long time to meet you, and now here we are. Just imagine that. You and me. Right here, of all places. Go figure."

After an awkward pause, he talked again.

"So. Where we headed?"

"Why do you talk like that?" I said.

"Like what? Grimesey said.

"Like you're English, or something."

"Ah that, right. Yeah, Gideon liked it. He said I sounded smart that way, always did my best work like that. You don't prefer it? All good, mate, maybe you'd prefer I sound like a cowboy from the old west."

He scrunched up his face, then he spoke in the most ridiculous cowboy voice.

"Howdy buckaroo, I reckon we best be fixin' to giddyup on outta here right quick. Whaddaya say, partner?"

Muggins and I looked at each other. I shook my head.

"No. Whatever that is, please stop it right now. And don't ever do it again."

"Ok, fine. Boston then. How about Boston? Are you ready for Boston?"

Grimes took another moment to compose himself. He took a deep breath and delivered, with his eyes wide open, his best Bostonian accent.

"Lobstah."

I blinked a couple times, not even sure what to say.

"No?" he said. "Oh, c'mon, that was pretty good."

"Yeah," I said. "Maybe just stick with the original. It's probably for the best."

"Alright then," he said, going back his English accent. "Suit your-self, mate."

"Yeah, I like that better," I said. "Let's stick with that."

"Right-o."

"So, which way do we go?" I asked.

I couldn't believe I was talking to my grandpa's pocket watch. It was a strange but pleasant distraction. As I spoke, I heard the rustling getting closer.

"Whichever way it is," I added, "we better go quickly. It sounds like the Shadow Pack is coming."

"Aw, blimey. You shoulda said something sooner, Logan. Look at me just blathering on, talking, yakking, spinning a yarn and all."

More rustling. It was a bigger group than before, and they meant business this time.

"Which way?" Muggins shouted.

"Sorry, far left! Take the far left path. And run!"

We scampered left as fast as we could into the thick of the trees, before coming to another fork.

"To the right, to the right," Grimes yelled. "Go to the right!"

"Not so loud, they're going to hear you," I said.

"Hard right!" Grimes shouted. "Hard right! And now to the left. Left, left, left! Go to the left!"

He was so loud. And he talked so much. I ran as fast as I could, trying to follow his directions. After a long painful sprint, we came out of the trees and into an open space. I slumped over for a second, completely out of breath. When I looked back, there was no sign of the Shadow Pack. But straight ahead of us, in the distance, I could see a castle-like building. It looked like a very important place with towers at the corners, iron grates on the windows and big wooden doors at the front.

"I don't hear anything," I said. "I think we lost them."

"We're almost there," Muggins said looking back over his shoulder. "Keep moving."

I looked down at Grimesy, still in my hand.

"Thanks, Grimes," I said.

"Ah, don't mention it, Logan. I'm always here to help, mate."

"I guess I'll see you in a bit," I said.

"Yeah, sure. Cheers, Logan."

I snapped the cover shut and put him back in my pocket. I felt bad about doing that, but what else was I supposed to do? He's a pocket watch, after all. Surely, he was used to it by now.

As we stood in front of the Council building, it looked much bigger, and more castle-like than I had realized. Muggins explained a few final things as we approached the entrance with its big wooden doors. It was a lot to take in, but I did my best to remember it all.

"Now remember," he said. "You're about to meet with the highest ranking and the most powerful officials in all of Cameria. When they address you, you dip your head with a little bow and show the proper respect for such authority. Every Camerian faction will be represented at this meeting. They don't always agree on everything, so things may get colorful. And loud. Be prepared for arguments, but don't argue with anyone yourself, regardless of what they say. You don't have any status here to argue with anybody. And if you talk out of turn, it will be viewed as highly disrespectful. So, listen carefully, answer questions precisely and don't speak unless you're asked to do so. Do you have any questions about any of that?"

"Yes. Can we go back home now?"

"No. Anything else?"

"No, that all makes sense," I said. "Answer questions directly, don't stray. Speak only when spoken to. Just like at school."

"Atta-boy. You're a quick study, Logan. Maybe you are a smart one, after all. Only time will tell."

The doors were guarded by two massive men in fancy uniforms. They looked like a special class of guard that only guarded the highest levels of royalty. It was easy to see why they got their jobs. You'd have to be crazy to try and pass them without permission. And good luck to anybody who tried. As we got closer, Muggins announced himself.

"Lord Muggins," he said as we approached. "I'm presenting this young man to the Grand Council. If we may, please?"

Without a word, the guards saluted his highness, Lord Muggins. They stepped aside and opened the doors for us to enter. As we passed, they tapped their spears on the ground and clicked their heels.

"Lord Muggins? I didn't realize you were such a big deal," I said without thinking.

I really needed to stop talking without thinking. This was important.

"Only in Cameria," he said. "And please don't make too much of it. It's just a title, after all. Nothing more than a title these days. So, let's just recognize it for what it is."

We walked into the main chamber, a cavernous room with gold accents, fancy paintings and ornately carved wood furniture. Our footsteps echoed as we walked toward the tall double doors at the other end. As we approached, Muggins casually waved his hand. He never touched them, but the doors opened anyway.

"How did you do that?" I asked.

"There's a time and a place for such questions, Logan, neither of which exist right now. Hold your queries for another time, please, and let us focus on the business of the Council."

Muggins wasn't exaggerating when he warned me about the Council. When the doors opened, it was chaos. Inside the room, fists pounded on the table and voices yelled over each other. A heated discussion was already taking place, and we walked right into the middle of it. The room was crowded, and the onlookers all had their attention focused on the center of the room. There was a table shaped like a pentagon in the middle, with one chair set at each of its five edges. Three of the seats were filled by some very important-looking occupants, and two chairs remained empty.

"Order," a voice yelled out from among the onlookers. The voice belonged to a tall, skinny man with a narrow face and a funny-looking mustache.

"We must have order," he called out again to nobody in particular.

I never got his name, but he sounded persnickety, as Mom would say. Uptight, and nasal, like he was talking through his nose.

"This meeting has not been properly convened," the persnickety man shouted. "Without Viceroy Smoak, leader of the Avian faction, and the Chairman of this Grand Council, no less, we lack a properly constituted quorum. This Council may not conduct any business in his absence. As the Junior Assistant Secretary to the Senior Parliamentarian of the Grand Council, I hereby demand order."

The yelling continued and he banged his hand on the table.

"Order, I say. Order!"

It was no use. The cacophony continued, even over the persnickety man's loudest objections.

"But the Light is being taken at a most extraordinary rate," one of the voices offered. "Without the Light, we are all doomed, don't you understand that? The stakes here cannot be overstated."

"The Qud Palmon Forest of East Cameria is over twelve-thousand years old," a woman at the table said.

She was older than Mom by at least ten years; a big, strong woman with hefty shoulders, meaty hands and a very sharp tone. And she was all business. The room quieted when she spoke, and all eyes turned to her.

"Without the Light, the forest will wither and die. When that happens, so too will its occupants. All of its people. All of *my* people. My proud and my noble people."

"Chancellor Pickelhaub," a voice responded. "Let us not rush to judgment and blame."

I was hard to keep track of who was who. But the woman at the pentagonal table was definitely Chancellor Pickelhaub. And she commanded respect.

"We have a process that must be followed, so let it run its proper course, shall we?" another voice added.

This voice came from a tall man with slicked back hair, sharp facial features, crystal blue eyes and a cocky smirk. I'd seen some cocky looks at school, but this was one for the ages. With just a glance, and a tilt of his head, you could see he thought he was better than everyone else. He looked around the table at the others—first at Chancellor Pickelhaub—then he turned to a man with white hair sitting across from her. The three of them sat at the pentagonal table, waiting for two more seats to be filled.

"Is that so? A process," the Chancellor said to the cocky man.

"I don't mean to blindly endorse her actions," the cocky man said back. "I'm merely asking the question: Is it possible that Karma is right? As a Council, are we not obliged to consider differing view-points and discuss such matters?"

"You don't speak for the rest of us, Adharma," Pickelhaub

snapped. "Qud Palmon faction rejects any such notion, and you would be well-advised to avoid anything even resembling the slightest modicum of support for Karma."

Adharma, the cocky man with the slicked hair, smirked and looked away from her. He spoke into the distance but didn't address anybody in particular.

"Again. I'm merely asking the question in fulfillment of our obligations as members of this Council. Is it not our duty, after all, to discuss and debate?"

I glanced to the other side of the table at the man with the white hair. He was quietly staring at me with a long, penetrating stare. He had milk-white skin, dark eyebrows, and pink eyes. He gave me a strange feeling, the way he looked at me and I wasn't sure how to feel about it. On the one hand, he seemed so holy, with an elevated sense of internal happiness, like the priests at St. Michael's. But there was something else I couldn't put my finger on. I could feel the judgment in his eyes. These people were so serious and so scary. Mercifully, he broke from his stare and turned to the woman, Chancellor Pickelhaub.

"I'm not saying that I endorse Karma's acts," the man with the white hair said. "But I do understand where she is coming from."

"Gabriel! Have you seen what she did?" Chancellor Pickelhaub barked back.

"She did unspeakable things," he admitted. "But the victims— well, I'm just not sure they were of the purest heart, if I'm being completely honest. Their actions were not always true to the Light. Not in any proper sense at all."

"What she did was unacceptable," Chancellor Pickelhaub said to Gabriel. "And she was properly banished for it. If we have any true interest in what's proper, let us at least be clear about that."

Gabriel, the man with the white hair, stared back quietly and considered the Chancellor's words. He seemed deeply attached to what he felt was morally right. But like Mom had said before, I wasn't sure I trusted his definition to be the same as mine.

Gabriel thought a bit longer and adjusted his position in his seat.

As he leaned forward, brilliant white wings showed behind him, extending from his back, clad in soft and shiny feathers like an angel. They fluffed a little as he settled back in his seat. Maybe he was an angel. Anything was possible at this point. And if he was an angel, then he must be good, right?

Something still bothered me, though. It's like the people you see on the news. The people that say and do really mean things, and then quote a verse from somewhere that conveniently justifies their action. They act as though saying the words give them a free pass. Like their actions were somehow required. But anybody watching knows they weren't. I wondered if he might be like one of those people, or if he really was as good as the words he used.

"What about Valkyrie," Chancellor Pickelhaub said. "Look at what Karma did to him."

"Had he been pure of heart," Gabriel replied, "perhaps he would have secured a more favorable fate for himself. As I've said many times, the Light would never harm a heart that is true. There is no dispute over Valkyrie's history."

Gabriel stood and leaned over the table with his hands placed firmly on its surface. His angelic wings stretched out, then tucked back in. His archer's bow sat propped against the back of his chair and a quiver hung at his waist, lit up from the inside.

He was just about to say something else, when a bird swept into the room from the main entrance. And when I say a bird swept in, I don't mean a sparrow or a blue jay. This thing was huge. With smoky grey feathers and massive clawed feet, it landed on the back of a chair, in one of the empty seats at the pentagonal table. The bird was four feet tall from head to tail, and its wingspan must have been seven feet across. As it landed, everything fell silent.

All eyes turned to the bird. In unison, they all placed their right arm across their belt lines and bowed. Muggins bowed, too. It was an impressive show of respect. Whatever this creature was, it was very important. I was trying to figure out why it was so important, when Muggins cleared his throat at me.

"Oh, sorry."

I put my hand on my belt and dipped my head, too, trying to look like everyone else. It felt ridiculous.

"Viceroy Smoak," the persnickety man said to announce the bird's entry.

"As you were," the bird said.

Yes, that's right. The bird could talk, too. First a pocket watch, and now this. And when I say he talked, I don't mean like a parakeet or a parrot. He had the voice of a grown man. A short-tempered grown man with serious business to tend to, and little patience for distraction. On his word, everyone relaxed their bows and stood back upright. Nobody in the room was surprised to hear the bird talk, except for me.

"You can talk?" I blurted out over revered silence.

I could hear Muggins groan as he lowered his head and wiped his hand down over his face. He was not pleased.

"Of course I can talk," the bird called Viceroy Smoak said. "And so can you. Not that you should. Not now."

"But you're a bird."

"Harpy Eagle, to be precise. Most days, anyway. Does that bother you, young man?"

I wasn't sure how to respond. The words, taken at face value, conveyed a sense of genuine concern. But his voice was angry. He glared at me with gloss black eyes, as his sharp taloned feet gripped the back of the chair tighter yet. His claws pressed deep into the grain of the wood. The feathers on his head puffed up and stood like a grey feathered crown.

"Perhaps this will make you more comfortable," the bird said.

Right before my eyes, it shifted its shape. His body stretched out, and his feathers began to fade, fluidly morphing into something else. His form poured down the back of the chair, and into the seat, as he gradually took on human form—not just any human form, but a very specific human form. The form of an old man in a red military uniform, like the old British redcoats wore. We had just studied them in history class that week, so I was familiar. And just like that, just like a dream, a redcoat was sitting in the chair looking wise and confident, stroking his bushy white mustache and waving a pipe at me. Had he always looked that way? Had I only imagined him existing in bird form? I just couldn't be sure anymore.

"You're a shapeshifter?" I asked.

"Well, you must be something of a genius," he said.

He looked around, addressing the room more generally.

"Look everybody, we have a young genius among us. Yes, of course I'm a shapeshifter, and I'm certainly not the only one. Not by any stretch."

"Order," the persnickety man yelled. "I demand it. We must have order."

"Yes," Smoak said, turning to look directly at me with an icy glare. "Let us have some order, please."

He had completely changed his shape, but his eyes were still familiar. Desperate, I glanced at Muggins for support, but he didn't look any happier.

"I'm sorry for speaking out of turn," I said. Then I bowed again.

Something about Viceroy Smoak's look made me do it. I felt like I had to.

"The floor now recognizes Viceroy Smoak," the persnickety man said. "Viceroy Smoak, you may address the Council."

"There's still one empty seat," I whispered to Muggins.

"Not now," he said, nodding toward Viceroy Smoak.

"I yield the floor," Smoak said, "I would like to hear from my colleagues first."

"As you wish, Viceroy," the persnickety man said. "The floor now recognizes Chancellor Pickelhaub, head of Qud Palmon faction, East Cameria."

The strong woman from the forest stood up from her seat again. She addressed the others at the table, but she was much calmer this time.

"As I was beginning to say, Karma has managed to activate the Lighthold and is actively taking the Light. This is a development that puts us all in grave danger. Not just me, not just the Qud Palmon faction, but every single one of us, all of Cameria, and likely beyond.

The Qud Palmon warriors are the fiercest defenders Cameria has ever known, and their loss would be devastating to all of us. If this Council and our alliance are to be of any value at all, then Karma must be stopped at once. Everything we have and everything we know is at risk. Karma's banishment should stand. With that, I yield the floor."

"The floor now recognizes Adharma, of the Proteus faction."

The slick-haired man with the cocky smile, Adharma, stood up again and addressed the Council. Muggins and I stood off to the side among the others, quietly watching.

"I made my position clear at our last meeting. Nothing has changed," Adharma said. "With that, I yield the floor."

Muggins grumbled at the words. Adharma whipped around, and pointed an angry finger at him.

"Silence," he shouted at Muggins. "You have no seat at this table. You lead no faction, and you'll silence yourself at once!"

Muggins stared at his feet quietly gritting his teeth. He rocked back and forth, trying to hold his words in.

Why was Adharma being so mean to him?

"The floor now recognizes Gabriel, of the Angelics faction."

Gabriel waved a hand to yield his time.

"My position is well known," he said.

"Very well," the persnickety man said. "The floor now recognizes Viceroy Smoak."

"Karma was entrusted with tremendous power," Smoak said, "and she chose to abuse it at every opportunity. She's made a mockery of her responsibilities, and she used the power she was given for nothing more than petty vindictiveness and self-enrichment. She was entrusted to maintain a fair and proper balance among us, to act as a force within a system designed to check itself. With such trust we also gave her the freedom to act. Freedom to make her own decisions. She abused that freedom at every opportunity. And now we understand she has also stolen precious artifacts, and is actively working against us. Working against this Council. Working against all of Cameria. Karma represents the single greatest threat to our collective existence. Our decision should stand firm. I move to adjourn on this issue. May I have a second?"

"I second the motion," Chancellor Pickelhaub said. "Let us now vote."

The persnickety man instructed them to submit their ballots, and quietly tallied them before making an announcement.

"This matter is now closed," the persnickety man said. "By a vote of three-to-one, Karma's exile has been upheld. Now, let us proceed with the next order of business—how to stop her."

"THE FLOOR once again recognizes Viceroy Smoak," the persnickety man said.

"Karma has gone rogue, in defiance of the rule of law. She has stolen the Lighthold and the Reflexor. The three standing Keepers of the Light have each met with untimely fates, and under circumstances we can almost certainly attribute to her hand. As it stands, no Keepers remain. Other than Karma, only a Keeper is capable of handling the Lighthold. If we want to stand any chance at all of recapturing the Lighthold, releasing the Light, and defeating Karma once and for all, then new Keepers will need to be identified. Without them, we stand powerless to act against her."

Muggins stepped forward out of the shadows.

"Permission to speak?" Muggins said.

"Permission granted," Smoak said. "But be swift, Lord Muggins, this Council has important business to attend to."

"The floor now recognizes Lord Muggins of the faction of—oh my. Never mind. Lord Muggins, you may proceed."

"First," Muggins said, "please forgive my interruption. This Council certainly recognizes that nobody chooses to be a Keeper, and nobody learns their gifts. Keepers are born. A Keeper's capabilities are far beyond the reach of any practice or desire. The gift is one of lineage, inherited from a family member. It can skip many generations. Centuries, even. We're very fortunate, however—"

"Lord Muggins, this Council doesn't need a history lesson from you," Smoak said, "so please move this along."

"Indeed, Viceroy. My apologies. Allow me to be brief. May I present to you Master Logan LeVec. Grandson of Gideon LeVec, our last and most recently departed Keeper. In my estimation, Logan is not only highly capable but perhaps one of the most powerful we've ever seen. Perhaps, I daresay, the most powerful Keeper that Cameria has ever known."

I was not prepared to be thrown into the spotlight like that. I was even less prepared for the laughter that followed.

Why are they laughing? Are they laughing at me? I think they are. No, they definitely are. Why did Muggins do this to me?

I had never wanted to run so badly in my life. I felt faint. I had fainted once before, and I felt close to doing it again. My knees were weak and my hands trembled. But Muggins stood by my side, reassuringly. As small as he was, he reached over and placed his hand on my knee.

"Relax," he whispered. "You've got this. You're going to be fine."

Then he continued.

"Logan's connection to Cameria is potent. And his beliefs and convictions are strong. I've seen it myself, firsthand."

"He's just a boy," Adharma said.

"Yes, well, about that. This boy, as you call him, he found me on his own. Nobody needed to convince him. Nobody needed to tell him or show him. And, whether he realizes it or not, he's already been well-trained. His mind is strong. His knowledge is vast. His abilities are likely unmatched. Gideon had tremendous foresight and did a comprehensive job in preparing him. This *boy* saw right into the portal. He saw right into the gateway to Cameria after my mere suggestion that it might be there. It was uncanny."

A rumble spread through the room as people whispered to each other.

"Is that so?" Smoak asked in a serious tone. "After a mere suggestion?"

"Absolutely. His abilities are stronger than any I've ever seen, bubbling at the surface and just waiting to come out."

"You said the same thing about that other boy," Smoak said, waving a confused finger in the air. "What was that boy's name, anyway?"

"Timothy," the Chancellor reminded him.

"Yes, of course. Too-Bad-Timothy. Such a shame what happened to that poor young man. *Bzzzt!*"

Muggins waved a dismissive hand.

"No, no, no. This is different. This is so much different. Logan even tamed a teaspoon dragon, and he did it in a matter of seconds. Seconds, I tell you. He has the gift, unlike any other."

"Impossible. Nobody can do that, not even the most gifted of Keepers has ever done such a thing."

"This is exactly what I'm trying to tell you. He's different. I saw it with my own two eyes," Muggins said. "It absolutely happened."

"It's true," I blurted out, proud that I finally had something to offer to the conversation. "He's right here. And I named him Smidge!"

Gasps echoed through the room, as I held Smidge up for all to see. Smidge sat upright in the palm of my hand like a puppy, with his tail hanging down.

Muggins cleared his throat. In my excitement to show off Smidge, I had forgotten that I still wasn't allowed to talk. The floor hadn't recognized me yet. Such an odd practice. I didn't really understand how a floor could recognize anything. It was just a floor, after all. They weren't my rules, however. I was just expected to follow them.

"I understand your doubts," Muggins said. "But what choice do you have? Look outside. It's already begun. It's happening whether you like it or not. What else will you do to stop her?"

Viceroy Smoak took a deep breath and released a long, tight sigh.

"Young man," Smoak said.

He turned in his chair and leaned forward, looking right at me when he spoke. His eyes were cold, and his voice was indifferent.

He's going to put me on the spot. What do I do?

"Do you have any idea what the Lighthold is?"

I froze. My tongue turned to carpet and sawdust filled my throat. My lips went numb. I probably would have run, but my legs trembled like quivering gelatin.

"Young man, I asked you if you know what the Lighthold is."

Muggins nudged me.

"Say something," he said.

Nothing came out.

"Young man?" Smoak insisted.

Why is this happening to me?

"Young man, I asked you a question. Do you know what the Lighthold is?"

I managed to shake my head, to indicate I did not. It was all I could muster under such pressure.

"The Reflexor?"

My mind went blank. I shook my head again.

"Do you have any idea at all what we'll be asking of you? The danger involved?"

I sighed. Then I lowered my head and shook it slowly.

"Lord Muggins, I'm afraid you've wasted this Council's time."

"Yes," Adharma said. "Very disappointing. Send him on his way. And with haste."

"Wait," Muggins said. "I'm not wrong about this. In Gideon's honor, I demand that you keep consideration open. This is a lot for him to handle. Just give him a chance to get his wits about him. I'm not wrong about this, not this time."

"Words we've heard before," Smoak said. "But in fact, you were. But solely in Gideon's honor, this Council will meet again in seven days. And Lord Muggins, you and your apprentice had better come prepared next time. Dare not waste any more of this Council's time."

Muggins bowed in respect. Then he cleared his throat at me.

"Oh right," I said. "Sorry."

I bowed my respects, and we left the room as fast as possible. Gabriel followed closely and slammed the chamber doors behind us."

"I'm sorry I let you down," I said.

Muggins waved me off.

"It was a lot to ask. I should apologize to you for putting you in that position. It wasn't fair and I should have used better judgment."

"So, it's over? We're done? What about the Light?"

"It's not over," he said. "You heard Viceroy Smoak. We have seven days to make it right. There is more work to be done, but you'll have to do most of it. I can only guide you."

DARKNESS CAME MUCH SOONER than I had expected. We spent the night around a campfire, eating food and bundling up in blankets that Muggins pulled from his bottomless bag. Smidge had a feast of his own. Muggins filled me in on who everybody was and told some of the most amazing stories about himself and Grimes and my grandpa. When morning broke, it was another long hike back to the burnt tree.

As we stepped back into Grandpa's back yard, it only took a second. I heard my mom frantically yelling my name. I ran toward her voice and, when she saw me, she ran straight for me.

"Logan, where have you been? You scared the daylights out of us."

"I was just out back, in the woods."

"Honey, we came home early this morning from Aunt Agnes' house. Since you weren't home, I just figured you had spent the night at Teddy's. You forgot to tell Bryce you wouldn't be home, by the way."

As if he would've listened.

It was weird. They didn't even notice Muggins, like he wasn't even there. For them, I guess he wasn't. They didn't believe in such things, as they'd told me so many times before.

"We came back here to pick up a few things from the house," she said. "And we were surprised to see your bike out front. I got so worried when we couldn't find you anywhere. What were you doing out there?"

"I was just having an adventure out back," I said. "In the woods. Checking on things, like Grandpa used to."

"What do you mean by *checking on things*?"

"Well, there is a tree out back, probably the oldest tree in the entire woods. During a big storm a while back, it got hit by lightning. And get this. The lightning opened a secret portal to a magical land called Cameria. I went inside and I saw the most amazing things."

Mom stood quietly with her hands on her hips, and her head tilted. She turned to Dad. Dad stared back.

"Don't look at me," he said. "This is your father's influence."

Mom knelt next to me.

"Logan, honey, Grandpa said a lot of things. But they weren't always true all of the time. I loved him dearly; I really want you to know that. Just like you did. But you can't follow his example. People expect you to tell the truth. You know that, right?"

I considered pulling Smidge out of my pocket to show her, but I decided against it. It would only lead to an argument about what he really was or where he really came from. This wasn't the time. Besides, if she couldn't see the portal or Muggins, then maybe she wouldn't see Smidge either, even when I held him up in front of her face. Would she just see empty hands, and accuse me of making things up? How would I explain that? It wasn't a risk I was willing to take.

"But I am telling the truth," I said.

She sighed.

"I don't want you going out there anymore. Ok? It's dangerous. I want you to stay completely off Grandpa's property until you can tell the difference between truth and fiction. Do you understand me?"

I wasn't sure how to respond, so I just nodded. She leaned in and gave me a big, warm mom hug.

"I'm so glad you're alright," she said.

"I know it's only been a day," I said. "But I sure missed your hugs."

I remember holding on to that one a little bit longer than usual. Over her shoulder, I could see Muggins walking off into the distance, looking at me. He gave a kind wave before fading away. He knew I needed to focus on this, and I would see him again soon enough anyway. At least I hoped I would.

6

My alarm clock jolted me from a sound sleep.

Monday already?

The weekend had gone by so quickly, mostly consumed by family errands, and I didn't even get to spend any time with Ginny. She must have had one of those weekends, too. Just as I'd get home with Mom, Ginny was leaving to go somewhere and just as she got back, we were leaving again. We would wave and smile as our cars passed on the street, but I really just wanted to sit under the willow with her and tell her about the things I had seen. I couldn't wait to tell her about Smidge.

Wait. That actually happened right?

I dashed over to my sock drawer and pulled it open.

Phew.

Smidge was there, curled up in a pile of socks, sleeping comfortably. He woke up looking like a happy kitten—groggy and wobbly, but excited to see me, so glad he could barely contain himself. He ran up my arm, onto my shoulder and nuzzled under my chin the way he does.

"Well, pal, it looks like rain today," I told him. Not that I really thought he cared.

After I dressed, I put on my jacket and Smidge curled up in the inside pocket. I grabbed the snakeroot blossom out of the drawer, gave him a good sniff, and tucked it into my pocket. When I got to the kitchen, Mom had already made breakfast.

"Wow. Nutella-stuffed French toast on a Monday?" I said.

"Sure, why not?" she said. "I was feeling ambitious this morning. Eat up, and don't be late, honey."

I sighed.

"Yes, I know," she said soothingly. "Your perfect attendance record is already tarnished with a single tardy. But that shouldn't stop you from giving your best effort every single day."

"I know," I said, as I inhaled the last bite of my French toast. I scraped the last bit of Nutella from the plate and licked my fork. "Thanks for breakfast, Mom. I'm gonna go. I'll ride my bike today."

"So early? Are you sure? It might rain."

"Yeah, I'm sure. I'm ready to go. So, I might as well go."

"Ok," she said confused. "Have a wonderful day, sweetie."

She kissed me lovingly on the forehead, and in the same motion shoved me out the door, turned on a heel and yelled up at my brother.

"Bryce, are you out of bed yet?"

I couldn't wait to get to school to show Smidge to Ginny. Teddy and James, too.

Luckily, I caught Teddy and James at the bike racks. I showed Smidge to them right before class. Luckily, they saw him right away, which was a relief. I hadn't considered what to do if they didn't see him until the moment I pulled him out. Ginny wasn't there yet, so I didn't get the chance to show her. When school was over I finally go to show her, and Smidge made Ginny squee.

"Oh my gosh, he's so cute," she screeched. "Can I hold him?"

"He's actually pretty nervous," I said. "Just pet him for now. He's just a pup, and still pretty shy."

She reached inside my jacket and gave his head a soft stroke.

"Oh. My. God. I'm usually not the jealous type," she said. "But I've never been so jealous of anything in my entire life. I want one so bad that I can't even explain it. Where did you even get him?"

A group of kids walked toward us. James and Teddy had already told others about Smidge. I had asked them not to, but they did anyway. I pulled my jacket shut as the group approached.

"Hey, I hear you claim to have a baby dragon or something," one of them said. "Sounds like a steaming pile of shit to me."

"Hey, easy," I said.

Another kid nodded his agreement. He didn't believe it either. Then I heard a voice from behind. But it wasn't just any voice. It was Chet Masterson's man-voice.

"Give me a break, that's no real dragon, don't be such a douche," he offered, without even seeing Smidge.

"What do you know?" I asked. "Have you even seen him?"

"Nope, don't need to. It's just a skink. Or a Mexican Alligator Lizard or something. This wise-guy is trying to pull a fast one. Don't listen to anything he says, he's totally full of it. He's probably just pretending he has a stupid dragon in some lame effort to make himself popular, or something stupid like that. Typical Logan the Loser."

Chet was never the most eloquent of my classmates. But here and now, knowing what I knew, he sounded like a complete fool.

"You're wrong," I said.

Then he smacked me in the back of the head, way harder than usual. So much harder than necessary to make a point.

"Quit telling lies, Logan. Nobody likes a big fat liar."

Once again, everyone within earshot, except Ginny, laughed. To be honest, I never found Chet funny at all, even when he picked on someone else. That wasn't very often, but it wasn't funny then, either. Maybe the others simply laughed out of a deep-rooted fear of his wrath; or the fear of becoming a have-not, like me. I was never sure why Chet had such an issue with me. Maybe he didn't like when other people got attention at his expense. It had to be all eyes on Chet. His parents did that for him, so he expected everyone else to do the same.

Satisfied that he'd gotten the reaction he wanted, Chet walked off mumbling something under his breath. I couldn't make it out, but I'm sure it was rude. As Chet left, so did everybody else. The Chet show was over, and people could return to their normal lives. A horn honked and Ginny looked over.

"My mom is here to pick me up," she said. "I'll see you later."

"Ok," I said. "See you soon."

She ran off to get in the car, and I started home, pedaling half-heartedly. It was a long ride, and I spent most of it wondering how I ended up being Chet's favorite target. Today hadn't gone the way I had hoped, and I realized I'd probably never be a *have*. But honestly, just being an invisible sounded pretty good right now. Anything was better than being an eternal have-not.

WHEN I GOT HOME, I went to my room, shut my door and fell into my bed. When the morning had started, all I wanted to do was go to school and share what I had seen in Cameria. But by the time the day was over, all I could think about was getting away from everyone. All of them, except for Ginny.

I wanted to go back and take her with me. Being there made me feel like I had special value. Not like here. As I lay there, quietly staring at the ceiling, Smidge crawled up the blanket and curled up on my chest, laying his head down with a relaxed huff.

"I don't know Smidge," I said. "I'm not really sure why I found you, or what I'm supposed to do with you. But I'm glad you're here. I don't expect you to understand what I'm saying. But I sort of grew up with people, mostly my mom, telling me how special I was. So, I've always figured I was special somehow. But just to them, you know? Because we're family. Everybody thinks their kid is special. I might only be twelve, but I understand that much. I never expected anything like this, though. The Grand Council, Cameria, you, Muggins. Any of it. Nobody did, except for maybe Grandpa."

Smidge picked his head up and looked at me, as if to say something. Then he huffed and laid it back down.

"What does it all mean?" I asked. "What am I supposed to do?"

He didn't answer, of course. He just snorted through his nose and fell asleep on my chest.

"Some help you are," I said.

"The thing about Teaspoon Dragons," Muggins said, appearing from nowhere.

"Ahh! What are you doing here?" I shouted.

"They're not big talkers. They actually don't talk at all. I'm not sure if you've picked up on that yet."

There he was, looking up from the floor, in his crumpled brown suit. Liver spots on his pale scalp showed through his sparse white hair. I was especially stricken by the white tufts of hair growing off the tips of his floppy ears, as he stood there holding his cap in his hand.

"Could you at least give me some warning that you're coming?" I said. "Or announce yourself when you arrive?"

"Now, what fun would that be?" he said with a chuckle. "I love to watch your face. Your reactions are priceless!"

"*Blaahhhhh*," he exclaimed, waving his arms in fake surprise, and laughing to himself.

So, this is what it had come to. Now, even Muggins was poking fun at me.

"Knock it off, Muggins. I'm really not in the mood today. What do you want?"

"You have questions," he said pointing at me.

Then he pointed at his chest.

"I have answers."

"Yeah, but how do you even know that?" I said. "Like, how can you possibly know?"

"What an interesting question," he said. "You know what? Nobody has ever asked me that before."

He shrugged.

"It's just what I do, I suppose."

"Ask me something else. You want to know why we've come together. Why I took you to the Grand Council so ill-prepared, and why they turned you away. You want to know why you're feeling so upset about being rejected from something you never even asked for in the first place. You're wondering why you care. And you want to know how you can possibly fix it all in just one short week. How am I doing? Am I close?"

"Um. Yes?"

"Ah, that's excellent," he said, swiping a finger through the air. "And the answer is simpler than you think. You already know everything you need to know. You just don't realize it yet."

"I don't understand."

Muggins scratched his head, thinking for a second. Then he looked up again, with lights in his eyes.

"What do you call the rash you get from brushing up against a prickle-thorn bush?"

"Prickle-thorny-itis, why?"

"How do you know that?"

"I just one of Grandpa's silly stories. It sounds ridiculous, though."

"And how, exactly, would one treat Prickle-thorny-itis?"

"Grandpa said you have to lick the slime off the back of a racer slug. Or else your skin gets really swollen, all red and bumpy like a giant raspberry. But that's just a story."

"Is it?"

"Yes, totally."

"Then why are we talking about it?"

"I don't know. You brought it up."

"Would you eat the fruit of a cankle-berry bush?"

"Absolutely not."

"Tell me about the fruit."

"Well, supposedly, it smells and tastes like the most delicious thing ever."

"Then why not eat it?"

"Because the fruit is sacred to some, so it's strictly off limits. You shouldn't even pick it, regardless of whether you intend to eat it."

"Have you ever seen the fruit?"

"No."

"Then how do you know all this?"

"Grandpa's stories."

"Oh, interesting," he said. "And according to Gideon's silly stories, do the Avians get along with the Angelics?"

"No way. They are sworn enemies. But they have a fragile truce to help keep the peace. Their truce is so fragile, he says, that it could be broken by as little as a stray drop of rain."

"Very good. And how would you get rid of a Rampart? With a bloodstone or a Pixie's Whistle?

"Bloodstone for sure. Bloodstone seems like just a rock to us, but Rampart's hate the smell of it. The high pitch of the Pixie's Whistle would only make it angry, and it might even attack you."

"Now tell me about the Lighthold. You know what it is, don't you?"

I nodded.

"Sure. It's a flawless neo-carbonite crystal, shaped like an icosahedron. A perfectly shaped twenty-sided crystal, about the size of a basketball. It's imbued with magical properties, including the ability to hold an infinite amount of Light or energy. It can even store magical energy, under the proper circumstances."

Holy cow, did that really just come out of my mouth? How did I even know that?

"Atta-boy. Very good," Muggins said, with a long, slow clap.

He sounded pretty happy with himself.

"And the Reflexor?"

I thought for a second, and it came to me. I actually did know what it was. I couldn't think of it under the pressure of Smoak's interrogation. But now I remembered.

"It's a reflective device. A complex set of mirrors and lenses. It was designed by Mephistophenes, to help light dark places, but he found a more powerful use for it. The arrangement of the mirrors is perfectly tuned to capture and channel ambient light and energy—like the Light in Cameria. The lenses and mirrors reflect and concentrate the light into a single beam to send it wherever you want."

I gasped in shock.

Once again, how did that just come out of my mouth? This is bananas.

"Very good, Logan. Very good, indeed, young man. And with the Lighthold and the Reflexor together, what might somebody do with them?"

"I guess you could use the Reflexor to send light straight into the Lighthold. For storage and later release."

"Impressive."

"Oh my god," I said. "Is that what's happening with the dark spot?"

Muggins wiggled his bushy eyebrows.

"Why don't you come outside with me," he said. "Let's go through a couple of exercises."

MUGGINS SHOWED me a lot about myself this afternoon. Things I never knew. He was really smart, like my second-grade teacher, Mr. Belding. Muggins was good at pushing me without making me feel pushed. He was good at building me up without letting me realize that's all he was doing. Just yesterday, I was dreading going back to the Council. I had been looking for ways to avoid it, in fact. But now I felt better about it. I was kind of looking forward to it, actually. Not to be cocky or anything, but I was actually feeling ready for this. And I still had a few more days to work with Muggins on our preparations. Regardless of what happens when we go back to Cameria, at least I'll get a break from Bryce and Chet Masterson. Today was quite a day, I would say. But a bigger day is coming.

7

———

S aturday morning, already. School was rougher than usual this week, since we were wrapping up some big units and preparing for two important tests at the same time. If you add that on top of living with Bryce, and all my training with Muggins this week, I felt a lot of pressure. The responsibility that came with a higher calling was a heavy burden to bear.

All the time I spent with Muggins made me think about Grandpa more than usual. I realized then that I had missed him quite dearly. Some days I just felt numb and didn't think of him much. But then I would get overwhelming flashes out of nowhere that brought an intense feeling of missing him and wanting him back; wanting more than anything for him to be here and to help me with this.

I even dreamt about Grandpa one night. We were sitting on his porch talking about Cameria and the importance of my role. It was so good to have him back. Seeing him in that dream, hearing his voice and his encouragement, gave me one of the most overwhelming senses of joy I've ever felt. It was so comforting and wonderful to see him, even if it was only for a moment, and only in a dream. I can feel that feeling now, just for thinking about it.

I was getting ready to go meet Muggins and had just finished tying my shoes, when I heard a knock at the front door. When I opened it, Ginny Mason's emerald green eyes were sparkling at me like a beautiful bag of gems.

"Hi," she said, as I pulled the door open. "What are you doing?"

"I'm just getting dressed," I said. "What are you doing?"

"I don't know. Nothing really."

Then she smiled and raised her eyebrows, like I was supposed to understand something. Something that shouldn't need to be said out loud. But I was never very good at that, so she had to say it out loud anyway.

"So, if you're not busy, then, you know, maybe we can hang out. Today. Just you and me."

Are you kidding me? Of course we can.

"Yeah, sure," I said. "Just for a little bit, though. I have to check on some things."

I know what you're thinking. Important plans with Muggins. Meet out back at the tree this morning. Grand Council, and all that. But cut me some slack here. I just wanted to spend a few minutes with her. Can you blame me? It's entirely possible that Ginny was the single greatest friend I'd ever had. I can't explain it, and maybe I've said this before, but when she's around, literally nothing else matters. There's no pressure. There's no judgment. It's just easy comfort and good feelings, all the time. And I liked that. I *really, really* liked that.

With Smidge nestled comfortably in his favorite pocket, I grabbed my coat, and we headed out to sit under the willow for a few minutes. We talked, we laughed, and before I knew it, Smidge had curled up on Ginny's chest as she lay on the lawn telling me a story about the time she got gum in her hair. As she finished, she abruptly changed the subject.

"You never told me where you got him," she said.

"Well, it's not too far," I said. "Just out back behind my grandpa's house."

Words can't describe how hard it was having this knowledge, knowledge of Cameria and everything else inside of it, and not being able to share it with anybody.

"Not far?" she said, "Well, exactly how far is it?"

"Just a quick bike ride, really."

She sat up, cradling Smidge in her arms. Her face beamed with excitement.

"Well, then, let's go! You *totally* have to take me there. Let's go right now!"

Crap. Things are about to get complicated.

"I don't know," I said awkwardly.

"Well, why not?"

"I just, I don't know. I tried to explain it all to James and Teddy, but they thought I was crazy even after I showed them Smidge in real life. My mom thinks I'm making it all up. And you saw how Chet was yesterday, at the bike racks. I don't need you turn on me too. That would be too much for me to handle."

"I would never!" she said. "Come on, just show me. Please? I'm dying to see it!"

"You don't think I sound crazy talking about this stuff?"

"Of course not. Why would I? I wonder about things like that all the time. Haven't you ever daydreamed and just imagined new worlds, secret worlds, magical worlds? Worlds so much more amazing than this little town could ever be?"

"Imagine? Yeah, I guess you could say I've imagined it."

"Well, me too. I do it all the time. Moving from place to place every time my dad gets transferred for work is hard," she said. "I don't think you realize. I've spent way too much time being the new kid. Too much time feeling uncomfortable. Too much time trying to find my place and make new friends among kids who've known each other since kindergarten, only to end up moving again and starting over. It's hard trying to fit in with people who've lived in the same neighborhood their whole lives, and played soccer together every year since they could walk."

"Yeah, I know what you mean."

"And honestly, sometimes I think it's more interesting to pretend I'm somewhere else. To imagine someplace really amazing and magical. Someplace where unbelievable things happen. Please don't tell anyone, but sometimes I just sit in my room alone, and pretend to be there."

"Where?"

"A magical place, a place that only exists in my imagination. I can always go back there, no matter what house I'm living in. I mean, this is nice and all, but what if there really was a door to a whole different world and you could just walk right through it? How amazing would that be?"

"Well, it would be pretty amazing," I said. "Believe me."

"It really would."

Then she sighed.

"I'd much rather go there than do what I have planned for later. I'm supposed to stay the night at Katelyn's house. I don't really want to, but my parents are going out to dinner. They're pushing me to put in the effort to make a new friend. I've made and left so many friends behind already that, at this point, trying seems useless. We'll probably end up moving again in another year, anyway. Just like we always do."

"I really hope not," I said.

"Me too. Then I'll have to start all over again. I told my mom I'd go to Katelyn's, just to get her off my back. But I'm thinking I might stay at Kaylee's house instead. It's a short walk, and what's the difference, really? The best part is that Kaylee spends most of her time on her phone. I don't have to put much effort in, I can just take a book with me and relax. I've stayed over before. She's not all that bad. I could probably hang out with her if I really had to."

"If you had to?"

"Yeah, that's right."

"What about me. Do you have to force yourself to hang out with me?"

Her face changed and lit up warmly. It was that sweet Ginny smile —so reassuring and honest.

"No, of course not," she said. "Not at all. I like hanging out with you. It's so easy."

"Ok, good," I said. "Because I like it, too. A lot."

I blushed as the words left my mouth. But, as usual, Ginny somehow made me feel comfortable again.

"You're somehow different," she said. "I don't know why. But ever since that day in class, when you finally decided to talk to me, everything has been so easy. It's like I've known you my whole life. Like you've always been there, somehow. Like a cousin I haven't seen in years, but when we get together, it's like we were never apart. Maybe that's what it is. Maybe we're distant cousins."

She giggled at the thought, and her giggle sounded like angels singing. When Ginny laughed, everything got better.

"Do you want to go see it real quick?" I said. "The spot where I found Smidge? I can take you there."

Her eyes shot wide, and she leaned in even closer.

"That. Sounds. *Amazing*," she exclaimed as she shoved my shoulder. "Show me!"

"Fine. Let's go."

~

I CLICKED my tongue to call Smidge over, and he climbed back into my jacket pocket. With Ginny on my handlebars, I pedaled straight to Grandpa's house. I dropped my bike near the porch and we dashed out back to where the tree is.

"This is it," I said, pointing. "This is the tree. I found Smidge just inside, in a bush."

She stared at the tree awkwardly.

"You found Smidge in a bush inside this tree? I don't understand," she said.

"I know it sounds weird, but it's just inside there. Like, right through there."

I pointed at the bush. I could see it plain as day from where I was.

"Right there?" she asked. "On the burn mark?"

She looked puzzled.

"I don't get it."

"Oh right, you don't—Hold on, this will help."

I tried to channel my best Muggins. I even tried to imitate his voice.

"Just believe it," I said, with ridiculous confidence. "Then you'll see it."

"What in the world are you talking about, Logan? Are you ok?"

Oh, good lord man, you're talking gibberish.

So, I tried again.

"Believe," I said, waving my hands with preposterous flair.

I must have sounded like a crazy, two-bit carnival hypnotist. My heart raced and my breath got short as I realized how insane I must have sounded. Now, even Ginny would think I was nuts. Maybe I was. Maybe I was imagining it all. Maybe everyone else was right, and I was just too crazy to realize it. I panicked.

"This was a terrible mistake," I said. "I'm so sorry. I never should have brought you here."

I turned to walk back to my bike.

"Let's just go," I said with despair. "Forget I said anything."

But she put her hand on my shoulder and smiled. Her eyes glimmered in the low winter sun.

"Logan, relax," she said. "Just take a breath, and tell me what you wanted to say."

"Fine," I said.

I took a deep breath and pointed back at the char on the tree. By now, my words were weighed down by self-doubt, and I wasn't even sure I believed in them anymore.

"This is a door, a portal. It's the entrance to a great and magical land, the land of Cameria. Just right through there. It's kind of like those three-dimensional pictures; you can't see it at first, but then suddenly you can, and you can't believe you didn't see it before."

She looked like she was starting to believe what I was saying, but she also seemed unsure.

"I know," I said. "It's weird. But hear me out. You probably just see a twisted burn mark on a twisted old tree. But me? I see the doorway to Cameria, a whole new place. A *secret new world*, as you put it. I can see it right there, right now. I couldn't at first. I had to let myself believe it was there; and when I did, there it was. The lightning opened it. If you just believe me, if you just believe it's really there, then you will see right past the charred wood like I do. It's like looking through a window, right into a whole new world."

She turned and looked again.

"Um, Logan. It's—"

Ugh.

"Sorry," I said. "I knew it. This was a terrible idea. You don't see it. You think I'm crazy, just like Teddy and James and everyone else."

"No," she said. "I see it just fine. And it's absolutely amazing."

WE STEPPED INSIDE and stood on the rocky ledge overlooking Cameria, but something was wrong. Cameria was changing into something very different than I had remembered.

"I can't believe this place," Ginny said. "Look at all of this, it's incredible."

"It is," I said sadly. "But it's also not."

"What do you mean?"

"Something has gone very wrong," I said.

"There used to be a rainbow at the falls, but it's gone now. The meadow floor used to be green and lush like something from a movie. But it's brown and spotty now."

The wind blew waves through tall dried grass, and trees that had once been bursting with life and leaf had gone completely bare. Not like fall when the leaves drop. These trees were decrepit and ugly— brittle and dying. I looked toward the mountains at the dark spot on the horizon. It was double the size it used to be. The whole of Cameria was getting darker.

"Uckh," I said. "This is not good. This is actually very bad."

"What's the matter?"

"Look, I can see why you think this is amazing now. But you should have seen it before. It was so much better. And apparently, I'm the one who is supposed to fix all of this."

I was interrupted by the sound of a new voice that was not Ginny's.

"Well, well, well. So nice of you to show up."

"Muggins, you startled me."

"And you disappointed me. You're late. Today is a big day, Logan. How could you be late for something so important."

He paused and looked at Ginny.

"Now what in the world is she doing here? How did she even get in here?"

Ginny scoffed, then she crossed her arms and cocked her hip.

"Rude!" she shouted, rolling her eyes.

"Sorry, Muggins," I said. "I lost track of time. I brought her with me. I just wanted to show her the spot where we found Smidge."

"That's very unlike you," Muggins replied. "She shouldn't have come here."

Muggins sounded grumpier than usual.

"Uh, Logan," she said.

Ginny was visibly uncomfortable, and I could understand why. Muggins is a sight.

"What is that thing you're talking to? And why is it talking back?"

I didn't get a chance to answer her. Muggins stepped in between us, placed his arm across his belt and bowed his respects to her.

"Lord Muggins of Codspire," he said. "And it is my immense pleasure to make your acquaintance, Miss—"

"Ginny," she said.

"Yes, Miss Ginny, of course. Please forgive my rudeness. Logan speaks quite highly of you. It's quite the pleasure to finally meet you in person."

I was so relieved. I thought he'd be angry. But he was actually very polite about it.

"Likewise," she said.

"Now, if you'll please excuse us, Miss Ginny, we must part company with you. We have some very important business to tend to, and I wish you luck on your return home. It's back that way, so just be on your way now. Please, and thank you, and all that polite nonsense we're supposed to say. Now off you go."

Then he turned to me.

"I don't think I need to explain what's at stake, so let us be on our way. Nice to have met you, Miss Ginny. Fare thee well, and safe travels to you."

"What do you mean *fare thee well*?" I asked.

"Certainly, you don't expect to bring her on such a journey. Time is short enough as it is."

"Well, I hadn't really thought about what I expected. But we can't just leave her here. We have to take her with us."

Muggins looked up at her, pointing a finger.

"*You* should not have come here, Miss Ginny. This is not a safe place for you, and you've put yourself in great danger by coming. Us as well."

He looked her up and down, studying her slender, bony frame.

"You'd be little more than a snack for the shadow pack."

Then he turned back to me and started walking.

"She can come at her own risk. But I won't be responsible for what happens to her. That's between you and her. And let it be known that I am none too pleased about this, Logan."

8

Well, of course she came with us. Try and stop her. Muggins was clearly annoyed, but not even the crankiest Muggins could just leave her there. Not even on his worst day. He might get huffy now and then, and he might fuss a lot, but he's not a complete ogre.

"How are we doing on time?" I said. "We won't be late, will we?"

"We are fine on time. For now. But I had hoped to get there early, for some final preparations. So, let's move it."

We started down the same path Muggins and I had traveled before, the open path that ran parallel to the river below, and eventually meandered its way down to the meadow floor.

"Careful," I said to Ginny. "Watch your step."

The hill was steep, with some bushes to the right, and a rough ledge on our left. We were making good time up to the point where we heard a familiar noise: Rustling in the bushes.

"Do you hear that?" I said.

"I do," Muggins replied. "I can't tell how far they are, but it sounds like they're coming fast."

The rustling got louder, and the first one emerged from the bush. Then a second, and a third. They backed us up against the ledge. I looked down at the water flowing below and it was about a ten-foot drop. The wolves crept closer, growling, and the one with the scarred-over eye snapped its teeth.

Ginny gasped and flinched, and that made me flinch. As I did, the brittle ledge gave way under our feet. We slid down the loose dirt of the hillside, and into the river. The strong current swept us downstream and as I tried to steady myself long enough to catch a breath, the frothy rapids rolled me end-over-end again.

"Ginny," I called out, trying to keep my head out of the water

She didn't respond. But I heard Muggins' voice not far away from me.

"We have to get out of these currents," he said.

But we washed even further downstream.

"We're going in the wrong direction," he yelled. "The Council is the other direction. We have to get out immediately!"

"What do I do?" I yelled, gasping for air. "It's so fast!"

"As soon as you can, swim to the bank on the right."

He strained to talk through the splashing and rolling.

"We'll collect ourselves at the river's edge."

I was powerless against the current. Bryce used to grab my hands and make me hit myself when I was younger, screaming 'stop hitting yourself' in my face the whole time. There was nothing I could do to stop it then, and I had even less control now. I was approaching a bend to the left, and the water looked smoother there. It was my best chance to scramble to the bank.

"Now, Logan," Muggins yelled. "Get over where it's smooth."

I paddled with all my might. I made some progress, but the current whipped me back to the middle. I tumbled down a small ledge of frothy whitecaps and over some rocks. The waterway split, and we were swept into a tunnel.

"Hang on to your hat," Muggins yelled. "We're in for a heck of a ride."

I wasn't even wearing a hat. But he wasn't kidding about the ride. Once we entered the tunnel through the side of the hill, the rocky river floor got smoother, like a water slide carved from stone. We swooshed to the left, then back up the bank to the right. We dropped down a steep descent, then hooked hard left again. We swooshed up the side once more as we zoomed around a corner, and picked up even more speed as we went.

I should have been more afraid. In the river, I was terrified, but this was strangely fun. Eventually, my ride came to an abrupt end. Without any warning, I found myself flying though the air, ejected from the end of the stony slide like a human cannonball, and hurtling down to a shallow pond down below. I landed first, and Muggins splashed down next to me. Water poured out of the tunnel, splashing down on top of us, and filling the pond until it poured over the side to a whole new descent. Muggins and I sat in the pond for a moment, collecting our wits.

"I've never done anything like that," I shouted. "That was awesome!"

"Don't be so excited about it," Muggins said. "The currents run very fast. We've come a very long way in a very wrong direction. We've lost a tremendous amount of time, I'm afraid. I don't know how we'll get to the Council in time, and I'm concerned about what that means. Now, where has Miss Ginny gone?"

There was no sign of her.

"Ginny?" I yelled.

Nothing.

"Ginny?"

A second later, I heard a scream from above. It was a girl's voice, and it was getting closer. Ginny shot out the end of the slide, flew through the air and splashed down between us.

"That. Was. *Amazing!*" she shouted, splashing her hands down in the water for emphasis "Let's go do it again!"

Muggins wasn't having it. I could tell by the extra-harsh grumble. Ginny looked over the edge at the next descent.

"Do you think there's another slide?" she asked. "Let's go. We have to go. Let's go right now."

Neither I nor Muggins shared her enthusiasm. We were in deep trouble.

"What's the matter?" she asked.

But before I had a chance to explain, I saw something out of the corner of my eye. I looked up to the rocks above and saw an animal peering down at us. I was worried it might be a shadow wolf again. But it wasn't. It was a snowy lynx, with beautifully marked fur. The lynx crouched down as I looked at it. I couldn't tell if it was hiding to stay out of sight or getting ready to pounce. It stared at me for a moment, growling, before it backed away from the edge and ran off.

"Did you see the way it looked at me?" I asked. "Not like an animal. Not curious. It had a look about it. Like it knew me. Like it knew who I was, and it had to get someone."

"You're being paranoid," Ginny said. "We probably just scared it. Three of us, one of it."

"Don't be so sure," Muggins said.

Smidge crawled out from my inside pocket, up to my shoulder. He shook the water off like a dog, then sneezed and blew some sparks out his nose.

"Sparks," Muggins said. "That's encouraging. He might be an incendiary."

"What do you mean?" I asked.

"Smidge. He could end up being an incendiary, a fire-breather. Teaspoon Dragons come in many types, different capabilities among them. Each teaspoon dragon is born with the full complement. But they usually end up favoring just one, over all the others."

"Really?" Ginny asked enthusiastically. "Fire? Like, real fire?"

"Yes. Absolutely."

"Oh man, now I want one even more," she said, ready to burst. "Where can we find one? I have to get one."

"As Smidge matures," Muggins said, "those sparks could become flames. If he's not an incendiary, then perhaps a sonic—able to shatter glass, wood, stone, or even bones with powerful rings of sound. Or a kryoplume. That's the opposite of an incendiary. They breathe icy clouds that freeze everything in their path. And then there's caustics. I shouldn't forget caustics. They can blow misty sprays of acid that dissolve the toughest armor. Or locks, or whatever else, you know—flesh included, of course. Very, very dangerous. You have to be extra careful with those."

"Are you serious with this?" I asked.

"Certainly, you're not questioning my honesty. What reason would I have to lie?"

"Sorry, I'm not. I'm just surprised. That's all."

"Last, of course, is the Night Terror, touchy creatures, fierce as all get out. They lull you to sleep with a soothing, whistling hum, like a sweet little baby dragon lullaby. But once you're under their spell—nightmarish hallucinations, the likes of which you've never imagined. It lasts until they release you. It could go on forever if they wish. Eternal torture."

"Right," Ginny said. "So, like I said before. Where can I get one?"

"That's complicated, young lady. As Logan can attest, it takes a fateful combination of luck and good timing, probably mixed with a little bit of tragedy, to get one. Not something we should seek out, if you know what I mean."

Ginny shook her head.

"No. I actually don't know what that means. Absolutely no idea."

She turned to me, looking for an explanation.

"I'll explain it later," I said.

Smidge tensed up. I could feel his limbs stiffen on my shoulder. His ears swept back, and his jaw trembled. The lynx reappeared from the ledge above, looking down at us. Smidge chittered as a woman strode up next to the lynx. She was tall and slender, with golden coco butter skin, and a sharp chin and nose.

Muggins sighed.

"Karma," he said. "I had a feeling you'd come."

SHE DIDN'T SEEM evil or horrible at all. She had a very motherly look about her, a doting face with kind eyes. Her eyes were gold in color, as was her hair. Not yellow or blonde, but like threads of actual gold. She wore a white gown and a flowing cape. From nowhere, a butterfly fluttered by. It was a meadowlark. A big one, with beautiful yellow wings and black swirls. It was an incredibly surreal moment.

"Well, what have we here?" she said, looking down at us. "Are you perhaps lost?"

Her voice was soft and sweet.

"Where could you possibly be headed, so far out this way? Don't you know it's dangerous in these parts?"

"I'm perfectly aware of the danger," Muggins said.

"Perhaps I can help," she said. "Where are you going?"

"Thank you, but I know the way just fine," he said. "I also know you don't intend to help at all."

She seemed genuinely insulted.

"Now, how could you possibly know that?" she said.

The words between them sounded mostly polite. But the tone cut deep, and it made me uncomfortable.

"I think she's trying to help," I said.

"She's not," he replied sternly.

"So where exactly are you headed with these poor, defenseless children? I wouldn't want to see anyone else get hurt under your watch. Haven't we already had enough of that, after all?"

"Anyone else?" I mumbled under my breath.

"Has there not already been enough suffering under your so-called *leadership*?" she asked.

Her tone grew sharper, and far crueler.

"Look at you, *Lord* Muggins. So small in size, yet so big with confidence. But, in fact, you're the Lord of nothing. The leader of nobody. Just a faction-less waste of space. Tell me. Why do you even bother to exist?"

Muggins winced, haunted by old memories—memories he hadn't faced for a while, and didn't care to be reminded of.

"That wasn't always the case," he said. "And you know it well. I don't need to explain myself or anything else to you."

Karma turned toward me.

"I see that look on your face. That look of boyish curiosity and youthful wonder. Has he not told you about what happened to the last group who put their trust in him? Be careful who you trust, or you may come to regret it."

There was something in her tone, more than the words themselves, something dark and sinister. This was the version of Karma that the Council had described. This was who the Council feared, and the raw cruelty in her voice sent a shiver through my bones.

Behind her, the meadowlark fluttered quietly in another loop. Its flight was aimless and beautiful and whimsical. It landed on her shoulder, and upon touching her, it froze—still, like a photograph. The beautiful yellow of its wings faded to ashen black. There was a faint crackle as it disintegrated, turning to dust and drifting away just as casually as it had arrived; into the flowing breeze as if it had never been there in the first place.

"If you don't already know," she said sweetly, flicking any remaining debris from her shoulder. "They're no longer here. Look around. It's just him. He's all alone, and utterly useless."

"That's enough," Muggins said angrily.

"The members of the Council are no better than you are. I will retake the role that rightfully belongs to me," Karma said. "Viceroy Smoak and all the other fools will each be dealt with in due course for denying me what is rightfully mine. They will pay for violating the Edict of Arno which states, as clear as day, that I should be Chair of the Council. I should be the one to rein over all of Cameria."

"Karma, it's not yours to take," Muggins said. "It never was. You broke the rules. You abused your powers, and you broke a sacred trust. You violated the sanctity of ancient artifacts, and all for your own selfish gain. The Council will never allow it."

"Is that what they've told you?" she said with a casual scoff and a wave of her hand. "Utter nonsense. Lies. Every bit of it."

She paused, then looked at me.

"You should know this. Hundreds of years ago, mine were a noble people. Powerful, independent and industrious. We were invaded and subsumed by Adharma's faction, our bitter rivals at the time. Our identities were destroyed, and our history was obliterated. All of it was erased from the books as though we never had our own existence.

I trace my lineage directly back to Mardagh, the greatest and most powerful leader we'd ever seen. A mixing of marriages defiled our lineage, and our culture was obliterated. But there was a faction within the faction, one that stayed true and did not simply blend or disappear into the will of our captors. The time has finally come for our rebirth, to re-emerge, strong as we once were, to retake our lands and to return to the glory taken from us centuries ago. The Council will kneel before me, or they will feel my wrath. So too will all who blindly follow them. You included, Lord Muggins."

"You're on the wrong side of history," Muggins said. "The portal was opened by the powers that be, to summon the Keepers and bring them in. They were intended to act as a check on you, to restore order and the rule of law that we all are used to, a circumstance under which we all flourish."

"Nonsense," Karma said, "We will return to power, stronger than ever."

"You're conveniently twisting old runes to satisfy your own misguided efforts."

"Let us just agree to disagree on this point, and allow history to be the ultimate judge on the matter. You should know I have some support within the Council. I'm not alone in this."

Then, suddenly, Karma looked at Ginny. It was a jarring look, as if she had suddenly realized something.

"Well, wait a minute now. You, young lady."

"Me?" Ginny asked.

"Yes, you. I'm very well aware of what you did last night. I believe you know that it's improper to tell lies, do you not?"

Ginny gasped. Karma knew something. And Ginny knew that she knew.

"Wait, what is happening right now?" Ginny asked. "But how could you know that?"

Karma reached up her flowing white sleeve and pulled out a

small silver mirror. It was old, like the antique mirror that my grandpa had on his dresser. She tilted the mirror at Ginny.

Ginny locked eyes on her own reflection and she went still. The sparkle of her emerald-green eyes was as dull as the rocks on the riverbank.

"Look away," Muggins said.

But it was too late.

"Silence!" Karma shouted.

Ginny sat frozen, completely transfixed, and she looked terrified at what she saw. She screamed out in pain, but she didn't look away. A red swollen welt rose on her arm. Karma thrust the mirror further toward Ginny, and Ginny screamed out even louder. A second welt raised on the side of her neck.

"Karma! Leave her alone," Muggins yelled. "This is precisely why the Council banished you."

He dunked his hand into the pond and swirled it through the air in a circle. In doing so, he threw up a wall of water between us and Karma. But the water didn't fall back down. It just hung in the air, suspended like a sheet of ice, breaking Ginny's gaze with the mirror.

"Over the edge," Muggins shouted. "Get over now, and head down the chute. Go!"

We dove over the side and began a new descent. It was a longer ride than he first, filled with twists and turns. Eventually, we eased into a long straightaway that flattened out and emptied into another pond. Alone again, we were even further off course than before.

"Are you ok?" I asked.

"I think so," Ginny said sheepishly.

She sat waist deep in the pond, soaked and sobbing, rubbing her arm and neck.

"Young lady, what was Karma referring to back there?"

"What do you mean?" she asked, as we dragged ourselves from the pond.

We stood on the bank, dripping wet as Muggins pressed Ginny with more questions.

"Did you do something you shouldn't have done last night?" Muggins asked.

Ginny nodded. I could tell from her face she was ashamed of being caught.

"I told my mother I'd finished all my chores and completed all my homework when I hadn't," she said. "But how could she possibly know that?"

"Do you lie or misbehave a lot?" Muggins pressed. "Break the rules often?"

"I wouldn't call it *often*," she said. "Just sometimes. You know. Now and then, here and there."

Muggins shook his head and pointed a bony little finger at Ginny.

"You should never have come here. You've put yourself in such unbelievable danger, Miss Ginny. Danger on a scale you've never imagined."

Ginny winced as Muggins checked her arm. The welts were swollen and raised.

"What did she do to you?" Muggins asked.

"Who?"

"Karma, of course. Now, who else would I be talking about?"

"I don't know," Ginny said. "I don't know how it happened. But when I looked into the mirror I was overcome. I could see myself. But not a reflection of me sitting in the pond. It was a whole different me, in a whole different place. Someplace dark and horrible. Karma was there, lecturing me about my behavior. She was lashing at me with something, a thin, bendy cane. I could see it happening. It was like an out-of-body experience, just watching myself being beaten, first across the arm, then the neck. It was horrible."

"Well, that's all very unfortunate," Muggins said coldly, "but you'd better pull yourself together in a hurry. You'll be fine soon enough. We have a long way to get back to the Council."

He looked up at us, and shook his head disapprovingly.

"You're both sopping wet."

He raised his hand and swept two lazy fingers in my direction. A gust of wind smacked me in the face, with a blast so strong it made my ears ring. The force knocked me over backward onto the ground. Ginny too.

Did Muggins just attack us?

"Hey!" I shouted, pulling myself back up off the ground.

I had reflexively defaulted to my oft-used, never-effective, go-to angry move. The reviled *hey* shout. And it was a good one, the best I had.

"Wait a minute; I'm totally dry," I said.

"Yeah, me too," Ginny said.

"Of course you are," Muggins said. "There's no need to thank me. But you're welcome, nonetheless. Now move it."

THE CONFRONTATION with Karma had worn me out. After hours of boring walking, I started to lose my patience.

"What time is it," I said. "I'm getting tired. And hungry. Are we there yet?"

Muggins grumbled.

I felt a jiggle in my pocket. Grimes was agitated, so I pulled him out and flipped the cover open.

"It's 9:01 p.m.," he screamed out. "And twenty-seven seconds, mind you!"

"Honestly," I said. "Why so loud?"

"Sorry, mate. I might be a touch hard of hearin'. And blimey, no, we are not almost there. We aren't even close. It's nearly a full day's walk to reach the Grand Council from here. A full day, I say."

My stomach fell.

"Everything is ruined," I said. "If we hadn't fallen into the river, we could have made it. Now what?"

"I think we'll be alright," Muggins said. "Always allow extra time, just in case things like this happen. You're lucky. I arranged for an extra day ahead of time with the Council. Viceroy Smoak was kind enough to agree; you know, given how woefully ill-prepared you were last time. No offense."

"Uh, thank you?"

"You're welcome, indeed. I wanted to get there early and take the extra day to help finalize your preparations. Settle you in. Give you some time to get used to being there. To relax, and not stress yourself out. I couldn't have you freeze up again like last time. That would be unacceptable."

"So, we have a whole extra day?"

"That's right. You're welcome."

"And when were you planning on telling me?"

"Just now. I literally just told you. Miss Ginny, you heard me, right?"

"I heard you," she said with a roll of her eyes.

"Good," Muggins said.

He looked around curiously.

"This looks like as good a place as any. We'll camp here for the night."

"Camp?" I asked. "With what? We don't have any gear."

"I brought some things in my bag."

"Sure, for yourself maybe. But what about us?"

"Oh, I have plenty."

He glanced around again.

"Yes, there. That's a good flat spot."

He held his bag out in front of him, with the top spread open. With a raise of an eyebrow, and a wave of his hand, a steady stream of equipment flew from his bottomless bag. A tent, blankets, pillows, lanterns, wooden logs, pots, pans, a kettle and food. Wonderful, wonderful food. One after the other, each of the items floated through the air to find its perfect place. With a snap of Muggins' fingers, the logs burst into a crackling campfire. The fire heated the kettle, which had found its spot on a hook just above the flame. Whole vegetables coasted toward the kettle and fell into uniform slices on their own, right before our eyes. The meat fell into bite-sized cubes that loaded themselves neatly onto skewers, each one perfectly arranged.

I should have been more surprised. But he did it all so casually, he made it feel normal.

"Whatever that is, it smells amazing," Ginny said.

"I know," I said. "I'm starved."

We dined like kings and queens, and with our bellies full of fire-roasted kabobs, we settled down wrapped in blankets around the fire.

"Muggins," I said. "I have a question for you."

"I may or may not have an answer for you, young man. But go ahead and ask it just the same."

"You keep talking about the Light. And Keepers. What exactly is the Light? What do Keepers actually keep?"

"That's two questions. Certainly, you know the difference between one and two, don't you?"

I sighed.

"I do. But can you just tell me?"

"Three questions now, oh my, far more than you bargained for. It's as if you'll never run out."

"I just want to know. Why can't you let anything be easy?"

"And that makes four. Honestly," he said. "Look. Keepers keep order, of course. And a few secrets. They keep balance. They keep equilibrium. Without Keepers, we get pandemonium. But most important, they are the Keepers of the Light. Without the Light, then Darkness. And right now, the hope is that they can keep Karma at bay. Do you follow me?"

"But it gets dark every night, and then the light comes back when the sun rises in the morning. What's so bad about darkness? We all get through it. Every single day."

"You're trying to apply concepts from your own home to things that exist here in Cameria, and, well, it just doesn't translate very well."

"What do you mean?"

"You said darkness comes when the sun sets."

"Right."

"But it's not right. That's what I'm telling you."

"Just explain it," Ginny insisted. "Just say what you have to say."

"Oh my, so many questions," Muggins said.

"Technically," Ginny said. "It wasn't a question."

"Fine," Muggins said. "It's dark now, is it not?"

"Yes."

"But do you recall seeing a sun today? Do you recall seeing it set?"

"Well, no, but why else would it be dark? That's my point. It's just dark, but it will be light again tomorrow."

He paused.

"Oh, the things you take for granted."

"What is that supposed to mean?" I asked.

"Answer my question," he said. "Did you see the sun set today? Did you see a sun at all?"

"I can't say that I actually remember seeing either, no."

"That's because here, the Light doesn't come from a sun. There is no sun. The Light is everywhere, it's everything, and it comes from nowhere in particular. The Light and the darkness I speak of are not the kind you're used to. It's not stars and shadows. The Light within Cameria is its very foundation, it's the magical force, the cosmic fabric, if you will, from whence everything else comes. The Light is that certain *je ne sais qua* that makes good things good. It's what makes happy feelings feel happy. It's what causes people to do favors without asking for anything in return. Here, for us, the Light is where trust comes from. And love. And respect."

He looked at me, then he looked at Ginny with a smirk.

Oh man, please don't say it out loud. Please, please, please.

"The Light is what makes your heart flutter every time you see Ginny."

He said it out loud.

Ginny blushed, and so did I.

"The Light," he continued "represents everything that is good and right, and fair and moral. And without it, the most profound kind of Darkness will be set upon us. Not just the darkness of night, or the darkness of a shadow, young man, but a complete darkness of existence. Judgment, prejudice, selfishness, blame. Lawlessness, lack of order. Failure of respect for other people. Greed, vindictiveness, hatred, and even war. Destruction for the sake of destruction. All of the bad, with none of the good. Without the Light, everything that is good will be gone. And it will all be replaced by something black and cold and ugly. Something unrecognizable by comparison. And it's not just Cameria. The goodness of Cameria spreads well beyond that portal's bounds. It spreads into everything you know, and even into things you don't know."

"Like what?"

"That's not the point right now. But may I remind you, you asked for one question, and, at present, I count six. Not including the one she asked. That one makes seven."

"I thought we agreed it wasn't a question," Ginny said.

"Fine. Six."

"But I don't understand. Why am I here? What does any of this have to do with me?"

"Eight questions now, my goodness. Look—the Cosmos likes balance. What goes around, comes around. As for Karma, well, she was supposed to be the cosmic vehicle through which that balance is achieved—personified and empowered. People do things and, if necessary, she can give out karmic responses. Cosmic payback, if you will, for people's wrongdoings."

"So, she has the power to punish people for their bad behavior?"

"In a manner of speaking, yes, that is what she is supposed to be doing. But fairly, and under certain rules and within reasonable bounds, of course. She stopped following the rules, however, and she ignored all the bounds."

"So, if she has so much power, why is there no check on her? Who checks Karma?"

Muggins chuckled innocently.

"Well, you do, of course," he said, as if nothing could be more obvious.

"There might be one other. I sense that may be true. But for now, you're it. Anyway, get some rest. Tomorrow we'll discuss the Grand Council. For now, though, you need to sleep."

"I. But. Whoa. That's a lot to process," I said.

It was late, and Muggins was right. As frustrating as the conversation was, I had no desire to argue with him. I was exhausted, and we could always talk more later. We filed into the tent and curled up into our sleeping bags. I wasn't sure if I would be able to sleep after the day I'd had, but it sure felt good to lie down. Really good. So good I don't even remember drifting off to sleep.

I WOKE up to the smell of breakfast cooking. The air was cold and heavy, but it smelled of the most delectable breakfast you can imagine. Ginny woke up right after, and we had the most delicious meal. I was enjoying my food just fine until it hit me. Today was a very big day. I was anxious about meeting the Council. What if they rejected me again? Worse yet, what if they mocked me? I quickly became consumed by self-doubt.

"What's going to happen at the Council today?" I asked.

"Same as before," Muggins said. "You'll be evaluated."

"And then what?"

"I sincerely hope that you pass this time and be anointed a Keeper of the Light. If you fail again—I mean, if they decide—Well, let's just say, it's my sincere hope that you will pass. How's that?"

"Fail? I failed?"

I'd never failed at anything.

"Let's not spend our time focusing on words and their meanings and all of that silly nonsense," he said, waving a dismissive hand. "Let's just pay attention to what lies ahead."

"What's he supposed to do, though?" Ginny asked.

Muggins grumbled at her question.

"Fine. Look. As legend has it, there were originally three. The Keepers of the Light. Anointed as such by the Grand Council many, many generations ago and entrusted with tremendous responsibility. It was a recognition that they were imbued with special capability at birth, well beyond the abilities of us normal folk."

Ginny looked down at Muggins curiously.

"*Us* normal folk?" she asked.

"Yes, exactly. You look confused, Miss Ginny. Have I confused you?"

"No, I'm not confused at all. Some of us might be. But it's not me."

"Splendid. As I was saying, there were three original Keepers. People do things they shouldn't do, and they make decisions they shouldn't make. Here in Cameria, Karma is meant to act as a check and set things back toward the middle where they belong. The Cosmos likes balance, like I said last night. It was a fine plan to start out, but she grew drunk on her own power. She showed beyond a doubt that she didn't care for the rules, or for balance or anything of the sort. She only cared for herself and what she could take, by abusing the power she had been entrusted with. Now, that's where you come in," he said, pointing a finger at me.

"Me?"

"Yes, that's right."

"I don't understand."

"Our wise old elders, generations before us, recognized the risk in giving her such power. Power meant to check others desperately needed a check of its own. Three at a time, the Keepers serve as checks on Karma, waiting to be called upon when needed."

"So, there are other Keepers on the Council that can help?" I asked. "That's great!"

"Oh, no. Absolutely not," Muggins said. "Keepers never reside in Cameria, the separation serves as a buffer, like a moat between a castle and its invaders. It's meant to avoid undue influence. The separation preserves their hearts and minds. It has to be that way. There should never be a time where a Keeper is called upon to do a job, only to be unable because their mind is clouded by a relationship or emotion. Keepers must keep the Light— that is all, and nothing more."

I shook my head, frustrated.

"So why can't the other two help us?"

"There are three, at the most, at any given time. That much is true."

He paused and looked at me.

"When one of the Keepers passes, only their descendent, hopefully somebody they've already properly trained, can assume their role. The Council has no power to seek out new Keepers. It must rely on a properly trained volunteer to step forward and assume that role. Gideon was it, Logan. He was the last."

"You said there were three. What about the others?"

"They're all gone. Now we have to start over with a whole new class of Keepers."

"With me? All by myself?"

"Maybe. Possibly. Well, yes, most definitely. At least for now. Does that trouble you, young man?"

"Yes, it troubles me. Why do I have to do this all by myself? Let's just go find two more."

"A lot remains to be determined, Logan. But time is incredibly short, as you can see. We desperately need a new class of Keepers, a new generation. Hopefully, you will be the first. I sense there may be a second. We still need to find a third. Well, what I should have said is that a third needs to *come forward*, just like you did."

"I came forward?"

"Yes, of course you did. Even if you didn't realize it then, when you went looking for me in that drawer, that was the first step in your pursuit. You did come looking for this, whether you realize it or not. There's no going back now."

"But I didn't come looking for this. I didn't ask for any of this. I just came looking for you."

Muggins pointed up at me.

"Exactly! And I am part of all of this. Don't you see? This is your destiny, Logan, whether you accept it or not."

"What about Ginny, and the welts on her arm and neck? Karma was standing there looking down at us. She never moved. She never even touched Ginny. Can she do that to me, too?"

"But she did touch me," Ginny said, "I could see it in the mirror."

"Absolutely," Muggins exclaimed, again pointing a crooked little finger. "That's what I'm telling you."

"Exactly what?" I said.

My frustration grew.

"She was here, and in the mirror? At the same time? Like a parallel universe?"

"Not exactly, no. But something like that, yes. Far too difficult to explain that right now, we have to get to the Council. Please, let us finish our breakfast and pack up, shall we? There's a long day ahead of us, a long day indeed."

WITH OUR CAMP PACKED UP, we set out on foot. As we hiked across the meadow, the light of day, dim as it had become, grew ever dimmer. It was shameful to see such beauty disintegrating right in front of us. And for what purpose? A selfish one.

"Is your arm ok?" I asked. "And your neck?"

"It stings," she said. "But I'll be ok."

"Muggins," I said. "What happened back at the pond? How did Karma do that to Ginny?"

"She's very powerful," Muggins said.

"But how does she use those powers? What caused those marks on Ginny? Karma wasn't even near her."

I felt bad for asking. I could see my questions were making her uncomfortable. She didn't want to be reminded. Maybe she was even ashamed of being caught and publicly punished. But I couldn't help it. My curiosity had gotten the better of me.

"When she shows you your reflection in a mirror," Muggins said, licking the last bits of breakfast from his fingers, "it's no ordinary reflection. When you see yourself in *her* mirror, the reflection you see is not the you that is standing there looking into the mirror. It's a more abstract reflection—an internal reflection on your past bad deeds. All your past misbehaviors. All the rules you broke. She knows about it, she shows it to you, and then she doles out her punishment. You know how people say you shouldn't do a certain thing, because Karma will come back to haunt you?"

"Yes."

"Well, that's exactly what they're talking about."

"But how?" I asked.

"It can be any punishment she wants. And it can be as harsh as she decides it should be. When Ginny looked into the mirror, she saw herself receiving some lashes with a reed. For others, it could be different. Karma decides. She does what she wants, when she wants."

"That's so weird," I said. "It's almost like what happened to Bryce with his car on Christmas Day. When he looked at himself in Mom's makeup mirror, his remote-control car exploded."

"It's not *almost* like that, Logan. It's *exactly* like that."

"No way! That's impossible."

"Is it?"

"But how can you even know about that?"

"Yes, exactly, how can I even know? It's an interesting question, isn't it? I know a lot of things. It's kind of what I do. You don't get to where I've gotten without knowing things. One other thing I know, and you probably should, too. Gideon didn't just catch a cold or a flu. When he went back to Cameria that day, he confronted Karma. Perhaps that wasn't the wisest of decisions. There was quite an ordeal that followed, and in the end, Karma placed a cursed illness upon him."

"Wait— What? Are you kidding me?"

"I wish I was."

"I can't believe she did that. Grandpa was right, Karma really is a—"

"Hey, watch it, now," Muggins said. "Mind your rules and clean up your language. You have to maintain proper behavior, and don't give her anything to work with."

"What is that supposed to mean?"

"Are you allowed to curse at home? I suspect not. Now, I have to say, every time my confidence is restored in your smarts, young man, you say something peculiar that raises new questions in my mind all over again."

"Rude!" Ginny said, shaking her head. "So incredibly rude."

"Look, it's very simple, so I'll just lay it out loud for you in simple terms. Every time you do something wrong, every time you break a rule, every time you do something you shouldn't do, Karma gets a chance to give you some payback. Ok? So don't break the rules and she's powerless against you. That's it. That's why I have so much faith in you, Logan. You've done right all your life. You have a strong moral compass, you follow the rules, you're a good boy. That will all be a tremendous strength against her. When was the last time you broke a rule of any kind?"

"I can't really remember. I usually try not to. People say I'm no fun. I'm not living my life. That I should be more like them and take more risks and break more rules. Live a little, they say."

"This is my point. Gideon lived a long life and made some choices that were not always the best. He left himself vulnerable. Now, I don't mean to speak ill of him, he was a great, great friend of mine and a great and loyal Keeper. But he had some weaknesses, some vulnera-bilities—some cracks in his armor, if you will. You, on the other hand —you may not realize it, but your greatest strength actually lies in your youth and inexperience. Your lack of living, as your friends put it. You haven't had a chance to make as many mistakes. And that makes you vastly stronger against her. Far less vulnerable."

"You really believe that? You really believe in me?" I said, waving a hand toward the impending darkness. "To deal with all of this?"

"Of course I do. One hundred percent. I wouldn't have brought you here if I didn't. The Grand Council may not realize it yet, but I do. You are our last, best chance to defeat Karma. There is no other way."

"Aren't there rules for her? Why doesn't she follow them?"

Muggins chuckled kindly at my suggestion. I realized as soon as I said it how naive it sounded.

"Not everybody follows the rules, Logan."

"So, there's just me now? That's the plan? I'm sorry, Muggins, but that seems like a really bad plan."

"So how do we stop her," Ginny asked. "How do we take back the Light she's already stolen? I mean, look around, it's already kind of gone. So, what do we do?"

"It's nothing we've had to address before. I have some ideas, as do others on the Council, but nothing is certain yet. First, we need a Keeper. We have Logan. Karma will probably have Kismet and the shadow pack on her side. And, more than likely, the Vapes as well. It will be a lot to overcome."

"Kismet?" Ginny asked. "Vapes?"

I sighed a long sigh.

"I'm so not ready for this."

"I'll explain in good time. For now, we just need to get back to the Council," Muggins said. "We can't be late. They won't look upon it favorably. Grimes, how long before we reach the Grand Council?"

Grimes rustled in my pocket, and I snapped him open.

"You're definitely going to be late," he screamed. "You'll never make it in time! No chance at this rate! No chance whatsoever."

Muggins winced. I couldn't tell what bothered him more—our tardiness, or Grimes' screaming.

"Walking isn't going to do it," Muggins said. "We'll need faster transport if we're going to make it. Let's find another pond."

"A pond?" Ginny asked.

"Yes, this direction. Come quickly."

❧

MUGGINS LED us down a path through the meadow, among the rolling knolls. In the distance, a lone Qud Palmon guard marched, keeping watch over the perimeter at the forest's edge. His body was bulky and strong, like an Orc, with a squat lower body, thick muscular arms and massively oversized hands. His fist must have been triple the size of my head. His barrel chest and broad shoulders were clad in plate armor, but with the way he moved, he didn't seem to notice it was there. A heavy sword hung from his belt.

"Stop right here," Muggins said. "Don't move a muscle."

As the guard patrolled, members of the shadow pack approached him from the distance, cold-blooded killers in all their vicious noth-ingness. He drew his sword and held it at the ready while they circled, but they closed in tighter, nonetheless. As he waved his sword, a fog appeared behind him as if from nowhere. The misty cloud flowed from the forest's edge and filled the gap between the guard and the trees.

"Oh goodness," Muggins grumbled. "A vapor is forming. This is very, very bad."

"What's so bad about fog?" Ginny asked.

"A fog is fine, Miss Ginny. But that's not fog, that's a vapor. A vapor is something different altogether."

"Is it, though?"

"Absolutely. Keep low and out of sight, Miss Ginny. You too, Logan. And do as I say."

The vapor grew thicker, and the shadow wolves persisted. The guard swiped his sword, but it passed through their nothingness with no effect.

In the distance behind the guard, a glowing blue spot pierced through the fog, just a tiny point of blue light emerging from the vapor.

"Look away from it," Muggins said. "Look away from the blue light. Don't stare. Whatever you do, don't stare at it."

It was such a beautiful blue light. A happy, pleasant, tranquil shade of blue. Stunningly beautiful, coursing elegantly through the soft white mist. I felt so relaxed, like I was floating, and my body tickled from head to toe. I'd never seen anything so simple that made me feel so happy and so good. All I wanted was to get closer to it. To stare at it longer. To feel more of that feeling. Then the spot of light emerged from the vapor altogether, and behind it was a terrifying creature. The beautiful blue spot of light was glowing in the palm of its hand.

"It looks like a plague doctor," Ginny said.

"No, you have it backwards," Muggins said. "That's a Vapor Wraith. Plague doctors look like them. The Wraiths are born of the vapor, and they materialize from nothing. They enchant you with that glowing ember of light in their palm, and then they steal your breath away before you even realize what's happening."

"Then what?" Ginny asked.

"No breath, no life. It's really quite simple." he said. "Seldom seen, the Wraiths became legends of their own making. It was once believed that they could steal away disease. The earliest plague doctors modeled their garb after the Vapor Wraiths—Vapes as we sometimes call them—with heavy black robes, and begoggled masks. They did so in hopes of taking on magical curative abilities. They believed disease could be coaxed out of the victims by the disguise."

"Did it work?"

"In fact, the Vapes did no such thing. The only thing a Wraith will coax out of you is your breath, right out of your lungs. And they'll steal your life away."

Muggins' voice slowly faded into an enchanting tune; harps perhaps, and my vision went dark. I couldn't see anything but that cool blue glow, glimmering against a backdrop of pure blackness. It got closer, grew brighter, and the calm and happy feeling grew even stronger. I reached out to grab it, but as I did, it started to move away from me, deeper into the darkness. I tried chasing it. But no matter how hard I tried, I could never get close enough to match the feeling of that first wonderful glance.

I felt a rude jolt. Daylight punched through the darkness, and I looked down to see Muggins. He had grabbed my leg and was violently shaking me from my trance. My head was cloudy, and I felt disoriented. I pointed to where I thought I had been just a second ago.

"How did I get all the way over here, from all the way over there?"

Muggins had that look.

"I told you not to stare at it, right?"

"I tried, but I couldn't help it. It was just so magical. It felt so good to look at it."

"You're lucky to be alive," Muggins said. "And if I hadn't reached you when I did, it most certainly would have stolen your breath. You were walking right to it, you nincompoop. Now, get back behind the knoll and stay out of sight!"

The happiness wore off, and calm shifted to crankiness. I pushed

Muggins away from me, and he fell to the ground. All I wanted was another short glimpse of the beautiful blue glow, but he was keeping me from it. That stirred a rage inside me that I'd never felt before. He grabbed my coat and pulled me down, close to his face.

"Look at me, Logan."

"Knock it off," I said, as I tried to push him away again. "Get the hell away from me!"

That's right. I said it. And nobody was more surprised than I was. I could see myself pushing him and I could hear myself saying the words, but I barely even recognized the person I had become. Muggins stood back up and dusted himself off.

"It will wear off in a moment," he said. "You need to have some patience. In the meantime, I'll try my best to do the same."

"I feel dizzy," I said.

"I know. Just keep looking at me," he said. "Stay calm and don't try to do too much. Give it a minute to wear off."

He pulled some blue tinted glasses from his bag and put them on my face, which helped calm me down. With my rage having passed, I felt terrible for the way I had treated him.

"I'm sorry for what I said. I don't know what came over me. I never talk to anyone that way."

"It's fine," Muggins said. "They possess an incredibly potent magic, it's a powerful charm. Once you're in its grip, it's hard to break free. Look out there and you'll see what I mean. It's time you understood the true power of what we're up against."

"But you told us not to look," Ginny said.

"The lenses will keep him safe for now," he said, handing her another pair. "Stay down low."

Another Wraith emerged from the vapor. Its long black smock flowed and dragged across the ground as it stomped toward the guard. The blue spark glowed brightly in its palm as it marched toward him.

"Why isn't he doing anything?" I asked. "He should do something."

"He can't," Muggins said. "It's already too late."

"Why can't he do something?"

"You know that feeling you felt staring at the blue light?"

"Yeah."

"We call that light the Spark of Aramore. He feels it too, just the same as you did. He has no desire to stop looking, no matter what price he pays for doing so. It feels too good, and he'll give anything for just a few more seconds. Even his own life. You would have done the same if I hadn't stopped you."

The Wraith shoved the guard to the ground and knelt beside him, with its knee on his chest and its hand held just above his face. The Spark of Aramore hovered right before his eyes, fixing him in its hypnotic trance.

The Vape pulled back its smock and opened a metal tube on its belt. Like steam from a hot cup of coffee, a wispy mist rose from the guard's mouth and floated casually into the tube. When it stopped, the wraith capped the tube shut.

"That's it," Muggins said. "It has stolen his breath. And with his breath, his life. May the gods be kind to his soul."

Muggins turned to look at me.

"That's it?" I asked. "He's gone? But he didn't even try to fight it. Why didn't he fight back?"

"The Wraiths' power lies not their ability to fight, but their ability to take the fight out of others. An enemy who won't fight back is easily defeated. The trick with Vapes is finding a way to keep the fight within you."

"How do you do that?"

Muggins was about to answer when two men emerged from the tree line. They were not Qud Palmon, they were just two ordinary people. And they were walking toward the Wraith and the fallen guard. It only took me a second to recognize one of them.

"That's Adharma, the cocky guy from the Council. What is he doing here? And who is he with?"

"That's Kismet," Muggins said uneasily. "Kismet is a devout loyalist to Karma, and he's something of a shepherd of the Shadow Pack. The pack obeys Kismet's every command, and they don't do a thing unless he says so. A more interesting question is why Adharma is here with him. This is a troubling development."

As the men approached, the Wraiths dissolved back to a vapor and faded from sight. Adharma knelt next to the guard's body and studied his face. He looked at his armor, his boots and his sword. He even pulled back his lips and examined the guard's teeth. Then he bowed his head, closed his eyes and gradually assumed the guard's form. Having taken the precise form of the Qud Palmon guard, Adharma stood up and marched back into the forest.

"Wait," Ginny gasped. "What just happened?"

"Interesting," Muggins said. "Well, for one thing, we just learned that Adharma is a shifter. Beyond that, I'm really not sure. Either he's secretly working in favor of the Council, or—"

"Or what?" Ginny demanded.

"Or he's secretly working against it."

9

———

"There's nothing more we can do for him. We need to get back on task," Muggins said, sounding more worried than usual. "We need to find transport soon, or we'll never make it back in time. Let's move closer to the water."

We veered off and cut a path across the meadow floor toward the main river. But the further we walked, the boggier it got. The ground grew moist and squishy under my feet.

"Aw man," Ginny said. "My shoes will be ruined."

"It' so humid," I said.

"And what's with all the bugs," Ginny said, sounding disgusted. "The farther we walk, the worse they get."

As I swatted at the flying insects lingering around my mouth and eyes, Muggins raised his nose in the air and sniffed. I couldn't tell what he was sniffing for, but something rotten was in the air.

"Yes, that's it. We're getting close, keep walking."

He paused to survey the meadow ahead of us, then grunted and shook his head.

"It's getting darker, and the damage is getting worse," he said. "You two stay right here, I'll be back."

He trotted off and disappeared over the backside of a knoll, while Ginny and I sat and waited.

"I'd rather be back under our willow," she said. "It's gross and sweaty here, and my clothes are sticking to me."

"Yeah, me too," I said. "But this is important."

She nodded.

"Speaking of which," I said. "Do you remember the conversation we had under the willow? You know, where you wanted a magical door? To a magical world?"

"Yeah," she said.

"Well? What do you think so far?"

"It's unbelievable," she said. "This is all just so unbelievable. Everything about it."

Then she paused, and the sparkle in her eye dimmed.

"What's wrong?" I asked.

"That was really scary back there, with Karma" she said.

"Yeah. I bet."

"There's so much to understand," she said. "This place is unlike anything I've ever seen. But it also feels familiar, like I've been here before. Or like I've always been here all along. Or maybe I somehow belong here or something. I can't really explain it."

I nodded.

"I get it," I said. "I feel the same way. It's totally weird, right?"

"Totally."

"Now, can I ask you something?" she said.

"Sure, anything," I said.

"Does your heart really flutter?"

A knot formed in my throat.

"Sorry, what?" I asked, with a crack in my voice.

I'd heard her just fine. But I was stalling for time to try and compose myself. I was hoping she would lose interest and move on.

"What Muggins said. I mean, I'm just curious. Does your heart really flutter every time you see me?"

I considered the question and gave the most honest answer I had.

"Yeah," I said. "It does. It really, really does. Every single time. Is that weird?"

"No," she said. "Not at all."

And then, without warning, she leaned right in and kissed me. Right on my lips. Soft and warm and wonderful. Nobody had ever done that before. She leaned back and looked at me, beaming, like she had just given me the greatest gift on earth. I felt an awkward pressure to return the gift, but what if I did it wrong? The pressure froze me. So, we sat there, staring awkwardly.

Oh my god, somebody please say something. Anything. Nobody? OK, I'll do it.

"What was that?" I asked stupidly.

"Oh my gosh, I cannot believe I just did that," she said. "I'm so sorry. Was it really that bad? I've never kissed a boy before. Did I do it wrong? It just seemed like the right thing to do."

Then it hit me. It wasn't just me. I realized that she felt every bit as awkward as I did. She was just as nervous and self-conscious as I was. What a relief that was.

But as to her question—was it bad? How would I know? It was my first kiss. The truth is that it wasn't bad all. Not as near as I could tell, anyway.

"Hmm. I can't remember. One more, just to see?" I asked.

I leaned in just as Muggins reappeared at the top of the knoll.

"Here we go," he interrupted. "I've found our transport. Two burbles, at our service."

He stopped abruptly.

"Now what in the world are you two doing down there?"

"Just talking, mostly," I said.

It was true. We mostly were.

"Yes, talking. I see," he said. "Fascinating talking posture you have."

He walked down toward me as I sat in the grass. He stepped into my lap, stood on my legs, and leaned in close to my face. His hands were on my shoulders and his crooked nose nearly touched mine.

"Is this how we talk now? Am I doing it properly? Let's talk, Logan."

"Knock it off, Muggins," I said. "Jeez, whatever."

I brushed him aside and pulled myself up. He'd brought a pair of strange-looking animals with him. They stood calmly, chewing grass, without a care in the world.

"You call that *transport*? What are we supposed to do with them?"

"We'll ride them, of course. Silly boy, what else would you do with a pair of burbles?"

"I'm not really sure," I said. "They look ridiculous."

The burbles resembled an unfortunate cross between a horse and an elephant, with long sweeping backs to sit on, and stubby little trunks that were just barely long enough to scoop up the pond muck they were so fond of eating. Their skin was sun-starved pale, the color of the mushrooms at the grocery store. They had jiggly, low-hanging bellies and gigantic backsides with well-defined cheeks that waggled back and forth with every step, like garbage bags full of gelatin.

"Ride them," I said. "You want us to ride those things?"

"Yes, of course," he said. "Burbles are tame, kindly creatures. They roam wild, but they're actually quite friendly once they have a belly full of pond muck. It's always best to find them at the water's edge. That's a little trick you might want to tuck away for later. Good chance they've already eaten that way. Off we go now."

We mounted our preposterous steeds. Ginny rode one, and Muggins and I shared the other.

"Just keep the wind in our face, and don't sit still for too long," Muggins said. "Avoid tailwinds at any cost."

"Why?" I asked.

"How can I best answer this? Well, burbles are prone to volcanic flatulence. With a steady diet of pond muck and not much else, they get the breeze a lot. The wind, if you know what I mean. They are very gassy is what I'm trying to tell you. They fart a lot, okay? There, I said it."

"Gross," Ginny said.

Muggins chuckled.

"Gentle creatures, yes. But truth be told, they stink to high heaven. How do you think I knew these two were so close by? I could smell them a hundred yards off!"

He made a clicking noise with his mouth, and the burbles started to walk. Thankfully, they were a lot faster than they looked, and we were on our way.

RIDING THE BURBLES, we cut our own path through the tall dried grass. It had been at least an hour, before I noticed it. There was so much darkness and destruction. So much of Cameria's beauty had vanished in favor of rot and ugliness. Pondering the landscape, I felt a bite and swatted at my neck. It had been a while, and the bugs were much less of a nuisance than where we found the burbles. It was still muggy, but the bugs had mostly gone away.

The hills on either side of the meadow grew steeper and turned to rough canyon walls. As we rode, we must have passed a hundred of those sacred cankle-berry bushes. The berries were a bright, beautiful shade of red, so plump and juicy.

"How are you feeling, Logan?" Muggins asked.

"I don't know. Hungry, I guess. Seriously, why can't we eat a few of those berries? I mean, they're literally everywhere."

"It's just not allowed, young man. The berries are sacred to the Qud Palmon. It was determined long ago that the berries were so delicious — so good, so satisfying — that they're too good for us to eat. We're not worthy of their wonderful nectar."

"That seems unfair, if you ask me," Ginny said. "It's so good that nobody can enjoy it?"

"Only the gods are worthy of enjoying such a delectable treat. That may seem silly or unfair to you, but in the eyes of the Qud Palmon, it would be a high crime to eat them, or even to pick them for that matter. They must be left for the gods, and only the gods.

Those are their laws. Our job is not to understand them, but only to respect them."

"That's not helping," I said. "Now I want one even more."

"Me too," Ginny added.

Smidge popped up out of my pocket and chittered his cautious disapproval.

"Sorry, Smidge, it just seems like a waste, that's all I'm saying."

"I understand why you would think that," Muggins replied. "Relax, though, we'll take a break soon and get you some food. How are you feeling otherwise? About the Council and all."

"Mostly just nervous," I said. "And confused, maybe."

"Well, don't tell the members of the Council that," he said. "They're expecting you to be bold and brave and amazing. Heroic, even. I'm sorry, but nervous and confused just won't do it. They'll be terribly disappointed."

"Not helping," I said.

"And you, Miss Ginny," he said. "How are you doing, young lady?"

"I'm fine," she said, with hesitation.

Neither of us was fine. I knew it, and I was sure she did too. I looked around at all the destruction and sadness. Muggins was right. I never should have brought Ginny here.

"Hey Muggins?"

"Yes?"

"If the Council wants me to be one thing, and I'm actually the total opposite of that thing, then why are you taking me there?"

Muggins chuckled.

"How you feel and what I know, those are two different things," he said. "My hope is that how you feel and what I know will both line up at the right time. Whether you believe it or not, whether you believe in what you are, that's up to you. But I know," he said, tapping his temple wisely.

A thought occurred to me. Could it be possible that, after all this, I was just mindlessly following a crazy man on a pointless quest that I had no hope of ever winning? There was no way to know. But

Grandpa had put a lot of faith in Muggins. That had to count for something.

We approached a wooden bridge. That's when I realized how quiet it had become. There were no more crickets, and, thankfully, no more biting flies buzzing around. No dragonflies or birds either. No nothing. Not a single living creature anywhere in sight, besides us and our burbles.

Muggins made a clicking noise with his mouth, and the burbles stopped in front of the entrance to the bridge.

"Now, listen up, you two. I need to explain something to you before we cross this bridge. I need you need to understand how serious I am. What I'm about to say will rouse your curiosity— perhaps pique your interest. It will probably put some ideas in your head and make you want to do certain things."

"Go on," Ginny said.

"In fact, once I tell you what I'm going to tell you, you'll probably want to do the exact opposite of what I told you, because I told you not to. But it's very important that you don't. Can you do that?"

"Yes, of course," I said.

Muggins looked at Ginny crosswise. She rolled her eyes while he stared at her.

"Yes, me too," she said stubbornly. "I heard you, you know. I don't know why I have to say it out loud."

"Good. I'm glad we're on the same page. Now, this bridge is going to take us across the Blackpool."

"The what?" Ginny asked.

"The Blackpool," he repeated. "It's a mystical pond thousands of years old. And I use the term *pond* loosely. Looking straight across it, you would probably think it is filled with a black liquid."

Ginny and I nodded our agreement.

"Yep."

"And if you think that," he continued, "you're dead wrong. It's nothing of the sort. The Blackpool is an infinite abyss filled with the blackness of a million stolen lives. Whatever you do, mind my advice on this. When we are on the bridge, do not look down. Do not look directly into the Blackpool, no matter what you do."

"Why not?" I said.

"Excellent question!" he said, pointing at me. "When you look into it and see yourself in the Blackpool, your reflection will rise up out of the blackness and pull you in, right down through to the other side. Many an unwary traveler has let their curiosity get the best of them. Some think they are too smart or too fast or too strong to suffer such a fate. The Blackpool hasn't always been this big. But with every new victim, it grows a little bigger."

"That sounds horrible," Ginny said. "What happens then?"

"I don't know," Muggins said. "Nobody has ever made it back to tell."

"Oh," she said.

"Do you know the saying 'curiosity killed the cat?'"

"Yes, of course."

"Good. Don't be a cat," Muggins said wagging a finger. "Do you understand Miss Ginny? Don't be a cat."

She nodded.

"I understand."

"Wonderful. And don't be any other animal either. Do you see any walking around?"

He was right. The bugs that were so thick and annoying at the other pond were completely absent here.

"Anything that gets close enough eventually spies its own reflection," Muggins said. "I hope you can show more wisdom and restraint. If you don't listen to me on this, I can't help you."

I didn't fully trust myself not to look. I had always been inquisitive by nature.

"Why can't we just go around?" I asked.

"The Blackpool runs right up to the edge of those hillsides. You can see how steep they are. The burbles would never be able to walk it. They're not mountain goats, after all. And going around is too far. Even with the burbles' speed, that would take days that we don't have. We'd never make it to the Council in time. So this is it."

He made the clicking noise again. On his cue, our burble waddled forward onto the bridge. It was time to go, and we were crossing, whether I was ready or not. As the burble stepped onto the rotting wooden platform, Muggins raised his head and looked to the clouds. He stared at the sky and whistled to himself as he gave the burble a gentle kick to hurry it along.

The rails were barely wide enough for the burble to fit through, and the boards creaked under its tremendous weight. I couldn't help but wonder what it looked like, down inside the blackness. Could it be black liquid? Was it really just an abyss? Would I see through the surface to a bottom, or would the blackness go on forever?

I could take just a quick little peek. The quickest of the quick. I could glance over, and look away in an instant, all in one sweeping motion with my neck. I wouldn't even stop. I'd be very fast, for sure. I was building up the courage to try when Ginny's burble stepped onto the bridge behind us. The wood creaked harder, and the bridge leaned.

"Oh my gosh," Ginny gasped.

The burbles calmed themselves after a few nervous stutter steps and some odd snorting noises. They plodded along, paying no mind that the bridge seemed ready to collapse under their massive weight. Fear swirled in my mind. What if a hand was reaching up out of the Blackpool to grab my leg and pull me in? What if it already had a grip on my burble, and I didn't know it? How could I avoid something that I didn't see? Indeed, it would certainly be safer to check.

My pulse raced. Fear took over, and paranoia ran rampant. I was sure I'd be pulled in at any moment. I looked over my shoulder at Ginny. She was stiff; the tendons at her elbows showed through and her skin was pale white. The bridge creaked and strained with every step. Her eyes were shut so tight, creases formed at the corners. She'd never looked so frightened.

Don't look down. Whatever you do, Logan, don't look down.

I turned forward again. Muggins was still looking at the clouds and whistling when I noticed something. A bird was flying toward us from far off in the distance. It dipped and rose again with each flap of its wings. It disappeared from my peripheral vision as it passed us, but given the angle, I knew it should have landed on the Blackpool by now. But I didn't hear the splash I expected. I didn't hear anything. If it landed, it would be there, just over the side, and if I peeked, then I would know for sure.

"Eyes forward," Muggins said with a well-timed reminder. "Remember what I told you."

It was unbearable. For something called a *pool*, the thing was enormous.

A board split underfoot. Our burble lurched to regain its balance.

"I need to get off this bridge right now," Ginny screeched.

"Me too," I said.

"We're almost there," Muggins said calmly. "Just a few more steps."

10

_____

A s we neared the end of the bridge, Muggins dug through his bottomless bag, pulled out a small bottle, and tied a string to it.

"Eyes forward, you two," he said. "Pay no mind to me. Keep your eyes forward, just like before."

He threw the vessel over the side of the bridge, staring at the clouds as he did. It fell over the side and its weight pulled the string tight against the rail. Without saying a word, he pulled the string back, and placed it back in his bottomless bag.

After a few more steps, we finally made it across to safety.

"Muggins," I asked. "Why is Karma taking the Light? What is she planning to do with it?"

"The Light is a potent force; it's what makes this place the wonder it is. By taking it, she deprives us all of that same power. And in so doing, she concentrates that power under her control, to use however she chooses."

"Are you sure there's nobody else who can do anything about it?" I asked innocently. "You know, besides me?"

"I believe the answer lies within you, Logan. The Council will see it this time. I have great confidence in that."

"A twelve-year-old Keeper against the all-powerful Karma?" I asked. "That doesn't feel like a very fair matchup."

"She's not all-powerful. She has limits. And I agree that three Keepers would be better. Even two, if we're not being picky. Two are definitely better than one. And a little bit of experience on your part would also be valuable," Muggins said. "But we don't have such a luxury."

"Very smooth," Ginny said. "Nice one."

"Be that as it may, you can still do what you need to do alone," Muggins said. "With proper guidance, of course. And sufficient determination. Perhaps some luck. I'm pretty sure about that, anyway. Look, let's be honest. It's not like we have any choice at this point."

If Muggins was trying to make me feel better, he had failed in the most profound possible way.

"I'm afraid," I said after a short period of silence.

"Afraid of what?"

"Afraid the Council will reject me again. Or even worse, that they'll approve of me, but I'll just end up letting everybody down. What if I don't have what it takes—what if I fail?"

"Oh, Logan," he said. "The only true failure in life is failing to try at all. The Light burns deep within you. You are a candle, small but bright, flickering defiantly at the center of tremendous darkness. But you flicker, nonetheless. Let your flame shine bright, and you will wash away all the darkness she brings."

"That's like what my mom always says."

"A lot depends on you," he said. "I know this is a tremendous burden, but we will get through it together."

"Hey, Muggins?" Ginny said.

"Yes, Miss Ginny?"

"How is he supposed to release the Light?" she asked. "And what is Karma waiting for? She's taking it, but she's not doing anything with it."

"For now, she's only taking it. You are correct, Miss Ginny. Releasing it though, that's an interesting challenge. One solution could lie in something Logan's grandfather once possessed."

"Really?" I asked.

"I can't say for sure, but it's a strong possibility. Maybe. Yes, well, I think so, anyway. It's called the Starlact. Karma needs it, but she can never be allowed to have it. If she gets it—with her powers plus the captured Light—she would be unstoppable. It would enable her to use the Light she captured as a weapon of unequaled force. We would never stand a chance."

"Keeping the Starlact away from her is one thing," I said. "But if the whole point is for me to release the Light with it, how am I supposed to do that?"

"If I'm correct, the Starlact will enable you to do your job, to unlock the Lighthold and release the Light. But you can never lose possession of it. In your hands, it's the solution to all our problems. In hers, the beginning of the end."

I gulped.

I didn't even have it yet, and I was already worried about losing it.

~

At long last, we finally arrived at the Council building, and thankfully dismounted our burbles. As I walked around behind my burble, it let loose an eggy blast without warning. And I'm not just talking about a little poot, either. I'm talking about a full-on, hair-blowing, paint-peeling, cheek-flapper. My hair blew to the side, and the sound echoed off the hillside. And the smell—it was like Bryce's PE socks filled with tuna fish and rotten eggs, baked in the sun for a week. It was even worse than our bathroom, after Uncle Bob had a big meal.

In what I can only describe as a moment of profound weakness, one of life's rarest moments, I actually wished that Bryce was there, just so I could let him crop dust me. It would have been a breath of fresh air by comparison. I pulled my shirt up over my nose and walked around the front to get away. But it was no use. The cloud was spreading and there was no escaping it.

"Hey!" I shouted, pointing a stern finger at the burble. "That is really gross. Do you know that?"

Its stubby snout twitched as it looked down at me. It felt no shame, and, honestly, had no idea what I was talking about. Its snout twitched again, but more actively this time. Without warning, it sneezed and shot burble snark all over my chest. It was on my face and in my hair. I tried to wipe it away, but it was too thick and voluminous. It was as if I'd been coated in hair gel.

"Well, this is just perfect," I said. "And what are you laughing at?"

It wasn't Muggins' usual chuckle, but a hearty belly-laugh. He laughed so hard he almost fell off. He had seen it coming, and he didn't even warn me.

"You'll get used to it," he said. "Actually, no you won't. You'll never get used to it. They really are disgusting creatures. Anyway, we'd better get in there."

"Right now?"

"Absolutely. But before we do, you need to do something about your appearance, young man. You are presenting to the Council, after all. You can't go in there looking like that."

He waved two fingers at me and blew most of the snark off. My hair was still slimy, but I combed it over with my fingers the best I could. It wasn't ideal, but it would have to do.

"I'm not ready for this, Muggins," I said.

"You're ready. You've always been ready," Muggins replied. "You were ready the first time I brought you here. You just didn't realize it. Everything you ever needed was already within you."

It was like presentation day all over again, but a thousand times worse.

"Can we reschedule? I need more training, and you can teach me."

"I didn't teach you a single thing, Logan. Everything you needed to know, you already knew. I just helped you realize it."

"Really?"

"Of course. What did I really teach you? What new piece of information did I actually give you?"

I shrugged.

"Not one bit. It's all right there within you, and it always has been. Do you remember the portal at the tree? All you had to do was believe in it, and there it was, right?"

"Yeah, I guess so."

"Well, this is no different."

"You're going to be great," Ginny added. "Believe in yourself, Logan. I believe in you. So does Muggins."

"There you have it," he said. "What more do you need? Off we go now."

Muggins prodded us ahead. There was no turning back. As we walked to the door, the burbles happily trotted off in search of a pond to refill their bellies with muck. The burly guards at the gate greeted Lord Muggins with their highest respects and waved us in, tapping their tall spears on the ground and clicking their heels together as we passed. As we approached the Council chamber, Muggins waved his hand gently. The doors opened wide again to welcome us in.

"Wait, hold on. What just happened with that?" Ginny asked.

But before anyone could answer, her voice was drowned out by the argument among the Council members. They were louder and angrier this time. And the Council Hall had more people than before. Lots and lots of observers. The persnickety man glared at me.

"What exactly do you mean by coming before this Council looking like that, young man?"

"It's complicated," I said.

He sniffed and waved his hand in front of his face.

"Have you traveled here by burble?"

"Yes, sir," I said. "That's correct. I'm sorry about the smell."

"Indeed," he said. "Indeed."

⁓

WITH FORMALITIES COMPLETED, the Grand Council reconvened, and Muggins presented his case as to why I should be anointed.

Adharma caught my eye, and more reflexively than anything, I spoke. Involuntarily. It just jumped out of me.

"It was you. I saw you at the edge of the Qud Palmon forest," I said.

"Silence," Adharma said dismissively. "Point of order."

The persnickety man repeated his call while Muggins elbowed me in the leg.

"Point of order, indeed. Master LeVec, the floor has not recognized you," the persnickety man said. "This council has rules. You'll abide by them if you know what's good. Speak when spoken to, and answer the questions asked of you. Nothing more, nothing less. Do you understand the instructions I've just given you?"

"Yes," I said with a nod. "Sorry."

He seemed more frustrated than usual.

"Good then, and we're glad you've come. To be perfectly honest, I think the Council members had their doubts about whether you would actually show up, given what happened the last time."

Viceroy Smoak cleared his throat. The persnickety man had obviously said more than he was supposed to, and he quickly retreated.

"Of course, yes, my apologies Viceroy Smoak. Be that as it may, the boy is here now, and the Council may proceed with its business. But no more outbursts. Are we clear on that?"

"We're clear," I said.

Ginny looked surprised at our exchange.

"You've been here before?" she whispered.

"Yeah," I said. "I've been here. But—*shhh*."

She cocked her hips to the side, and her jaw dropped open, insulted that I had just *shushed* her. I shrugged an apologetic look, but what was I supposed to do? The Council had its rules, and I didn't want to screw anything up. Not again. Not if I could avoid it.

"Very good," the persnickety man said. "The floor now recognizes Chancellor Pickelhaub. Chancellor Pickelhaub, you may proceed."

"Thank you," she said, staring across the pentagonal table at me.

She looked serious.

"Lord Muggins has asked this Council to anoint you a Keeper. A Keeper of the Light, of all things."

Snickering echoed through the chamber.

"Let me ask you, young man. How do *you* feel about that?"

"Honestly?" I said. "I'm really nervous."

Muggins groaned. But it was the most honest answer I could give.

"That's understandable," she said in a more calming tone. "This is a tremendous responsibility."

"I understand."

"And the stakes here cannot be understated, not even a little," she went on. "Happiness, imagination, new ideas. Decency, cooperation, hope and common courtesy. All the ideals we think of as parts of a normal, functioning society are borne from the Light. And today, they are all at grave risk."

The moment she paused, a rancorous debate broke out. The persnickety man waved his arms and shouted in a failed attempt to restore order. The Council members tried to listen, but there were too many voices. Some of the voices actually sounded sympathetic to Karma; supportive even. But most were not.

"Silence," Viceroy Smoak demanded.

Silence fell upon the room, immediately obeying his authoritative voice.

"Thank you, Viceroy," Chancellor Pickelhaub continued, seeming to address everyone in the room, "All those things come from here. They come from the Light. We established this Council as a system of governance, to provide a united leadership across all the factions of Cameria. To work together as a single body and to watch out for the good of all, unmoved by the desires of a loud but singular self-interest. This is the way it has always been since the Eight Days War and this Council has successfully preserved the peace until recently."

She turned to address the other side of the room.

"I implore all of you, let us not abandon our work now."

Then she turned back and addressed me more directly.

"Do you understand what you'll be agreeing to, young man?"

"I do."

"And you agree to do this willingly without any improper influence or pressure?"

"I do."

"The strength of Qud Palmon alone is not enough. Our forces can defeat vast armies, but not a single one of us, not even all of us together, has the power to release the Light from the Lighthold. If this young man possesses the gifts of the Keepers, then we desperately need his help."

"I had my doubts, to be sure," Adharma said in his cocky demeanor, "but having had the time to consider this issue, I have no further questions of my own. He should be fine. I'd go so far as to say he may be the most perfect choice we could possibly hope for."

He smiled at me. Could he actually be on my side after all? Perhaps. I was less sure about Gabriel. It was all so confusing.

Despite that, for a fleeting moment, I felt like one of the *haves*, like the kids at school who have the right friends and everything always goes right for them. I wasn't a have-not here, and I certainly wasn't an invisible. This was new to me, but I liked it.

The persnickety man interrupted.

"May I remind the Council that votes are not meant to be discussed out loud and will be tallied by anonymous written ballot."

"Noted, and thank you," Viceroy Smoak said. "The Council shall proceed accordingly. I will say, however, that I do not take much comfort in asking this young lad to assume such a dangerous undertaking. It's a lot to ask of anybody, let alone a tender young man aged only twelve."

"What choice do you have?" Muggins said defiantly. "What choice do any of us have?"

"We always have a choice," Smoak said. "Always. In everything we do."

"Point of order," the persnickety man said. "Let us now hold the vote."

I looked over at Gabriel, with his snowy-white hair and silken wings. He had some doubts. I could see it.

"I do believe it is possible that he has the purity of heart we need in a Keeper of the Light," he said. "But I am troubled by his youth and inexperience."

He looked at me again. His gaze was penetrating, as if staring into my very soul and pondering my true worth. I shifted uncomfortably.

"The time has come to post your ballots," the persnickety man said.

He walked around the table with a silver bowl, collecting the ballots from each of the four leaders seated at the pentagonal table. The fifth seat was still vacant.

Gabriel's doubt lit a fire inside me. They could judge me all they wanted, but I knew I could do it. I was pretty sure, anyway.

The members of the Council whispered to each other with looks of concern. The room was otherwise silent as the onlookers sat on edge, watching with quiet anticipation.

The persnickety man collected the Council's ballots in the shiny silver bowl. He placed the bowl on a nearby table and read them aloud.

"One vote in favor," he said, setting the ballot down next to the bowl.

"And one against," as he read the next.

My heart sank.

Someone voted against me. That sucks.

"One more in favor," he said. "The vote now stands at two in favor, and one against."

He pulled the last ballot out of the bowl.

I could barely breathe. I was near fainting. My knees wobbled, and my head started to spin.

What if it's a tie? Where is the fifth Council member, and why don't they ever show up?

"One in favor," he announced. "This Council, by a three-to-one vote, has anointed Master Logan LeVec a Keeper of the Light. Godspeed, young man. May the Light be your guide in all that you do."

Then he mumbled more quietly:

"You're going to need all the help you can get."

It didn't matter, though. I was glad they had approved, but curious who had voted against me. I looked crosswise at Gabriel, but he didn't let on.

The persnickety man opened the drawer of a nearby cabinet and retrieved a small silver chest. He opened it and removed a fancy pin, walked over to me and pinned it to my shirt.

"This is the emblem of the Keepers. Wear it with great pride, young man. You are one of them now, and we welcome you to their ranks. Be safe, young Logan, and do well. We're all counting on you."

WE BOWED our respects to the members of the Council, and Muggins shoved me toward the door.

"Come with me," Muggins said. "We need to have a discussion. Right now. You too, Miss Ginny."

"What do I do now?" I asked.

"You start by listening very carefully and following my directions."

We left the main chamber through a side door, and followed a long hallway. At the end of the hallway was a door, and behind the door, a staircase. We climbed the stairs up one of the corner spires, the highest fixtures of the building, which let out to a balcony at the top. The view fromt he balcony was astonishing.

"What do you see?" Muggins asked, pointing into the distance.

"What do you mean?"

"I mean out there. What do you see?"

"I see a lot of things. The meadow, The Blackpool way over there. I see the hills near where we came in from my grandpa's yard, and I can even see the tops of the trees of the Qud Palmon Forest. The Light is dim, but I see them all. What are you asking me?"

Ginny innocently pointed to a dark spot on the horizon.

"I think he might be talking about that," she said.

"Oh. Right. It's so big now."

We were closer to the dark spot than I had ever been, and I could see it much better. A tall and jagged building sat on the top of a rocky outcrop. It was like a castle, but a hazardous and uninviting one composed of giant shards of volcanic glass or obsidian—black, jagged, sharp and menacing.

"That," Muggins said, "is Karma's lair. I want you to look more closely at it. Tell me what you see."

I squinted into the distance. There was something strange above the glassy black complex—something hovering above it, something swirling, like the little tornado that forms when you drain the bathtub. All the Light in Cameria was being collected, somehow draining away from us right down into the heart of her lair.

"How is she doing that?" I asked.

Muggins pulled a telescope from his bottomless bag.

"Use this," he said. "Take a closer look."

"Karma is literally stealing the Light!" I said. "All of it."

Smidge popped out of my jacket pocket at this mention of her name, chittering angrily. But then he made a different noise, one I hadn't heard before, something akin to a bark; but not a bark because Teaspoon Dragons don't bark. He snapped his head as he made the noise, and a visible white ring flew from his mouth. The ring rushed through the air, like the cloud that forms in front of a jet when it punches through the sound barrier. It struck the stone railing, and when it did, it shattered a portion of the rail, blowing a circular groove straight through it.

"Hmm. Fascinating," Muggins said. "He could be a sonic, after all."

"Sonic?" Ginny asked.

"Yes, and what a treat that would be. Sonics are far more rare than incendiaries. Only time will tell, though. He's powerful, to be sure, especially for his tender young age."

Smidge snorted and chittered again before calming down and ducking back into the quiet warmth of my pocket. I raised the telescope to my eye and focused on the point where the bottom of the funnel disappeared into her lair. Atop her jagged fortress, a tall turret rose from one corner. At the top was a complex mechanism, a complicated assembly of lenses and mirrors, hundreds of them gathering the Light from every direction, redirecting it all down the turret in a single concentrated beam.

"That's the Reflexor, isn't it?" I asked.

"It is," he said. "Your knowledge is far more vast than you realize. She's using the Reflexor's capabilities to redirect the Light."

"And then what?"

"I would ask you the same question. Do you have any ideas of your own?"

"She has the Lighthold down inside, doesn't she? She's using it to capture the Light."

"I believe that's correct."

"Oh, man."

"Spot on. My sentiments exactly."

"What is she going to do with the Light she captures?" Ginny asked.

"To start, she will just deprive us of it, I imagine. Without the Light, we all become weaker against her. That's the point, really. She is taking that which makes us all strong, in order to make us all weak. It's easier to impose your will on a weakened enemy, after all."

"Like the Vapes?"

"Yes, just like the Vapes."

"But what is her will?" I asked. "What does she want?"

"That remains to be seen. But she'll likely turn it against us. Left unchecked, the concentrated energy captured in the Lighthold could be used as a weapon. That can't be allowed."

11

We arrived back down at ground level and walked to a nearby downtown area.

"How are you feeling about all this?" Ginny asked.

"I don't know," I said. "But somebody has to do something, right? You see what's happening."

"Are you up to it? You seem nervous."

"Oh, I'm nervous, alright."

Muggins stopped abruptly in front of an old restaurant, the Slippery Chicken.

"Follow me," Muggins said as he nodded and turned in.

The inside was nearly empty, apart from one man sitting with his back to the door, but he didn't look up as we approached. Muggins pointed.

"Over there," he said, motioning toward the man who sat alone. "At the table next to him."

I pulled out my chair and sat back-to-back with the man. He never acknowledged us.

"What have I gotten myself into?" I murmured under my breath. "I never should have come here."

"That's not true," said the man who sat alone.

He stood up and turned around.

"I remember you. You were at the coffee shop. You could hear me whisper from all the way across the shop. Your hearing must be extraordinary. How do you do that?"

"He's what we call a Listener," Muggins said.

"I didn't hear you whisper at all, Logan. My gifts do not give me any special ability to hear the spoken word."

"Really?"

"No, of course not."

"You read lips?"

"No, no. I'm a Listener, not a reader."

"Then how did you know?"

"It's quite simple. I listen to your thoughts."

I shot back in my chair, stunned.

"Careful with the name-calling," he said. "And no, I'm not a freak. Not here, anyway. But I understand why you might think that."

Wow. He really does listen to my thoughts.

"Can you please stop doing that?" I said. "It's creepy. But I guess you already know that. So I don't need to tell you."

"Yes, I do. And no, you don't."

"His gifts are, shall we say, highly valuable," Muggins said with a chuckle. "As are yours. Each in their own way. Everyone has their own unique value here in Cameria."

"I have some news that may be of interest to you," said the man who sat alone.

Then he looked at Ginny, and sighed.

"Yes, I can hear yours as well, young lady," he said. "If I can see you, I can hear them. You'd do well to bear that in mind."

"Oh my gosh, that's so crazy!" she yelled.

"Shush," Muggins scolded. "Not now."

Ginny was even more annoyed at being shushed by Muggins than she was by me.

"Someday you'll take me seriously," she said.

"Don't mind them," Muggins said dismissively. "Let's talk business. What have you learned?"

"Well," the man said, "it's just as we'd suspected. They've infiltrated the Qud Palmon and are sowing seeds of doubt, trying to stir up trouble. A revolt within their own ranks is brewing, division within the Qud Palmon. Their hope is that the in-fighting among the Qud Palmon will serve as a distraction from what is important, rendering the Qud Palmon a less formidable foe against any real enemy, while they continue to fight among themselves."

"Who?" I asked. "Who infiltrated?"

They both ignored me.

"It would also appear they are pushing the leadership to wage war against other factions," he continued. "A classic case of divide and conquer. One way or another, their intentions are clear—to divide the member factions against each other, break up the Grand Council, and conquer each separate faction individually. They want to tear the whole Council down, brick-by-brick. It's working so far."

"Divided, we fall," Muggins said quietly.

"Precisely."

"I appreciate you letting me know. And the others we discussed?" Muggins asked.

"My sources tell me they've been placed in the Hall of Tortured Souls. Far from certain, but a very distinct possibility."

"Poppycock," Muggins said. "They can't be prisoners. They're safely in hiding, waiting. They have to be. It's just a matter of where and how to find them."

The Listener grunted with a hint of disbelief.

"Have you been to see Jarvis?" the man asked. "He may have more information."

Muggins hesitated.

"I haven't, but I'll be sure to make my way," glancing over at Ginny and me. "Perhaps at a more appropriate time."

"Very well," the man said. "Is there anything else I can do for you?"

"No. Just let me know if you hear anything else."

"Of course," he said as he stood up to leave.

"For what it's worth," the man said, as if listening to Muggins' thoughts, "I really don't think abandonment is in their nature."

Muggins sat quietly, looking despondent.

"I've lost my appetite," he said to us. "But you should get some food if you're hungry."

WITH OUR HUNGER SATISFIED, Muggins rushed us out the door and down the road.

"Where are we going now?" Ginny asked impatiently.

"Look," he said. "Against my better judgment, I think we need to visit Jarvis. He has some information I desperately need, so when we get there, please follow my directions if you'd be so kind. Can you do that for me?"

Muggins seemed crankier than usual. Maybe it was Jarvis, or maybe it was something the Listener said. I couldn't tell.

"Muggins?" I asked.

"Yes?"

"My grandpa called you Muggins, the magical toolbox troll."

"I'm aware," he said, as we walked.

"He said you helped him with things."

"Indeed, I did. That's quite correct."

"Like the treehouse in his yard."

"Yes, also correct."

"And that you were a friend of his."

"True as well. Gideon was a good friend. A very good friend, in fact."

"But there's more to it than that, isn't there? A lot more."

Muggins stopped.

"Now, what do you mean with a question like that? What are you getting at with this?"

"I just feel like there's more to it. More that you're not telling us. Like when you just waved a finger and blew us dry after we fell in the river. Or how you open the doors at the Council building with the wave of a hand. Or why everybody here pays so much respect to a little troll that builds treehouses in my grandpa's back yard. No offense, but why would they give you so much respect if that's all there was to it?"

"There's far more to it, if you must know. And I have certainly spent my days doing more than building treehouses. Of that, you can rest assured. That is merely an occasional escape, to clear my mind of larger concerns."

"So, what else do you do?"

"Right now, I spend my days trying to find my family. My people. All of them. I search every day for vindication, and I hope every day for forgiveness."

"Where are they?" I asked. "Your people, I mean."

"I've been trying to figure that out for some time now."

"You don't know where your family is?" Ginny asked.

"At the moment, no. But I intend to find them."

"How can you not know where your family is?" Ginny asked.

"It's complicated."

"Do you feel sad that you can't find them? I know I would. That would be awful."

Muggins didn't answer right away.

"I feel a lot of things about it, Miss Ginny," he said somberly. "Sadness? Yes. Definitely sadness. With every day that goes by, my shoulders are weighted with a most profound sadness. One you could never possibly imagine. Angry? Yes, that too. Guilty, regretful, vengeful? Yes. All those things. Every single day."

"What do you think happened?" Ginny asked.

"I lost them all in the Eight Days War. Every single one of them."

"Did they die?"

"I don't think so. But I also don't know for sure. It all happened so quickly, and the casualties of the war were massive, unlike anything in our history."

"You fought in the Eight Days War?" I asked.

"Oh yes. My involvement was considerable. To say that I fought in the Eight Days War would be an understatement like few others."

His lip quivered as he stared into the distance.

"At some point, during the ninth day, I presume, I regained consciousness in a desolate battlefield. By that time, everything was quiet. I was badly injured but still alive, surrounded by others who were far less fortunate. I was, in effect, alone. I don't know what happened, but they were all gone. Every single one of them. Some perished on the battlefield, but it was only a fraction of our numbers. The rest—well, I don't know. It's been my life's mission to find out ever since. My people were a peaceful people for the most part. I would like to believe that they went into hiding to avoid the atrocities of war. But if they did, they've stayed in hiding ever since, even during the period of peace that has followed—The New Spring, as we call it. I've been searching for them ever since. Searching for redemption and forgiveness."

"Redemption from what?" Ginny asked. "What do you want forgiveness for?"

"This may surprise you, but many moons ago, I used to lead a faction of my own. It was one of the oldest and most revered in all of Cameria. We were the Elementalists. Our numbers were great, and our strengths were second-to-none, not even the great Qud Palmon. Our enchantments rivaled their brute strength twice over, or at least that's what I told myself. I led my people into a great war that spread more broadly as other factions got involved. In the end, my ill-advised aggression had taken on a life of its own. It quickly developed into the Eight Days War. When all was said and done, my people were lost. My wife, family, our land, everything. Everyone I ever knew or loved."

"That's awful," Ginny said.

"Perhaps they perished," he continued. "Or went into hiding. Maybe they've just turned their backs on me, silently banishing this old fool without even having the decency to tell me, while living happily in my absence. I just don't know, but I hope to find out some-day. If only I could tell them how sorry I am—that alone would be good enough. For now, though, I walk alone."

I knelt beside him and placed a consoling hand on his shoulder.

"I'm so sorry," I said. "I had no idea."

"There's no reason you should have," he said. "This is my business to deal with, not yours."

He took a long, deep breath.

"So, for now, I spend what time I have left searching for their forgiveness. But I also fear that there may be nobody left to give me the forgiveness I seek."

"When you kill Karma, and we release the Light," Ginny said, "Then maybe they'll come back to you."

"One can only hope," Muggins said. "But I have no intention of killing Karma. You should understand that now."

"But you keep saying she has to be stopped."

"She does. Karma has found herself on the wrong side of the Light. I believe I can bring her back. I mean no harm to her at all, if I'm being honest. War and death and killing are awful-sounding ideas to me. It was a hard-learned lesson, as I hope you now understand. One I won't soon forget."

"But she's so evil," I said. "She's ruining everything. And look what she did to my grandpa."

"An unfortunate circumstance, to be sure," he said. "But one that lends itself to correction."

"So, you think you can fix her?" Ginny asked.

"That is my hope, yes. To bring her back. To fix her, as you say."

"Why would you show her any mercy at all? Look at what she's doing."

"Her past is a troubled one, but she didn't ask for any of this. Karma was an unlikely product of an unexpected love, born of a forbidden relationship between two members of rival factions. It was during the early days following the Grand Council's formation, in the time that followed the Eight Days War. Factions became more defined and distinct. More separated and individualized."

"I see," Ginny said.

"As a consequence, sadly, it became clear that Karma had no place she could truly call home among either of her parents' factions.

No home on one side, and no home on the other. She belonged to neither, and quickly became an outcast."

"She never had a real home?" Ginny asked. "I kind of feel bad for her."

"I felt the same way you do. And I had a lot of influence then, much more than I do now. I recognized her strength. I secretly took her in, and I mentored her."

"You have a real soft spot, don't you," Ginny said. "For all your tough appearances, you do a lot of really nice things. You're actually very kind, deep down."

Muggins smiled.

"You're very kind to say so. I appreciate your words. But you left out naive. After some time, she rose to prominence within the Council and assumed a minor leadership role. A helper of sorts. An enforcer, if you will. She was installed in a position of great power. They relied upon her to use her gifts to help maintain balance among the individual rivalries to help maintain the peace."

"What went wrong?" I asked.

"All power tends to corrupt, and absolute power corrupts absolutely, as they say. Soon, she strayed from any moral tether she may have felt and began acting on the wrong side of the Light."

"What happened then?"

"Things progressed quickly. Before long, she unshackled herself completely from the burden of the rule of law. Feeling unbound to any expectations about her placement in peaceful society, she grew hungry for more power. She grew selfish and mean, downright cruel, in fact. She had been elevated to a position of tremendous strength and influence within the Council, and had influence over the lives of everyone in Cameria."

"Are you saying she used to be good?" I asked.

"In a manner of speaking, yes. In the Eight Days War, not only did my entire faction disappear, but so did vast groups of others, including both of Karma's parents. She was left with nothing. Out of my own guilt, I took her in and guided her. In a not-so-indirect way, I am responsible for what she has become. Other members of the

Council objected. They didn't want to install her to such a position of strength without proper checks. She hated the Eight Days War and the destruction it wrought, and she vowed never to let it happen again. At the first hint of unrest among factions, she sought out those who caused trouble and one fateful day, she made her position clear. She sent a strong message to show everyone else how things would work going forward."

"What did she do?" I asked.

"It started with Kleber the Strong. He was a notorious Qud Palmon warrior and an elder statesman, highly influential among his people. He was unhappy with the bargain of peace that followed the Eight Days War and he was hungry for a greater share of the Camerian lands than the bargain had provided him. He pulled together some of his top lieutenants and planned a coup to put things back where they were before."

"Did they succeed?" Ginny asked.

Muggins shuddered.

"I should say not. Karma learned of his plans, and at the tender age of sixteen, she visited him to dissuade him from such aggression. As the story goes, he shooed her away with no respect at all. She presented him with a mirror, the origin of which is still the subject of much debate. Some say it was a gift of the gods. Others believe that it is imbued with strange nomadic magic. Others still attribute its powers to the darkest and most dangerous forms of sorcery."

The mirror.

"There are as many theories about its origin as there are stars in the sky. But one thing is certain. There is no denying its capability, as you now know."

"So, what happened to Kleber?"

"She showed him his reflection. But what he saw was a reminder of all the wrongs he had done in his life. All of it, all at once. The violence, the thievery, the back-stabbing betrayals. There are many versions of what happened after that, but nobody disagrees about this: Kleber the Strong's cries of pain, and his pleas for mercy, were heard at the most distant edges of Cameria. From the deepest, darkest reaches of the Qud Palmon Forest to the grassy huts of the Elementalists to the misty ledges of the Skycliffs where the Avians live. When children woke from their sleep to ask what happened, parents blamed the howling of coyotes or the squeaking of a door. But we all knew his cries announced the dawn of a new era for Cameria. From that day forward, things would be different."

"And they just let her go on after that?" Ginny asked.

"For a while, it worked just fine. But as Karma strayed further from the way of the Light, it became clear there was no getting her back. And now we have this, much of it my own responsibility. We all have regrets to some extent, but you might say I have more than most. So now I work to fix it."

"I don't really know what to say," I said. "I've never had to deal with anything quite that big."

"You don't need to say anything," Muggins said. "Like I said, its my burden to bear. But that's enough of that. That's Jarvis' place at the end. Remember what I told you before. I prefer not to take you in here, but I don't think I have a choice. Just listen to what I say and follow instructions. Are you clear on that?"

"Yes, got it," I said.

"And you, Miss Ginny?"

"Yes," she nodded, "got it."

12

"I feel weird," I said. "I don't really want to be here anymore."

"Is our important work of saving Cameria boring you, young man?"

"No, it's hard to explain," I said. "I'm not bored. I just don't want to be here. Like, I don't feel like I care about what we're doing."

"I feel it too," Ginny said, "like something is sucking the happiness out of me. And if you look around, everyone looks like they feel the same way."

Muggins grumbled.

"I knew it wouldn't be long before this became an issue. Be strong, you two. That's exactly what she wants. Keep your minds strong, and don't give in. We've come too far for that."

"I guess," I said half-heartedly, trying modestly not to give in.

Ginny was right. People on the street were feeling the same way. They talked about it, but nobody knew what to do. Sorrow and despair flowed from their lips as I overheard two men complaining.

"The Keepers never should have left us like this," one said.

"Selfish and unfair," the other said. "Downright cowardly, leaving us to fend for ourselves in the face of such evil."

"Death to the Keepers," the first one said. "Should they ever dare return. But I don't suppose they'd ever have the courage."

"Death to the Keepers," the other agreed.

"But they didn't abandon Cameria," I whispered to Muggins, careful not to let the two men hear me. "They didn't abandon anybody. My grandpa would never do that. Don't they know that?"

Muggins looked at me.

"Perhaps, but sometimes it's easier to sit back and blame others than to step up and put the effort in to fix things yourself. The Light is draining. And this is a tragic but direct consequence."

"That is so unfair," Ginny snapped.

"Yeah," I said. "Seriously."

"I don't disagree with you," Muggins said. "It's a shame, and that's why I need you to stay strong. Don't let her win."

The silhouettes of the forest and mountains in the backdrop were cold and jagged. Trees once lush with leaves and birds turned gnarled and grey, leafless and lifeless. It wasn't hard to imagine how quickly the Shadow Pack's numbers must be growing, displacing all the good wildlife. Cameria grew uglier by the minute, and I wondered for a moment if it was just here; or if perhaps the darkness was spreading past the tree into my grandpa's yard toward my family.

"It's just around this corner now," Muggins said. "That's where we'll find Jarvis."

We came around the corner to find an old wooden building. It was weathered and creaky-looking, with a sign above the door that read *Jarvis Mallefactor, Puppeteer.*

INSIDE THE SHOP, the wooden floor squeaked under my foot, while candles set a soft orange glow upon the room.

"I don't like it here," I said.

"Ditto that," Ginny said. "So creepy."

"Ew," Ginny said, pointing up at the wall.

String puppets hung from hooks, and dramatic, ominous

shadows fell across their faces. Dozens of them hung limply, gawking down at us blankly.

"They look so lifeless," I whispered. "But also ready to spring to life at any moment."

"Right?" Ginny whispered back. "Like if you look away, they'll jump down at you."

"Exactly," I said. "But that's not possible, is it?"

"I sure hope not."

"Why don't you two just focus on me," Muggins said. "Just do as I say."

Deep in thought, a man sat behind the counter, screwing a small metal loop into the wrist of a wooden puppet. The man was heavy-set with big, flappy lips, overly puffy cheeks, and a wild beard. He threaded a string through the loop and tied it down tight. With his knot finished, he looked up at us, and quickly shoved the puppet into a cupboard below, out of sight, and quickly closed it.

"Well, how about this," he said, leaning on the counter and staring at us. "If it isn't Lord Muggins."

"Jarvis," Muggins said.

"Ooh, I like the look of this one," he said nodding toward me with an icy gaze. "He would make a good puppet."

He looked me right in the eye and stared in a way that made me extremely uncomfortable. But different from the uncomfortable that Gabriel made me feel. Very different.

"Can I make a puppet of you, little boy?"

"I don't think we have time to sit and model," I said with forced laugh. "While you carve me out of wood."

"Who said anything about carving?" he asked.

Jarvis grabbed my arm with a firm grip. It was far too tight for any well-intended purpose. He turned me side-to-side and looked me over carefully, front and back, up and down, mussing my hair with his free hand.

"Yes, indeed," Jarvis said. "This one would make a very fine puppet."

Then he turned to Ginny.

"And her too. A splendid set, the two of them together. Yes, I like that idea. I like that very much."

"Hands off," Muggins said.

I didn't like the sound of Jarvis' voice one bit. I looked back to the walls again at the dozens of string puppets that dangled from their hooks. Their limp, gangly bodies stood in sharp contrast to their faces. Sheer terror, frozen in time. Each face looked like a snapshot that had been taken at the height of its own mortal fear. One, in particular, caught my eye. It was modeled after a boy who was probably my age and had a haircut much like mine.

He turned his head toward me as he hung there. At least I thought he did in the moment. He stared down at me, as if he knew what might happen next. His frown turned even sadder. His eyes shifted away from me when Jarvis started talking again.

"Yes, I can see it now," Jarvis continued, still looking me over. Then he reached for Ginny. "With these two I could put on a splendid show, a very good one indeed. Perhaps my best yet. It's always better when they're made together, you know, at the same time. Never underestimate the value of timing."

"I said hands off," Muggins insisted.

Muggins sounded more fierce than usual. He pushed his way in between us, to separate me from Jarvis' grip. Jarvis stepped backward, cautiously.

"No need to be impolite, now," he said. "I was just making polite conversation. But that's fine. You have other things on your mind, I can see that now. We can strike a deal later if that's what suits you. You go first."

He looked over at me again. It still didn't feel right.

"I'm not here for anything of the sort," Muggins said. "But I am here to collect a favor from you. You still owe something of a hefty debt, do you not?"

Jarvis huffed.

"What sort of favor?" Jarvis asked.

"I'm looking for some old friends."

"Yes, I know that. But they're not here, as you can very well see. Is that it? Is it deal time now?"

"I didn't ask if they were here," Muggins said. "I intend to find them, and I understand you may know their whereabouts."

"Yes, I see. People talk. It's been a long time now. But some say they've been put to work, forced labor, you know. In the mines, digging white iron out from the Arkan tunnels. Deep below ground, hardly ever seeing the light of day."

"I've been to the mines," Muggins said. "There's no trace."

"Well, if not there," Jarvis said. "Then likely they've taken to hiding and just stayed there. Or, perhaps, just perhaps—"

He paused, reluctant to speak the words that would follow.

"Some say they're in the Hall."

"The Hall?"

"Yeah. You know—The Hall of Tortured Souls."

Muggins winced at the words, shaking his head in disagreement.

"Can't be."

"Sorry to say it, but you did ask. Is that really all you came here for? I don't think I've said anything you didn't already know."

"You're wrong," Muggins said.

"Yeah, you're probably right," Jarvis said. "The Hall is where she puts the absolute worst of them—horrible place. I can't imagine it myself. It would be a real shame if they were there."

Jarvis shuddered at the thought.

"So that's all? Nothing more you need?"

"No. It's not all."

Muggins paused.

"You're aware that she's taken the Reflexor and the Lighthold."

"Yes, I know."

"I need to know how to unlock the Lighthold. How to release the Light."

Jarvis laughed another hearty laugh.

"You don't," he said quite simply.

"Nonsense."

"No, I mean it. And you'd be crazy to try. The power is far too great. You'll sooner catch lightning in a bottle than safely handle the Lighthold," he said with a laugh. "And if you can do that, maybe you stand a chance. Otherwise, just forget about it. Try it, and I guarantee that you'll end up like that one kid, Too-Bad-Timothy. You know what happened to him, right? *Bzzzzzzzzzt.*"

Muggins winced.

"Only a Keeper can handle such tremendous power," Jarvis said.

But I'm a Keeper. This is great!

Muggins glanced at me. I was just about to let Jarvis in on my secret when Muggins started talking really loudly in an intentional effort to drown me out.

"Fine, I'm not a Keeper," Muggins shouted. "But if I was, what would I do? Theoretically speaking, of course. How would I handle it in such a case?"

Jarvis was shocked by Muggins' outburst. I was, too. Jarvis studied Muggins curiously before answering.

"Well, you would need a key. You would need a Starlact."

"Go on."

"The Lighthold is imbued with the Magic of The Ages. It's the oldest and most powerful magic known to Cameria. You couldn't possibly break it."

Muggins huffed arrogantly.

"That's right. Not even you, the great Lord Muggins. And I mean no disrespect by saying it. It's just a simple fact. It's pointless to even try."

"So you say," Muggins answered. "That's never stopped me from trying before."

"Yes, of course. And we know how it usually turns out, if you know what I mean."

I really wanted to tell Jarvis I was a Keeper and just get on with our business. Why debate our lack of a Keeper when I was, in fact, a Keeper? I pondered Muggins deception when my eye was drawn back up to the wall for reasons I still can't explain. The string puppet was staring down again, right at me, right into my eyes. This time I was certain of it.

He shook his head, ever so slightly. It was subtle, barely even noticeable. But it was there. He was signaling *no*; I shouldn't trust Jarvis.

"I've been wanting to enlist the Council's help," Muggins said, "but something doesn't feel right. I can't put my finger on it, but something is going on, something well beyond their words. Something they choose not to discuss in the open."

Jarvis smiled knowingly and shook his head.

"You wanted a favor," Jarvis said. "I'll do you a favor. Have a seat and let me show you something," he said, pointing to a table and chairs near a corner of the room.

Muggins climbed up and stood on the seat of the chair, leaning into the table's edge with his hands. Ginny and I took our seats as Jarvis blew out his candles. Only the soft glow of the oil lamp at the table's center shone on our faces. He lit a match, took a puff of his cherrywood pipe, and exhaled softly, forming a thick cloud that hung in place, swirling above the oil lamp.

He motioned with his hands to shape the smoke into something else. I could see an image within it, but the image made no sense. It was Adharma infiltrating the Qud Palmon. As I stared into the smoky swirl, I saw snippets of conversations, things Adharma had said and done.

"Adharma has been spreading false stories," Muggins said. "He's creating distrust among them, undermining Chancellor Pickelhaub, and the rest of the Council. He's been purposely creating division and revolt within the Qud Palmon, and elsewhere, too. All across Cameria."

Jarvis grinned at Muggins' realization.

"Welcome to the party, Lord Muggins," he said. "It's so nice of you to join us."

I couldn't believe it myself. Adharma wanted them to overthrow the Chancellor, to remove her from Qud Palmon leadership, and replace her on the Council with somebody he had chosen.

"So, it's true. Adharma is cooperating with Karma, after all," I shouted.

"He is cooperating with her," Ginny added, "but the Council is standing in the way!"

"That's why Adharma took the form of the guard. He's pretending to be one of them, spreading lies among leadership in the meantime."

Muggins groaned a familiar groan.

"I've seen enough," he said. "I understand now."

Jarvis slowly waved his hand through the cloud, and the images fell apart, back into thin wisps of smoke.

"And back to my original question now," Muggins said. "The Lighthold?"

Jarvis laughed again.

"It's like I said, you'll need a key. You'll need a Starlact. So there. I assume you now have everything you came here for, yes?"

"For now, yes. I have. Thank you."

Jarvis glanced at me again with a look that sent a chill down my back.

"Now, let's talk about these children."

13

"It's time for us to go now," Muggins said, nodding toward the door.

"But my collection," Jarvis said. "I need them for my collection. We were supposed to make a deal."

I pushed Ginny toward the door as Jarvis walked toward us. Usually, Ginny would be offended by this. But she wanted to get out of there just as badly as I did.

"Keep going," Muggins said.

"Come back!" Jarvis yelled as he followed us out the door.

We ran down the street, around the corner and out of sight. Jarvis was a large man, and had trouble keeping up. When we were safely out of sight, I leaned against a rail in front of a shop to catch my breath. As I panted, I heard a buzzing sound in the distance that I didn't quite recognize. I threw a rock into a tree toward the buzzing, hoping to shoo away whatever was making the noise. The buzzing became more active and animated but eventually slowed and quieted.

"I never should have brought you there," Muggins said. "I am so very sorry. I should have come alone. I know better than that. It's just that we were already so close. I was so desperate to get his information."

"It's ok," I said.

"What did he mean about needing us for his collection?" Ginny asked.

"Well, Miss Ginny, that's a conversation for a different time, I'm afraid. I wouldn't want to cause you nightmares unnecessarily."

"So where do we go from here?" I asked.

"You heard Jarvis. We need the key. We need the Starlact. Then we'll be able to unlock the Lighthold and release the Light."

"What is the Starlact?" Ginny asked.

"It opens the Lighthold," Muggins said. "But we don't have it. And finding it may be a bit like finding a needle in a haystack."

"What did you just say?" I asked.

"I said finding the Starlact will be like finding a needle in a haystack. Maybe even worse. Because I'm not even sure where to find the haystack. How do you find a needle in a haystack when you don't even know where the haystack is?"

"Hold on a minute. Could it be the start clock?" I mumbled to myself.

"Starlact," Ginny corrected.

"No, you don't understand. My grandpa mentioned something once when we were fishing at Mueller Lake. It was fall, and the leaves of the trees at the water's edge were yellow and red, and they reflected off the water. They were the reddest and yellowest I had ever seen. I remember that day so clearly. He was telling one of his more colorful stories, and I remember he said something. I didn't understand it then, but now it makes perfect sense. He said when darkness comes, the start clock will help restore the light. It didn't make sense back then, but I think I misunderstood. I think he was talking about the Starlact! He said when the time comes, I'll be able to find it in a safe place. I bet we can find it at Smerconish's. That's where he used to work."

"Why would it be at his work?" Ginny asked. "Why not here? Wouldn't it make more sense for it to be here, in Cameria?"

"I don't know, maybe. But I just have a really strong feeling that it's there. Do you trust me?"

She paused thoughtfully.

"I do."

"Let's get to Smerconish's then."

"Look how dim the Light is," Muggins said. "Are you absolutely certain? If you're wrong, we'll be done for."

"Yes," I said. "One hundred percent. Can you find some burbles to get us back to the tree?"

14

After a long and fart-filled burble ride, we hiked the trail back up to the edge of the cliffs where the tree was. I walked out through the portal, and I was back home, just like that. I stood next to the tree in my grandpa's back yard again, cold and quiet as it was, as if Cameria had never been. We ran through the woods toward the house to get my bike, and once we got to the porch, I stood my bike up on two wheels.

"Ginny, on the handlebars! Muggins, hop on my back. Let's go!"

I pedaled as fast as I could toward the old hardware store, and we rushed inside. The bell above the door tinkled as we walked in, and a tall man with a kind face approached us as we entered. It was none other than Henry Smerconish himself. He was the son of the late Mr. Smerconish, the store's namesake. Henry stood looking down at me. He wore a crisp green apron with pockets in the front, and his hands hung leisurely from the apron strings that looped over the back of his neck.

"Welcome in. How can I help you kids today?"

Ginny looked down at Muggins. Then she looked at me.

"Why doesn't he think this is weird?" she whispered. "You know, with Muggins."

"I don't know," I whispered back. "Maybe he doesn't believe. So there's nothing weird."

"We're looking for a Starlact," I said to Henry. "It unlocks the Lighthold."

"A Starlact?" he parroted back to us. "To open a *Lighthold*?"

"Yes, that's right."

"I sell a lot of things here," he said, "but that's the first time I've ever been asked for that."

"Do you have it or not?"

I regretted being rude, but what was I supposed to do?

"To be honest," he said. "I don't know. Can you give me a little more information, young man? Maybe I can look it up in the catalog."

He walked behind the counter and pulled a catalog the size of a phone book from under the counter. He plopped it on the countertop and flipped through its pages. My heart sank. This was an old-school store, and they did things the old-school way. There was no computer, just an old manual cash register, complete with a bell that rang when the drawer opened. And a paper catalog.

It won't be in the catalog. I can't believe I just wasted so much time coming here.

"So, can you give me a little more information?" he repeated.

"Hello, Henry," Muggins said, stepping forward.

"Evening, Muggins," came his reply. "Been a while now, hasn't it? How have you been, old friend?"

"I've been just fine, thank you for asking. And I hope you have, as well."

Henry nodded.

"The Starlact he's asking about. Gideon might have had one," Muggins said. "Or he made sure that one would be available in any case."

"Gideon, you say?"

"Yes, that's right."

"Oh, well why didn't you just say so. You all are in the wrong department, I'm afraid."

"Wrong department?" I shouted.

"Yes, you want the magical items department, things for Keepers. We call it Keeperwares."

Henry motioned to one end of the store.

"Keeperwares are all on aisle 21," he said. "Just past housewares."

"Are you kidding me?" I shouted. "This is amazing! Let's go!"

I looked up at the aisle markers above. We were standing at the end of aisle ten—paint department. My eyes tracked further down the main aisle. 18. 19. 20.

Aisle 20 was the last one.

Ginny scoffed.

"Rude!" she blurted.

"Oh, I get it now. You were teasing," I said. "I get that a lot. I should have known better. Thanks for nothing, Henry. We'll figure something else out on our own. Sorry to have bothered you."

I turned to leave.

"Well, I'm sorry to see you go, young man. Do what you feel you must. But I really do think you'll find what you're looking for down there, on aisle 21, if only you try."

"Enough with the teasing already. You made your point. You think I'm ridiculous. I get it. Just like everyone else. You don't have to rub it in. I'll just let you get back to work."

"Logan," Muggins said sharply. "Calm down for a minute. Henry is a friend."

"You'll also find some white snakeroot for your Teaspoon Dragon," he said with a shrug. "In case you need a fresh tuft. That's also on aisle 21."

Smidge poked out of my jacket pocket at the mention of the white snakeroot and sniffed the air trying to find some.

"Hey! How did you know about Smidge?" I asked.

"Don't trouble yourself with such questions, young man," he said. "Like I said. Aisle 20 is housewares, household items, mirrors and such. You're looking for aisle 21. Keeperwares."

I looked down at aisle 20 again. At the very end there was a collection of tall mirrors, all standing upright, leaning against the back wall. He sounded sincere, and I wanted to believe him. But if there was another aisle there, I sure couldn't see it.

"I can show you the way, but first I need to make sure you understand a few things."

"Yes. Whatever it is, tell me. We have to go. It's, like, an actual emergency."

"I don't have anything to tell you, just a few questions to ask."

"Ok, fine. Go."

"What is a skyhook?"

I paused. What a strange question.

"Skyhook? Pixies use them to hang things in mid-air. They literally hook onto the sky. If you have two of them, you can even make a swing right in the middle of an open space. No trees required."

"Very good. And the pixies are sworn enemies of what group?"

"The Giblins," I replied. "They're the worst."

"Don't you mean *Goblins*?" Ginny whispered.

"No, Giblins," I said back. "Distant cousins of Goblins, but they're much bigger and way more rude."

"And what is a Giblin's most notable characteristic, besides rudeness?" Henry asked.

"Greed, of course. Money is the most important thing to them. Nothing else matters."

"And to satisfy their greed, what is their favored currency?"

"Shmeldings, of course. But it's not their *favored* currency. It's the only one they'll trade in. Nothing else will do."

"You're so weird," Ginny said. "How do you know all this?"

I shrugged.

"My grandpa. His stories. They were all true, after all. Mom always said they were crazy, but they're not."

"They're not crazy at all," Henry said. "You pass, young man. And quite admirably, I might add. I'm glad you understand all of that so well."

Henry looked pleased. Maybe even proud. If not proud of me, then proud of my grandpa's clever teaching methods.

"Like I said, Keeperwares are on aisle 21. Just on the other side of that mirror."

He pointed to one mirror in particular, among the many on display. It was larger and nicer than the rest, with an old-world look to it, dark stained wood and dramatic, deep carving, like it may have been around for hundreds of years. Now that he had pointed it out, I could tell there was something special about it.

I stepped toward the mirror and touched my hand to its surface. Or tried to, anyway. But as I reached out, my hand went right through. The surface of the mirror wiggled and shimmered like a glossy bubble. My hand disappeared to the other side, all the way up to my elbow.

"Well, go on," Ginny said, nudging me forward. "Let's see what's on the other side."

"One last question, young man," Henry said. "Like anything else in this store, things on aisle 21 cost money. I keep the shop out here, of course. But aisle 21 is managed by Jothi."

"Jothi?"

"Yes, Jothi. He is, well — he's a Giblin."

"Oh," I said, with a mix of surprise and disappointment.

"Aisle 21 is Jothi's business. And Jothi is *all business*, as you might expect, understanding Giblins the way you do. Have you brought any Shmeldings with you?"

I patted my pockets.

Of course I hadn't. Why would I have? Where would I even get them?

"Um," I said.

Henry shook his head. It was the headshake my mom uses when she disapproves of something.

"I warn you now, Logan. Jothi doesn't take kindly to shoppers who are unprepared to pay. That will not go well for you. Not at all."

I looked down at Muggins.

"Why didn't you tell me?"

He shrugged innocently.

"Some things need to be learned, and not told," he said.

"What does that even mean?" I shouted. "Whatever. Where am I supposed to get Shmeldings?"

"Seriously?" Ginny added. "You could have said something."

Ginny and I both looked at Muggins impatiently. Smidge popped up and chittered at Muggins, signaling his own impatience. Then it occurred to me.

"I've got it. I have an idea. Follow me!"

WITH GINNY ON MY HANDLEBARS, and Muggins riding backpack-style, I rode out from Smerconish's, down the street, past my grandpa's house.

"Where are you going?" Ginny insisted.

"My house."

"What do you need there?"

"You'll see."

I had already been wrong multiple times up to this point. If I was wrong here, then it would mean ruin. I dropped my bike and ran up the porch when we got to my house. I rushed through the front door, hoping to check in with my mom, but also to do what I needed to do, and make a quick exit.

"Mom?" I called out.

No answer. It was strange that she wasn't home. Nobody was home. I checked the kitchen.

"Dad? Where is everybody?"

"Maybe she's shopping," Ginny said.

"No, she always shops on Saturday morning. Or on Tuesday afternoon, to get the things she missed on Saturday."

I pulled open one of the kitchen drawers and rummaged around inside.

"Do you need help finding something?" Ginny asked.

"No, I found it," I yelled, holding up a kitchen tool triumphantly.

"You're going to save Cameria with a can opener? God help us," she said.

"No, don't be ridiculous. Just follow me. You'll see in a second."

I ran down the hall to my bedroom and through the door and grabbed the coffee can bank. I shook it again, but it still didn't sound like there was much more inside than there ever had been.

"Oh no. It's supposed to be an interest-bearing piggy bank. Where's all the interest? There have to be some Shmeldings inside. Otherwise, we are totally screwed!"

"What?" Ginny asked.

"What if my mom was right? What if it really was just an old coffee can."

"Now is not the time to stop believing," Muggins said, appearing from nowhere as he often tends to do.

"Just believe," he said.

"What if this is all just craziness. Total nonsense. What if he really was just a crazy old man who told crazy stories?"

I shook the can.

"Listen to that. Just a couple stupid nickels and some change I added."

"Oh, Logan," Muggins said. "You know that's not true. After all that you've seen so far, you still have doubts? Look at who you're talking to right now. And by that, I mean me. I know you don't always understand me, so I want to be very clear on that point. I'm talking about me. Muggins, the magical toolbox troll."

"Yeah, I know. But what if I'm just dreaming? None of this seems like it can be real. How could it be?"

I shook the can again; then I shook my head in disappointment.

"How can it be real?" Muggins asked. "I don't know. That's for you to decide. Not me."

I turned and placed the opener on the can's lip.

"What did you expect to be in there?" Ginny asked.

"I — when he gave it to me — it's hard to explain," I said. "You'll just think it's crazy."

"Just say what's on your mind," she said.

I took a deep breath. It was Ginny, after all.

"Shmeldings. I think there will be Shmeldings in here. When my grandpa gave me this bank, he said it was special. That it was an interest-bearing piggy bank. I know that sounds nuts. It's just a coffee can with a hole in the lid. But he said if I put money in and let it sit, I would get more out than I put in. He said it was much better than what a regular bank pays. He also put in five special nickels to get me started. I don't know what made them special. He never really said. But he did say they were special. So, I'm expecting that when I open this can, those five nickels will have become Shmeldings. And the money I put in myself? I don't know. Hopefully, there's more now. I know it sounds crazy, but that's what's on my mind. And if I'm wrong, then we're totally and completely screwed."

I paused, waiting for her to laugh. I had heard myself talking. I knew how it sounded. Who would believe such a crazy story, anyway?

"Well, hurry up then," she said. "Open it up. Let's see what's in there."

"Right, of course. Sorry!"

I looked at Muggins for a sign of what he was thinking. He nodded a reassuring nod.

"Go on. Go for it," he said.

I squeezed the opener, carefully turning the handle. The lid popped up slightly as I came almost full circle around the rim. The inside was dark through the gap. I couldn't see anything past the narrow slit. I took a deep breath and reached toward it, placing my thumbnail under the lid.

"Come on, open it," Ginny insisted.

I lifted the lid slowly. When I did, it erupted like a money volcano. So help me, I've never seen so much money in my life. It just kept pouring up out of the can and spilling onto the floor. Fives, tens, twenties, fifties. And even hundred-dollar bills. A nonstop flow of coins and bills, just pouring and pouring onto my bedroom floor.

"Muggins," I shouted. "It's even better than Grandpa said it was! Open your bottomless bag."

He held it up, and I started scooping whatever I could off the floor and stuffing it in. One scoop after another. He looked at me with a puzzled look, but he kept holding the bag, nonetheless.

"Can you believe this?" I said. "It's still coming out!"

I shoved a few more handfuls in, but the excitement wore off when I came to a somber realization. I sat waist-deep in a treasure trove of money, and it was completely useless to me in the moment.

"What's wrong?" Ginny asked.

"It's just money," I said.

"And that's bad?" she said as it dribbled out. "This is unreal!"

"I don't need *this* money," I said sullenly. "I need Shmeldings."

The eruption eventually stopped, and the clatter of the pouring coins gave way to an ominous silence. I stood, and picked the coffee can up. I turned it over and dumped the last of its contents onto the floor. I dragged my feet through the pile, turning over bills and coins to find something I didn't recognize. But there was nothing unusual. I sighed and put the can back on the dresser. But when I set the empty can back on my dresser, it jingled like it still had coins in it. I picked it up and gave it a gentle shake.

Jingle-Jingle.

I peered down inside. There were five glistening coins at the bottom. Coins I didn't recognize. A currency I'd never seen before. They were thick and heavy and shiny and beautiful, like old pirate treasure or something from a museum.

"Could it be?" I shouted. "Could it really be?"

I tipped the can down for Muggins to see inside.

"Those sure look like Shmeldings to me," he said.

I scooped them out and shoved them deep into my pocket.

"Let's get back to Smerconish's!"

I DON'T EVEN THINK the bike stopped moving before we hopped off and rushed through the entrance. Henry greeted us at the door.

"Jothi is expecting you," he said. "Mind your manners, though, and be patient. Jothi can be a bit—crusty. Customer service is not his strong suit, if you know what I mean."

He chuckled to himself like he was in on a joke that I didn't fully appreciate yet.

"Good luck," he said.

Ginny nudged me toward aisle 21.

"Go on," she said with a nod of her head. "Get in there."

We stood in front of the fancy old mirror again. And there I was, looking right back at myself—a full-fledged, properly-anointed Keeper of the Light. I sure didn't look like much, certainly not what you might expect from the guy tasked with defeating Karma and saving Cameria from total destruction. I was barely five and a half feet tall, with mussed hair and scrawny little arms. Muggins stood on my right, Ginny on my left. Smidge-the-fearsome was tucked into a warm pocket, napping, and Grimes, the crazy talking pocket watch, was snapped shut and quietly tucked into the pocket of my jeans — my boys' medium jeans, with a stringy hole worn through the knee.

Look at us. What are we doing?

"Well, are you ready?" Ginny asked. "We have to go."

I thought for a second.

"Please remember, it's up to you to keep the Light." I whispered.

"What?" Ginny said.

"That's the last thing my grandpa ever said to me. It didn't make much sense to me when he said it."

"But now I understand. It's up to me now; or it's up to us, really. We have to do this. Together."

I put my hand on the mirror's surface, and it shimmered and wiggled again, to the point I couldn't see my own reflection anymore. I pressed my hand through, and then my foot, and I stepped entirely through to aisle 21. And what an aisle it was. Ginny followed closely.

"Holy cow," Ginny exclaimed.

"Whoa," I said. "This is incredible."

Aisle 21 was so long, I couldn't see to the end of it. So long, in fact, that the floor of the aisle had tracks laid down. And there was a motorized cart that ran from one end to the other.

"I don't understand," Ginny said. "How big is this store? We were just outside and it didn't seem that big. But this looks like it goes on for miles. How is that even possible?"

Muggins chuckled.

"This is aisle 21," he said. "The rules are different here."

"What rules?" she asked.

"All the rules, really. Most of them, anyway. Except for one or two. I don't know. I can't really keep track."

She stared awkwardly, mouth hanging slightly open.

"Here. Listen," Muggins said. "You know my bottomless bag?"

"Yes, of course," she said.

"Have you ever seen a bag like that before?"

"Of course not. Where would I have?"

"Exactly. I got that bag here. From Jothi. Do you understand now?"

"Kind of," she said with a shrug.

I honestly couldn't believe what I was seeing. Not only did aisle 21 run for as far as I could see, but the shelves rose so high, I couldn't see their tops. Perfectly symmetrical shelves, numbered and filled with bins or individually shelved products. This was the area that Henry had referred to as Keeperwares. And let me tell you, there was a *lot* of stuff here.

"There's only three Keepers at any given time, and all of this is for them?" I asked. "That's completely unreal."

"It's an important job," Muggins said. "They need supplies, and that makes this a very important place. Where else would they be able to find all this stuff, if not here?"

"Yeah, good point."

The shelf in front of me was labeled '*quantum locks.*' A sophisticated-looking device, presumably a quantum lock, sat on the shelf above the label. For such a fancy-sounding name, it looked like it was carved from wood, with interlocking wooden gears on the front of it. The shelf above was labeled '*musical note stationery and pens.*' The bay above that was filled with old leather-bound books. And just above that, a bin full of what I can only describe as potion bottles. Oddly enough, everything I could see cost one Shmelding.

Oh, thank goodness. I have five!

"This place is amazing," I said.

Then I was interrupted—and quite rudely, I might add. The voice was deep, and wet, as if the words were being spoken through a throat full of phlegm.

"What da hell you want?"

I turned to look to the left, and I instantly regretted it.

He looked like something I can only describe as big and strong with thick leathery skin. His face looked like it belonged to a radioactive frog or a mutant angler fish. But scarier. He had a wide mouth with big, sharp teeth protruding from his bottom jaw, out from under his lips. The teeth were long enough that they always showed. Even when he tried to close his mouth, those spiky teeth poked out past his lip. His eyes were black and lifeless, and set way too far apart for my liking.

This had to be Jothi. And Jothi was one of the scariest-looking things I had ever seen. While he waited for our response, he glared at us with an intense look of distrust, like I was there to steal from him. He stood behind the counter, cash register and all, with a dim yellow light shining down on him. If he was ready to help customers, he didn't look or sound very helpful. He picked up a notepad from the countertop and threw it at me. The notepad hit me in the chest and fell to the floor.

"Hey," I shouted.

"I said what da hell you want?" he shouted back. "You no speak English, or somet'ing?"

His loogie-laden voice was gross, and unlike anything I had ever heard. Jothi would have been terrifying in complete darkness, but seeing him by the light of day made it even worse.

Compose yourself, and be polite. Even if he's being a total jerk.

"I need a Starlact," I said.

He laughed out loud as the words left my mouth. At least I think he was laughing. He could have been choking on his own vomit. It was hard to tell.

"Oh, dat very expensive. You have Shmeldings? You no use money from out d'ere, in here."

He pointed to where we had just come in.

"Dat money no good here. You have dat money, you go back out d'ere and spend it. And get da hell outta my space."

I looked at Ginny, arms crossed and hips cocked in telltale disapproval.

"Please don't say anything," I murmered. "I have to keep this on track."

"Yes, I have some Shmeldings," I said hurriedly.

I jingled them in my pocket, and he recognized the sound immediately. I didn't even have to show him.

"Very good," he said, leaning in like a cat to catnip.

He flipped through a book on the countertop, studying it closely.

"Oh, dis t'ing," he said. "I remember dis t'ing. A good friend set it aside for safe keeping. Said for Jothi no lose track of it. Three twenty-seven forty-seven," he said in his gurgly voice.

"I don't understand," I said. "Is that the price? That sounds like a lot."

"Dat not price. Dat location."

He walked out from behind the counter, right toward me. I tried to get out of the way, but he caught me with his elbow as he passed.

"Hey," I shouted. "Why does everybody keep doing that?"

He didn't even look back. He just walked over to the motorized cart and opened the door. He looked back at us and waved a finger, motioning toward the inside of the cart.

"Git yer butts in. You wanna go, or what?"

"It's fine," Muggins said. "Go ahead."

We stepped into the cart and Jothi squeezed in with us, taking up all the remaining space. It was reminiscent of an old mine cart, with a couple of levers rising up from the floor. He grabbed a lever, squeezed the release at the top, and pushed it forward.

The base where the lever came up had a metal gauge marked with numbers. He moved the lever to 327, and it locked into place. The engine started chugging, and we rolled down the tracks. As we chugged our way down the main aisle, I saw that the towering shelves were numbered. Even numbers appeared on the left, odd numbers on the right.

"Do you think he actually has it?" Ginny asked, as we coasted down the tracks with a click-click-click.

"I sure hope so. I'm not sure what to do if he doesn't."

I couldn't believe the size of this place. It was like a whole world unto itself. Plants, herbs, elixirs, powders, liquids, caged animals I didn't even recognize. There were gadgets, tools, more books, personal storage bins and things I just don't know how to describe. I watched in amazement as they all sped by, and before long, we jerked to an abrupt stop.

The shelf to my right was numbered 327. Jothi pulled another lever. That caused the seating area of the cart to slide to the right with us in it. It clicked into a groove that went straight up the height of the rack.

"You hold on tight now, and no fall out. I no wanna clean up no mess," Jothi said. "I no like messes. Messes yucky."

He set the next lever to 47. Gears ground together, and we started our ascent: 1 then 2, then 3. I looked down over the edge as we went past 9. The cart shimmied as we rose up the column, and the tracks faded from view. I checked again and we were only up to 26.

"21 more? I might puke," I said.

"I'm begging you," Ginny said. "Please don't puke. If you do it, then I will, too. I cant' deal with that right now."

Metal ground against metal as we rose higher still, and the cart jerked to a noisy stop at 47. Jothi reached into the storage bay and tipped a bin forward to look inside.

"Hmm. Last one. You very lucky," he said. "But last one always cost extra. No hard feelings, right?"

"How much?" I asked.

He stared at my pocket.

"Five Shmeldings. You want it, or what?"

"That's all I have," I said.

He pointed at my pocket.

"I know. I heard da jingle-jingles."

"That's not fair."

"Jothi not here to be fair. Jothi here to make money. So, you want it, or what? Fine, never mind, I put it back and you go away now. Bye-bye."

"Wait," I said. "I'll take it. Five is fine, we have a deal."

"Very good," Jothi said, stroking his chin. "Very good, indeed. You pretty smart."

He put the bin back in its place and set the lever to zero. Gears ground together again, and we descended to the floor. When we got to the bottom, the cart slid back onto the wheels and Jothi set the other lever to zero. We were on our way back to the front counter until Muggins interrupted the journey.

"One more stop, please," he said.

"Now what you want?" Jothi grumped. "I got a business to run. Come on now! You just pay and get out of here!"

"Gideon had a personal storage bin here, did he not?" Muggins asked.

"Gideon? Who dat?" Jothi replied.

"Come on, Jothi. Gideon. You knew him well, I'm sure of that. He was a Keeper and a trusted ally to the Grand Council."

"Oh, dat guy. Gideon. He my old friend with Starlact. Why you no say so? Yeah sure, he have a bin. You want to go, I guess?"

"Yes, please."

Jothi reset the levers. We rolled forward, then to the other side. Jothi locked the cart into the side, and we rode up to 26.

"What you want from here?" Jothi asked impatiently.

"I wanted Logan to know about this. It belonged to Gideon before he passed. Logan has taken his place, now."

"Oh, dat's rich," Jothi said. "Dis little noodle replace Gideon? Come on now, don't make Jothi laugh."

Muggins gave Jothi a cold stare. To my surprise, Jothi actually changed his tone.

"Sorry about dat. I stop teasing baby Gideon now."

"Thank you. As I said, Gideon's bin belongs to Logan now, as do all of its contents, whenever he wants them. Could you pull the bin over, please?"

Jothi tipped the bin down so we could see inside.

"I'm not entirely sure what's in here, Logan, some things that belonged to Gideon," Muggins said. "I just thought you'd like to know about them. Some of this, you may find useful one day. Others you may just want to have for sentimental reasons. Regardless, this is all yours now. I'm sure he would have wanted to share it with you himself. But if you ever need anything from here, you come see Jothi. He'll take proper care of you, just as he did for your grandfather, Gideon."

Muggins looked at Jothi.

"You Gideon's grandson?" Jothi gurgled.

I nodded.

"Oh," he continued. "Sorry. Jothi not know. Jothi take good care. Really, really good care."

"Thank you for that," Muggins said pleasantly.

I took a minute to sift through the contents of the bin. There was an old photo of my grandmother, some strange tools, a locket on a leather strap necklace, and a whole bunch of other stuff I didn't recognize. As I sorted through, a soft glow rose up from the bottom of the pile, a glimmer of light shining through the gaps between every-thing else. I dug in, thinking it was an old flashlight that had switched on. But I pulled out a small glass bottle, corked and sealed with wax. A strange little light danced around inside, like a spark, just bouncing around off the walls of the bottle. I turned the bottle around to see the other side and was shocked by the label: *Lightning. March 3.*

"Holy cow," I blurted.

"What?" Ginny asked.

"He told me about this, but I thought it was just a figure of speech. I didn't know he actually caught real lightning in a real bottle."

"Oh, please. Nobody can do that," Ginny scoffed. "It's literally impossible."

"See for yourself."

I held the bottle up in front of her face, with the label facing out. The light danced off the gloss of her eyes as she studied it.

"Holy cow is right," she said.

"Muggins, can I take this with me?"

"Of course you can, Logan. It's yours, after all. Just be careful with it. Very careful."

I shoved it in my pocket.

"We go now, dat ok?" Jothi asked. "Busy, busy."

I wanted to spend more time with my grandpa's stuff, but I could always come back another time.

"Sure," I said. "That's fine."

Jothi moved the levers and took us back to the front, where he rang up my purchase.

"Four Shmeldings," he said.

"I thought you said it was five," I replied, for no good reason at all.

"Wow, tough negotiator," Ginny said.

"Jothi did say dat. But Jothi give to you for four dis time, because Gideon. Don't make Jothi change mind. Just pay up and go now."

"That's very kind of you, Jothi," Muggins said with a nod. "And for that we thank you. Logan, please pay him so we can be on our way."

I pulled four Shmeldings from my pocket and slid them across the counter. With our transaction completed, we were on our way.

As we left Smerconish's, I pedaled with all my might.

"Muggins, my legs are killing me," I said.

"It sounds like you could use a good tailwind to push you along," he said.

"Oh, man, if only. I seriously need a break."

"Very well, then," he said. "Why didn't you just ask?"

A strong gust of wind hit me in the back. And before I knew it, my legs were pedaling slower, but the bike was going faster. Eventually, I wasn't pedaling at all. We were just going — sailing down the street faster than I'd ever ridden before.

"Did you do that?" I asked.

"Of course I did."

"But how?"

"I have a gift with the elements, in case you hadn't noticed. I was right to think you hadn't. Yes, I can see that now. Such a seemingly gifted child, but you fail to understand the simplest things. I can't seem to figure you out."

"Likewise," I said.

Ginny looked back at me from the handlebars and rolled her eyes. I rolled mine in response. Then she smiled. What a wonderful smile it was. I knew we understood each other, without even talking. We were tuned to the same wavelength with this. We coasted down the street, driven by the the wind, and we arrived my grandpa's house in no time at all. I dropped the bike out front, and we ran out back, straight toward the old tree.

"Muggins, how did you do that? With the wind."

"I told you—I have a gift with the elements. You really don't listen very well, do you?"

"I heard you say it. But I hear you say a lot of things I don't understand. How do you do it?"

"It's really quite simple. Smoak is an Avian, and I am an Elementalist. There's not much more to it. Do you follow?"

"No, not really."

"Look. My faction, my people. We are, or we *were*, called the Elementalists. Most of us had a knack for manipulating the elements. Water, air, stone, metal, that sort of thing."

"Like *magic*?"

Muggins scrunched his face and shook his head.

"I wouldn't call it magic. It's more like a relationship. I need them to do certain things. And they do them at my request. Water and air tend to be the most cooperative. But other things can be convinced as well."

"Seriously?"

"Yes, of course, I have no reason to lie to you now. Some Elementalists were better at it than others. I just happen to be particularly good, better than most. Some say the best ever. I don't know, it's probably true, but it's also not for me to boast about it."

"Were there a lot of you? You know—before?"

"Oh yes, we were numerous. Large enough to have representation on the Grand Council."

He was proud, reflecting on better, happier times.

"You were represented on the Council?" Ginny asked.

"My people were. Yes, absolutely. Let me ask you a question. When we visited the Council, did you happen to notice that there were five seats at the table, but only four of them were occupied?"

"I did, yes."

"The fifth seat used to be mine."

"Are you kidding me?"

"Do I strike you as someone prone to kidding?"

"No."

"Good. Because I'm quite serious, in fact. You asked if I ever did more than build treehouses, and the answer is yes, I've done far more than that. Smoak, Pickelhaub, Gabriel and Adharma. There was once a time that I used to sit with them. Until the Eight Days War, that is. After all was said and done, the Council could no longer recognize me as a leader of anything. I was alone, a faction of one. A leader with no followers. Some of them openly mock me now. I don't blame them, really. But I plan to take my seat back at that table someday. More importantly, however, I have to find my people first. All of them."

"But what if they're all just gone?" Ginny asked.

Muggins cringed.

"I don't need to answer that now. Somehow, somewhere, I will find them, and I will beg for their forgiveness. And if I can't do that, I will die trying. For now, out of respect for the role I used to hold, the Council allows me to observe and participate in Council business, albeit in a far more limited fashion. I have lost my power to vote, of course. I just have to stand by, watch, and perhaps influence where I can. But that is all they will allow me to do."

He stopped abruptly, and his expression hardened as we arrived at the tree.

"Move it, now. Off you go. Time is no friend of ours."

Muggins walked through the portal and waved us in to join him on the cliffs. As I stepped inside to join him, I heard something behind me, like dogs barking. I looked back out, and a group of policemen led hounds into the woods on long leashes. They were coming right toward us, and they were coming fast. I wasn't sure what to do. I stood frozen, watching as they approached, wondering why they were there.

The dogs ran fast, with their noses to the ground, serpentining back and forth to stay on our scent. They were just a few feet away from us, but they ran right past the tree. The dogs doubled back and circled the tree, sniffing the ground around it. The dogs seemed confused, and the policemen did, too. They walked around the tree, looking up into the branches.

"The tracks just stop right here?" one of the officers said.

"Can't be," the other said, shining a light up into the tree, "but yeah, it sure looks that way."

"The hounds followed our scent here," Ginny whispered. "That's what they use them for. But the scent stopped at the base when we came inside here. So, they probably think we climbed up."

I looked past the policemen, toward my grandpa's house. My mom wasn't far behind, trudging through the woods, trying to keep up. She looked cold, loosely wrapped in a coat she had grabbed in a hurry, fighting to pull it closed while she called out my name.

"Logan, honey. Please come home. Where are you? Are you ok? We love you, baby boy."

She was staring right at me as she struggled to catch up. But she didn't see me. She was crying. She looked so scared, and her voice shook when she called my name.

"I'm right here, Mom. I'm ok!"

Then I heard a rustling behind us inside the portal. And a growl.

"Logan, are you out there? Where are you, honey? If you can hear me, please come home. We love you."

Her voice still trembled. I realized just how long we'd been gone. It had been a while since the last time she saw me. My bike was out front, and she knew I liked to explore the woods. She must have been so worried. That's why nobody was home when we went—they were at the police station filing a report.

"I'm right here, Mom!" I yelled again. "I'm right here."

I yelled as loud as possible, but she didn't hear or see me. No portal. No entryway to Cameria. Just an old, burnt tree. As I stood atop the rocky cliffs overlooking Cameria, my own mother had no idea I was there. She didn't believe, so in her mind, Cameria didn't exist. Therefore, in the moment, neither did I.

"This is terrible," I said, catching a glimpse of Cameria. "Ginny, are you seeing this?"

"Oh, I see it," she said. "It's awful!"

"Look at the darkness around Karma's lair," I said. "It's enormous, and still growing."

"What if it reaches the trees of the Qud Palmon Forest?" Ginny asked. "It's so close."

"That cannot be allowed," Muggins said. "We have to get to the Council building."

I looked down at my feet. The creeping darkness was spreading here, too, right across the cliffs, under my feet. It had even spilled through the portal, spreading out from the tree's base into Grandpa's yard.

I heard another sound, closer this time. It was definitely a growl. And it wasn't a police dog.

15

A shadow wolf burst through the bushes and leapt at my throat, giving up its shadowy form mid-leap. I flinched and ducked to the side, but its claws tore through my shirt and skin. Three gashes right across my upper arm. Muggins crouched in a combative posture and moved his hand in a circular motion. The branches of the bush took on new life, wrapped around its hind leg, then further up the leg and over its hips. Another wound around its snout, and two more wrapped around its torso. Muggins flicked his fingers back toward the bush. The wolf disappeared as the tendrils drew it back in.

"Are you hurt?" Muggins asked.

I looked down at my arm. Dabs of blood stained my shirt around the rips in the fabric.

"It's bleeding," I said. "But I'll be fine."

"The bush won't hold it for long, and others are surely close by. They always are."

"I need to go back. I need to let my mom know I'm here, and I'll come right back. I swear!"

"Absolutely not. I understand your wishes, but that's a terrible idea, plain and simple. The pack are nearby, you'll take them with you. You'll take them right out there, right to her. Is that what you want?"

"No, what I want is just to let her know that I'm alright. Just real fast. Did you see her?"

"I did. But I'm sorry, we just can't."

"But—"

"Let us be going now, and quickly. For Gideon."

Grudgingly, I agreed to go, looking over my shoulder as we walked, hoping she had some sense that I was alright.

"And don't fall into the river again, Miss Ginny," Muggins said. "We haven't got time for any more delays."

"Grimesy, what time is it," Muggins asked.

I pulled him out and flipped his lid open when.

"FORTY MINUTES PAST FOUR O'CLOCK," he shouted.

He paused and gasped to recover his breath.

"And you had better hurry!" he continued yelling. "All is not well. The Council has called a special meeting at precisely six o'clock to discuss important matters. You'd better be there."

ONE THING IS FOR SURE. Muggins has an amazing knack for finding burbles. He found pair of really fast ones this time. When we arrived, the Council building was busier than usual, and as we approached, I could hear the people out front yelling at each other, hurling insults back and forth.

"This Council need to stand down, and leave Karma alone," one of them yelled. "There's a reason this is all happening. And shame on you all for trying to stop it. It's the proper course, after all."

"You're out of your mind!" another voice replied. "She's ruining everything, can't you see that? Open your blooming eyes."

The kindness and respect that I had come to expect of Cameria's people had finally given way to simmering hatred. I pulled Grimes from my pocket and flipped the lid open.

"FIVE MINUTES TO SIX," he yelled out without me even asking.

"Oh, you just shut up over there," someone screamed back, "or I'll give you something to be loud about."

"Jeez," I mumbled.

I sheepishly tucked Grimes back into my pocket and tried to avoid making eye contact with the elderly woman who had just yelled at us.

"What is going on here, Muggins?"

"You remember what I told you about the Light? In its absence, what we end up with is—well, this."

"It hurts my heart to see this," Ginny said. "Why can't it go back to how it used to be?"

"It can," Muggins said. "But we'll need to release the Light first, and most likely confront Karma in the process. It's the only way."

A harpy eagle swooped down from the sky. As it approached the entrance to the Council building, it took the form of Viceroy Smoak, in his red-coat uniform, just in time to land smoothly and walk through the Council building entrance. He stood patiently waiting for the guards to open the door for him.

"Why don't you open it yourself?" one of the guards offered.

"I beg your pardon? Do not mistake my lack of a violent response for acceptance of your disrespect," Smoak said. "You're fortunate I have more important business to tend to. But you can rest assured, I will address your insubordination in due course."

"Come on, now," Muggins said. "Let's make a quiet entrance and duck in behind him."

Smoak opened the door, and we dashed in behind him before it shut, careful to avoid the people near the entrance.

Viceroy Smoak took his seat in the Council Chambers. Gabriel, Chancellor Pickelhaub and Adharma had already taken their seats. Muggins' seat remained empty, of course. The persnickety man quickly called the meeting to order, and the Council members wasted no time getting straight to business.

"With every tick of the clock that passes," Smoak said, "the Light grows dimmer. Soon, it will be gone completely. The Vapes are growing in epidemic numbers, and my sources confirm that the

Shadow Pack is as well. I say this with tremendous sadness, but I'm afraid we are rapidly approaching the end of Cameria as we know it."

"I would like to report that the Qud Palmon stand ready to fight," Chancellor Pickelhaub added. "But I cannot say it with much confidence. The fighting among our own leadership has caused a crisis in the ranks. Our soldiers are divided against themselves, and I can't say with any level of conviction what we could bring to a battle at this time."

"Gabriel was right to be wary," Adharma said. "It is plain to see. If only some of us had listened, we might be in a different place by now. The newly anointed Keeper has done nothing to help us. He is failing all of Cameria."

Ginny whisper-scoffed.

"Are you going to let him get away with that?" she said. "Stand up for yourself!"

"We're not supposed to talk," I whispered. "Don't you remember?"

"In our greatest time of need, yet another Keeper has failed us," Adharma went on. "Perhaps the time is upon us to finally explore a different path, and to embrace a different strategy. One with a better chance to preserve all that we have built."

But I didn't fail. I'm trying my best here. He's the one that's screwing everything up.

"Logan, say something," Ginny said in a voice that was now well-above a whisper.

I was so nervous. The floor hadn't recognized me, and I wasn't supposed to talk until they said I could. I wanted to say something, but my tongue had turned to wood.

"I have a solution to all your ills," Adharma continued. "All of *our* ills. It will involve a departure from past norms. It will require us all to embrace an uncomfortable compromise. There will be difficult change, but I daresay it's a small price to pay to preserve one's own existence."

"How many Avians are there?" I whispered to Muggins. "In Smoak's faction—are there a lot of them?"

"Thousands, if I had to guess. Possibly tens of thousands. Why do you ask?"

"I think I have an idea," I said.

"Hear me out," Adharma went on, pointing to the darkness outside. "and let us begin a new chapter. The dawn of a new day, if I may be so bold."

"What are you proposing?" Chancellor Pickelhaub asked.

Gabriel sat quietly, observing. Smoak was curious, but cautious.

"This Council was brought together for a purpose," Adharma said, "a purpose that it has since outlived. If there is any doubt about that, I invite you to take a peek out the window. I propose that you all follow my lead and allow me to chair this Council. Perhaps Karma could even join our ranks. Together, we can bring about radical change. Necessary change. Change for the better."

"Don't listen," Ginny yelled out without being recognized. "He's lying."

The murmur in the crowd fell silent. Adharma stopped talking and the people parted like the red sea, opening a clear lane between Ginny and the pentagonal table. The Council members stared at her in silent shock. Then their eyes shifted to me.

Oh my god. Oh my god. Oh my god. What do I do now? Think Logan!

"Um," I said.

"What is the meaning of this?" Smoak demanded. "Who is this young lady? How *dare* you interrupt this Council."

"Silence," Adharma yelled, pointing an angry finger at Ginny. "You have no business speaking before this Council. Not another word from you, or the consequences will be severe."

Say something, Logan.

"I—. I—."

"Well, what is it, young man?" Smoak demanded. "Never mind, we don't have time for this nonsense. Interrupt again and I'll have you dragged out of here. Adharma, please continue."

I managed to clumsily blurt out some words.

"Permission to address the Council?"

It was messy and unconvincing. But I got them out.

Why did you say that? Now you actually have to talk to them.

The persnickety man glanced at Smoak, and Smoak nodded his approval.

"The floor now recognizes Master Logan LeVec, Keeper of the Light."

"I'm afraid I have some bad news," I said shyly.

"Well, what is it?" Smoak demanded.

I looked at Adharma with his chin held high, glaring down his nose at me. He was defiant, as if daring me to say something, and all too confident that I didn't have the courage.

I'm tired of being afraid of what other people think. I'm standing up for what's right. You want to challenge me, pal? You got it. Watch this.

"Kismet," I said, "the master of the shadow pack has been summoning more and more shadow wolves, expanding their numbers way beyond anything we've ever seen. The vapes are growing in numbers, too."

"Yes, we are already well aware of this," Smoak said.

"Kismet has formed an alliance with the Vapes," I continued. "The Vapes, Kismet and the Pack—they'll all come together against this Council, and against all of your individual factions."

"Silence!" Adharma shouted.

"No, no, no," the persnickety man yelled out, "Master LeVec has the floor, and you'll let him finish."

"And Kismet has partnered up with Adharma, too," I continued. "They're working together on all of this behind your backs. And what's even worse, Adharma is also working with Karma. They're all working together, trying to split you up against yourselves. Adharma has even infiltrated the Qud Palmon guard. He's a shifter, and he's been working the inside. With the Light being as weak as it is, it's all become so much easier, too. It's all part of their plan. Like the saying goes—united we stand, divided we fall. They're dividing you all, so it's easier to make you fall. And now I believe I've run out of things to say, so that's all I have to say about that. Oh, and I'm sorry for interrupting. So, yeah. I guess I'm really done now."

I bowed an awkward bow for no apparent reason. Then it was

silent. Silent disbelief. Silent shock. Silent skepticism. Silent stewing anger.

Somebody say something.

Adharma slow-clapped at me, with his big, smug face hanging out.

"Bravo, young man, on a story well told. Extra points for creativity and effort. But you're wasting precious time, and you should leave this Council to its business. Off with you, now. Run along, go play outside or something. Let the adults handle this."

Are you kidding me? Nothing? Nothing at all?

"Not so fast," Smoak said. "Do you have any appreciation at all for the gravity of the accusations you've just made, young man? These are serious allegations, not to be taken lightly. Such words are not to be thrown about without some consequence."

"He's just a boy," Adharma said dismissively. "He knows nothing. It's nonsense. Send him away."

Smoak looked at Muggins.

"Do you vouch for the boy's allegations?"

"I do," Muggins said solemnly. "All of it. Every single word."

Smoak snapped his fingers at the persnickety man.

"Go fetch my Viggery from my office," he said.

THE PERSNICKETY MAN sprang into action. The sound of shoes clopping across the stone floor faded into the distance, down a long hallway. Viceroy Smoak sat quietly, looking me up and down, tapping his fingers on the table, staring at me as he waited.

Did I do something wrong? I must have done something wrong.

Adharma looked at me and mouthed silently.

"You'll pay for this."

The trot of footsteps came back toward the meeting chamber, and the persnickety man plopped a device into the palm of Viceroy Smoak's hand. It resembled a small telescope, but also, not really. More like a wooden rod, with an eyepiece affixed to one end, and a spherical crystal at the other end. Nothing in between, just the stick to keep them at a fixed distance from each other. Smoak peered through the eyepiece toward the crystal and mumbled something to himself. Then he handed the Viggery back to the persnickety man and let out a heavy sigh.

"Not only is she taking the Light," Smoak said. "It's just as the boy says. With the Light diminished, she's been sowing seeds of discontent. She's turning us against each other right before our very eyes, hidden in plain sight. To divide us as a union and to conquer us each individually. It's all true."

Gasps rang out among the observers.

"And Adharma, supposedly our sworn ally, has been helping her this whole time. How did I not see this sooner?"

Smoak turned his attention to Adharma.

"You've betrayed us all, and you'll be dealt with appropriately. But right now, we have to deal with Karma before it really is too late."

"Fools!" Adharma shouted. "You're already too late. The wheels are set in motion. The train has left the station, and it is speeding down the tracks at a frantic pace. If you are foolish enough to step in front of it now, well then, be my guest. I can't help you in that case. But if you join me now, perhaps you could be spared."

Smoak snapped his fingers again at the persnickety man.

"Summon the guards," Smoak said. "And be quick about it. Remove this traitor at once."

The persnickety man shuffled toward the door, but the doors burst open as he approached, knocking him over backwards.

Karma sauntered in unannounced, draped in flowing white gown trimmed in gold, with her golden hair and her golden eyes surveying the room with menace.

～

GASPS ECHOED THROUGH THE CHAMBER.

"Karma!" Chancellor Pickelhaub shouted.

Kismet followed immediately behind her.

"You can't just burst in here uninvited," Smoak said. "How dare you sully this most revered of halls with your corrupted presence?"

Smoak gently swirled into the shape of a woman, middle-aged with kind eyes, a soft voice and the face of a doll.

"Sweetheart," Smoak said. "You don't need to do this. Come outside with me, dear. Let's take a walk and get away from these people. We can get some sweets at the shop."

"Oh please," Karma said, with an evil laugh. "My mother? Is that the best you can do? That might have swayed me as a child. But now it's just pathetic."

Karma thrust her arm forward, and her hand emerged from her flowing sleeve to push her mirror toward Smoak. His eyes met his reflection, and he was knocked to the floor.

Muggins scanned the room with hurried eyes. There were books, cups, and a candelabra on a small side table. A collection of swords was also mounted to the wall near a painted portrait. He flicked his hands through the air. One by one, the objects flew through the air, hurtling toward Karma, pelting her about the head and chest, knocking her back on her heels. Cups, books, plates, all in sequence. The swords, however, never moved.

Muggins leaned forward, groaned, and pushed both hands forward through the air. The pentagonal table slid across the floor. It picked up speed as it slid closer, and it crashed right into Karma. She stumbled backward, and the table pinned her against the wall. Muggins glanced around for something else. But when he looked back, she flicked her mirror and caught his eye.

Muggins froze, expressionless. Without warning, he flew through the air backward, like he'd been hit by an invisible car. He fell to the floor and slid to the wall, where he lay motionless.

"Muggins," I yelled. "Are you ok?"

He didn't respond.

I turned to Karma, and as I did, she flashed her mirror at me. I winced, afraid of what might happen. I looked away as fast as I could.

"I'm sure I saw myself," I mumbled. "But maybe not, since nothing happened."

Karma groaned with frustration, pushed the table back, and stepped out from behind it.

"Enough of this nonsense," she said.

"What do you want here?" Pickelhaub demanded.

Chancellor Pickelhaub stood tall, refusing to be intimidated, and she needed Karma to know it.

"You have no business before this Council."

"Oh, but I do," she said. "I've come to allege a wrong. In fact, I've come to make a demand for satisfaction," she said.

More gasps rang out.

"Demand for satisfaction? *You've* been wronged?" Pickelhaub snorted. "I've heard some tall tales, but that's something else."

"Oh, but I have," Karma said. "Yes, indeed, a most foul and grievous wrong, I should say. And it was perpetrated by him!"

She pointed right at me.

Me? What did I do?

"He killed my precious Jynx. My snowy lynx. Unprovoked, he agitated an angry swarm of violet lancers so they would attack her. He threw a rock right at the hive as she stood below. My dear Jynx never stood a chance, and he is now responsible for her death! Honor's Law dictates that any man who causes death or damage to the livestock of another shall be put to death. As the Honors Edict dictates, you must grant me my satisfaction. Does anyone here dare to disagree with me?"

"But I—" I said confused.

"You threw the rock at the busy hive, just around from Jarvis' puppet shop. Do you deny this?" she said, daring me to say otherwise. "You heard the buzzing, and you purposely threw the rock, did you not?"

"I was just trying to keep them away from us," I said.

Silence fell across the room again.

"So, you admit your crime!" she said. "Honor's Law. Last I checked, it's the rule of this land. And it demands sacrifice. The perpetrator must be put to death."

I looked around waiting for somebody to disagree. Anybody.

They all fidgeted uncomfortably, but nobody would make eye contact, or say a word.

"What is happening?" Ginny whispered to me.

"As a technical matter," Chancellor Pickelhaub said. "If what you say is true, that is what the law requires."

My heart fell to my stomach.

"But," she continued, "Honors Law was never meant to be applied this way. It's not what the Elders intended. The Honors Edict was written generations ago, at a very different time to address very different issues. It was a time when killing livestock could jeopardize a farmer's ability to survive, as they might otherwise starve. You suffer no such risk here today!"

"No matter, it is still the law, and the law must be applied without compromise. I believe I am now entitled to choose an executioner. In the old days they would choose a family member to drive the point home. But I see none here, so I'll settle for an alternate."

This can't be happening. How is this happening? Muggins, I need you. Somebody do something!

Karma looked around the room. Most people there were unarmed. But Gabriel's bow was leaned up against the back of his chair.

"You," Karma said, pointing at Gabriel. "I choose you. Get up on your feet and be quick about it."

"You can't be serious," Ginny shouted. "Please don't do this. You can't do this."

The room buzzed as people began to understand what was about to happen. Gabriel stood from his chair and lifted his bow. His hand rested on his quiver, as it glowed with Arrows of Light.

Viceroy Smoak was visibly injured and struggled to pull himself up from the floor.

"Is Cameria no longer governed by the rule of law," he said, "and guided by the principles of the Light?"

"Don't you lecture me about what is right," Karma shot back. "I won't be denied."

"The law was never meant to be applied this way. You know that."

"Do you deny the text of the Honors Edict?"

"No, I do not. However, I do deny your interpretation. That was never the intent."

"Do you deny the facts presented to this Council?"

"I have no basis to dispute the information charged. Nor do I have any basis to confirm it."

"Then I have delivered a proper demand for satisfaction. It is this Council's obligation to deliver it to me. I believe the Council must now vote. May I have a motion to poll the Council?"

There was utter silence. I still had hope, but that hope was short-lived.

"Aye. So moved," Adharma said. "This Council shall now vote. On the issue of the grievous murder of Jynx, the snowy lynx, committed by one Master Logan LeVec, and the satisfaction sought under the Honors Edict, on the facts and circumstances presented, I vote to convict as charged."

"He's just a boy," Chancellor Pickelhaub said.

"The Edict applies equally to all occupants of Cameria without distinction. It applies without bias or mercy, does it not?"

"He's not from here."

"But he's here now, and he's broken our laws, and I presume you vote in favor as well, as you must?"

"It is what the law requires," the chancellor said hesitantly. "I have no basis to defy the Edict."

"It was never meant for this," Muggins said, groaning.

"Silence," Adharma barked back "Point of order. The floor has not recognized you."

My knees wobbled. I was ready to faint.

"The Edict demands that you punish your own," Karma continued. "I command you to right this wrong on my behalf."

"You are pure evil," Muggins said, his tone defeated.

"I repeat my demand," Karma said. "So, you may all live with the shame of it. Enjoy what you have for now, because this is just the beginning. My vengeance on this Council and your people will be swift and sweet. Now, let us get on with the matter at hand."

Karma motioned to Gabriel.

"Nock your arrow, and draw your bow," she said. "Now."

Adharma and Kismet charged at me. They grabbed my arms, dragged me across the room and pinned me against the wall with my arms outstretched.

"Let him go!" Ginny yelled.

Gabriel pulled an Arrow of Light from his quiver and raised his bow. He nocked the arrow to the string and squinted an eye, taking careful aim at my chest.

"Gabriel! Don't do this!" I begged.

He shook his head and spoke.

"Do not resist. In fairness, you should understand. The Light would never harm a heart that is true."

Now he's judging me?

"But his heart *is* true," Ginny pleaded, with tears streaming down her cheeks.

"His heart is truer than true. He's the kindest, sweetest person I've ever met."

"I didn't do anything wrong," I screamed.

The whole Council stood by, quietly watching. The sound of silence was deafening. Their laws, as they chose to apply them, required this, and nobody was willing to stop it.

Karma stepped closer to Gabriel.

"Now," she said in a dreadful voice. "Deliver me my satisfaction."

Gabriel's bow creaked as he drew the string tighter and let loose his arrow. It sailed across the chamber and hit me right in the chest.

Silence. Darkness. Nothingness.

16

When I awoke, the Council members stood over me, looking down as I lay on the floor. Smidge had crawled from my pocket and was chittering softly. He nudged my chin to wake me.

"What just happened?" I asked groggily.

"It would appear that you fainted," Smoak said. "Just as Gabriel's arrow struck you."

I looked at Gabriel.

"You shot me, you jerk! Why would you do that?"

"My quiver draws its arrows from the Light. As I said, the Light would never harm the pure of heart. I stand by those words, and you can see that I was correct."

"You knew it wouldn't hurt me?"

"*Knew* is a strong term," he said with a friendly grin. "I was, however, hopeful. I might go so far as to say quite certain. Yes, I was quite certain it would be fine. I had a good sense about you."

"Quite certain? That's one heck of a risk you took—with my life, no less."

Gabriel offered me a hand and pulled me up off the floor. Ginny ran over and hugged me around the neck so tight I almost passed out again.

"Easy," I said.

"Thank goodness you're ok," she said. "I was so worried!"

"Me too," I said. "And I'm glad you're ok, too."

"My intent," Gabriel said, "was to buy more time, so we could find a way to deal with Karma. But in the stress of it all, you fainted. That was a fortunate circumstance for all of us. I'm sure you would agree."

"But you shot me. After you voted against me."

"It was Adharma who voted against you, not me. Of that, I am certain. He sensed the threat you represented long before we figured him out. As I said, I meant no harm, and I was certain that none would come to you. I thought you understood that."

"Where is Karma now?"

"When you passed out," Gabriel said, "she looked down at you, lying motionless. Believing her demand for satisfaction had been delivered, there was nothing left to keep her here. She, Kismet and Adharma all left together. I don't know how we never realized they were all working together right before our faces."

"Where is Muggins?" I asked.

Nobody answered.

"Where is Muggins?" I demanded.

Ginny pointed uncomfortably at some overturned chairs. He was lying on the ground behind them, spread limply on the floor.

"Oh no!"

I rushed over to him and shook him.

"Muggins, are you ok?"

He didn't respond. I shook him again.

"Muggins, wake up," I pleaded. "Please wake up."

I shook him one more time, and he groaned and rolled to his side.

"Get your hands off me and stop shaking me, will you? I have enough problems already without you adding to them."

He was sore, and crankier than usual.

"Where did she go?" he asked.

"She left with Kismet," I said. "And Adharma. We were right

about her. We were right about all of it. They're all working together, and they have at least some of the Qud Palmon guard on their side. And the Vapes and the Shadow Pack are with them, too."

"We have to get to her lair," Muggins said.

"Viceroy Smoak, can you assemble your people, the Avians?" I asked. "All of them, all at once?"

"I suppose it's possible. I would need some of time to coordinate. What do you have in mind?"

"I'll explain it in a minute," I said. "Gabriel, can you do the same? Summon all the Angelics?

Gabriel hesitated.

"It's really important," Muggins added, "that we all come together here, despite past differences. We'll need you and the Avians to work together on this, no matter what. We all have to work together for the greater good."

"Yes, of course," he said. "In the name of the Light, it shall be so."

"Good, tell them to come together and wait for further instructions."

"Chancellor Pickelhaub, how many of your guards still remain loyal?" Muggins asked. "Do you have any way of knowing?"

"We have a clear understanding where our people's loyalties lie," she said. "I would say there are probably still several hundred who have not been corrupted."

"It's better than nothing," I said. "Here, look at this."

I scribbled out a couple of diagrams and shared it with them.

"I think this can work," Muggins said. "Can we count on you all?"

"Yes," the Chancellor said after a long pause. "I do think this can work. Indeed, I think it actually can."

"Agreed," Gabriel said.

Viceroy Smoak labored to look it over.

"Yes," he said. "Let's try it."

"Great. So, I know I just did a lot of talking out of turn and the floor didn't recognize me, or whatever, and I'm really sorry about that. But it was also really important, so I just went for it. I hope that's ok. We have a lot to do, so yeah. Thank you for listening. I'm not sure what else I'm supposed to do right now, and I'm in a bit of a hurry, so I'm just going to go now. So, ok, bye."

Then I bowed my respects and dashed out the door, with Ginny and Muggins close behind.

~

"ARE WE ALMOST THERE?" Ginny asked, as Muggins led our burbles across the valley floor.

In her defense, we had been riding for quite a while, but there was still a long trek to Karma's lair. Muggins bristled at her question, but he didn't say anything. He had that same look my dad gets when Bryce annoys him right before my mom steps in and smooths things over. It's usually better for everybody when she does that. But she wasn't here to step in this time. I missed her, and I hoped she was doing ok. She must have been worried about me. Wondering where I could be or what had happened to me. Suddenly, Muggins groaned and grabbed his ribs. He leaned forward and slumped over.

"Are you alright?" I asked.

He waved a hand at me to shoo me away, but it was clear he was in a lot of pain.

"Karma got me good," he said. "Perhaps we could all benefit from a short break, after all."

He made a clicking noise with his mouth and leaned to one side. The burbles veered off the path toward the river, toward a stand of trees that made for good shade. It would have been a great place to sit and drink lemonade with Ginny before Karma started destroying everything.

"Feels good to be off," Ginny said as she dismounted, wandering off through some bushes, reaching her arms above her head for a good stretch.

Muggins leaned weakly to the side, to slide off the burble. But his landing was clumsy, and he crashed to the ground.

"What did she do to you?"

"I'd rather not discuss it," he said. "I can fight through it, but I need some rest right now. Just a few minutes."

I helped him over to a nearby tree and leaned him up against it.

"Just relax right here," I said. "Just breathe and think about something pleasant. That's what my mom always says."

Muggins chuckled, but his chuckle became a loud, hacking cough.

"Sorry," I said. "Just relax. I'm going to find Ginny."

"Don't be gone too long," he said. "We need to get going soon."

I pushed through some bushes to find a path to the river's edge where Ginny had gone, and I bumped into her coming back toward us.

"Oh, there you are," I said. "I was wondering where you ran off to."

"I'm right here," she said with a little bounce. "How's Muggins? Is he still alive?"

"Yes, of course. He says he'll probably be fine. But he doesn't seem fine to me."

"Hmm," she said, looking around. "Interesting. It's pretty amazing here, isn't it?"

"Yeah," I said. "Unlike anything I've ever seen, or probably ever will see."

"Don't be so sure. You may see things that are even beyond this," she said. "So, do you think our plan will work?"

"It has to," I said. "There's no other way."

"How do you think it will all come together? I mean, in the end, how do we really pull it off? What do we do?"

"Muggins and I have it all figured out. It's like we talked about with Jarvis, we need to use the Starlact, we need a key, to open the Lighthold and release the Light. But before we can do that, we have to get into Karma's lair, and then we have to get past Karma, and then we have to find the Lighthold. But once we do all that," I said, realizing the sheer enormity of what was a head of us, "then we'll be fine. Smooth sailing. No problems after that."

We were in serious trouble, and I knew it. How in the world would I, little Logan LeVec, pull this off?

"And you have it, right? The Starlact?"

"Of course. We got from Jothi. You were there."

"I know that," she said. "I just wanted to make sure you still had it."

I patted the pocket of my pants.

"Yep. Right here."

"Good," she said.

She turned to the side.

"Look how those cankle-berries glisten in the light like little gems. So plump and juicy, I bet they're unbelievably delicious. I want to try one in the worst possible way. Will you pick one for me? Go on. Pick a good one."

"No way. You heard what Muggins said about them. We're not worthy, or whatever. It's a big no-no."

"But it looks so ripe and juicy and delicious. And I'm so hungry! I'll even share it with you, half for you, half for me. It's just a berry, after all. One little berry. Look at all the plants around. How much difference could it actually make?"

I shook my head.

"They're sacred," I told her more firmly.

They sure did look delicious, though. For all the darkness and ugliness that Karma had brought, the berries were still vibrant. The fruit was still plump and beautiful, like juicy little rubies, full of delectable nectar begging to be eaten.

"How about a kiss, then? Would you do it for a kiss? We can make a trade."

It was a generous offer. Tempting to say the least. Some might even say compelling.

Live a little, Logan. What's the worst that could possibly happen? That's what Teddy always says. Just live a little, why don't you. Have some fun. It's fine.

Smidge wriggled around in my pocket and popped his head out. His ears swept back, and his lips pulled back to bare his tiny little teeth. He chittered his clear disapproval at me, but as I stared into Ginny's glossy, emerald eyes I somehow lost myself. It was just one berry, after all. There must have been millions of them. And she was offering another kiss. Who would really miss just one little berry?

"Go on," she said more forcefully. "Don't you want a kiss? I'll make it a good one," she said with a tease.

"Um."

"What are you worried about?" she asked.

Smidge chittered louder. I stuffed his head back down into my pocket.

"Nothing, I guess. It's just a berry."

I plucked the ripest, plumpest, most delicious-looking berry I could find, and presented it to her proudly.

"That wasn't so hard now, was it?" she said, teasing me even more.

"I guess not," I said. "So, what do you say, are you ready to trade?"

"Close your eyes," she said with a giggle.

It was that free, uninhibited Ginny giggle. So fresh and so relaxed. I closed my eyes and leaned in, ready to receive my prize.

"You close your eyes too," I said.

Then I leaned in closer. As I did, I recalled our first kiss. That first magical kiss, so soft and warm. I didn't just feel the kiss on my lips. I felt that kiss everywhere, right through to my very core. It was pure magic, and I couldn't wait for another.

"Ready when you are," I said.

She giggled again. But it was different this time. Her sweet, beautiful Ginny voice was deeper. It was more masculine, and more maniacal. That delicate Ginny giggle turned into a harsh, throaty laugh. A mean laugh. A *man* laugh. I opened my eyes to see Adharma kneeling on the ground in front of me. He had his head tipped back, laughing even louder. I scuttled backward, out of his reach.

"You're no more dead than I am," he said. "I knew that Gabriel couldn't be trusted. I knew he was up to something. I couldn't figure out what it was, so I doubled back to check, and I'm so glad I did."

"What is happening right now?" I asked.

"You shouldn't have done that, Logan," Adharma said. "That was a sacred fruit. But you already knew that, didn't you? And you did it anyway. And for what? A kiss? You should be ashamed of yourself."

"Wait. You were Ginny? Why would you trick me like that?" I demanded.

I already knew the answer, though. I didn't need to hear it from him. He stood back up and walked toward the woods.

"There will be consequences," he said. "I'd do it myself right now. But Karma insisted on dealing with you herself. She was very clear about that. She'll be coming for you."

He disappeared into the bushes, his voice still laughing in the distance.

"Hey," I shouted in my angriest voice. "That's not fair, you jerk! You tricked me."

"Karma will catch up with you soon enough, Logan," his fading voice said. "That much is certain."

"Stop," I pleaded. "Please!"

I'd made a colossal mistake, and all for the hope of a kiss never received. Despair overcame me. I replayed the conversation in my head, trying to figure out what had gone so terribly wrong. Then I felt a tap on my shoulder. Startled, I spun around.

Ginny stood there. At least I think it was her. I pointed a serious finger at her, and yelled out the first personal question I could think of.

"What kind of tree do we sit under in my front yard?" I yelled.

She must have thought I was out of my mind.

"What?"

"What kind of tree? Tell me now! Say it, or so help me."

"Where we drink lemonade? It's a willow tree, of course. Who were you just screaming at?"

Relieved, I lowered my voice.

"Oh, I'm so glad it's you. We need to find Muggins. We have a big problem on our hands."

~

GINNY and I rushed back to Muggins. He was still sitting against the tree, meditating it seemed. He looked more peaceful than when I left him, and he looked more comfortable. I hated to interrupt him, but it was necessary.

"Muggins," I said.

He didn't respond.

So, I leaned in and yelled.

"Muggins!"

He sprang to life, startled.

"What in the world are you doing, young man?" he shouted back. "What is all the yelling about?"

"I picked one of the sacred berries," I blurted out with no warning.

"Now, why would you do such a thing? Did I not explain it to you properly?"

"Adharma tricked me."

"Adharma? But how?"

Smidge popped out of my pocket and stared at me with a disapproving look, as if to say 'I tried to warn you.'

Then he snorted at me. There were a lot of sparks in that snort. He must have been pretty angry.

"Well?" Muggins insisted.

"Sorry. Adharma is working together with Karma. And she sent him to do it."

"Do what? How did he trick you?"

"I'd rather not say right now."

"Logan."

"Ok, fine. Adharma shifted, and he pretended to be Ginny. Then he bribed me to pick the berry."

"Bribed you? With what? That makes no sense."

"Do I have to say it?"

"Yes, I need to know what we're dealing with."

I looked at Ginny with butterflies in my stomach.

"Do I have to say it *right now*?" I asked.

"Yes. Just spit it out, will you? What in the world happened?"

I took a deep breath.

"Adharma shifted so he looked like Ginny, and he bribed me with the offer of a kiss, ok? And I fell for it. I totally fell for it, and I picked the berry because of it. I'm so sorry! It was so stupid, and I can't believe I did that."

I wondered in that moment if your face can catch fire from embarrassment? Mine felt like it might. I snuck a sideways glance at her. I think she was blushing, too.

"Do you hate me now?" I asked.

"Oh, Logan," Muggins said.

He hates me.

"I really wish you hadn't done that. I told you not to give Karma anything to work with. Those berries are sacred."

"You did."

"Then why would you make such a terrible decision?"

"I know. I really know. It was so stupid of me. But there's something else I need to tell you."

"What is it?"

"I was talking, you know, pretty freely. Because I thought Adharma was Ginny. So, I might have told him I had the Starlact. And, you know, the whole rest of our plan, too."

"*Might* have told him?"

"No. There's no might about it. I absolutely, definitely told him. Almost all of it. Look, I'm really, really sorry about this, Muggins!"

Muggins smacked his hand to his forehead, and slowly pulled it down over his face.

"Oh, Logan. Not only does Karma know you're alive now, but she also knows our plan. You can count on that. Adharma will waste no time telling her. We had the advantage of her thinking you'd been killed. And now we've lost it."

Muggins stared into the distance.

"She knows we're coming straight to her. She'll be prepared for it now."

"I'm sorry," I said. "I really am."

～

MUGGINS STILL WASN'T his old self. We'd been riding our burbles toward Karma's lair for quite some time. The darkness was way beyond what it should have been. I pulled Grimes from my pocket to check the time.

"THE TIME IS 4:03 P.M." he shouted.

The sheer blackness at the base of the mountains was spreading across the meadow floor, and the meadow was narrowing as we approached the Blackpool. My stomach sank. We had barely made it across the first time, and now we were going to tempt fate by trying again.

"I hate this part," Ginny said.

The burbles trotted obediently toward the rickety old bridge, but someone stood at the entrance. When we got closer, I could see there were actually two of them, two Qud Palmon guards.

"Do you think they're friend for foe?" Ginny asked.

"That remains to be seen," Muggins replied. "We'll take it as it comes."

We arrived at the bridge entrance, where the guards stood watch. They were menacing, with their muscular figures, standing tall in full battle armor, blocking the entrance to the bridge with crossed swords.

"What business do you have here?" one asked.

The other thrust his chest out as if to invite a challenge.

"We'd like to cross, if you don't mind," Muggins said calmly. "I have a message to deliver."

After a pause and a sideways glance, they separated to let us through. One of them nodded for us to cross.

"Can we assume they are friends?" Ginny asked.

"Pickelhaub got the word out. It's working," I said. "The guards have assembled to help ensure our safe passage. It's all coming together."

"That's one possibility," Muggins said with a hint of caution.

As we gradually made our way across, the bridge groaned under the weight of the burbles. Ginny's voice squeaked with every little rock.

When we got to the other side, two more guards emerged from the darkness. They stood at the end, swords pointed at us, blocking our way.

"Adharma has already gotten to them," Muggins said. "I was afraid of this."

"Give me the Starlact," one of them said coldly.

"There's no chance of that," Muggins said. "It's simply not going to happen."

The guard banged the post holding the end of the bridge with his giant fist. Everything shook.

Did something break? Whatever you do, don't look down, Logan.

Startled, the Burbles stutter-stepped in place. But with rails on each side, and enormous guards in our way, there was nowhere to go. The bridge rocked harder under their feet as the burbles stomped in place.

"It's going to break," Ginny screamed. "We're going into the Blackpool!"

The guard banged the post again.

"Give me the Starlact," he screamed at me. "Now!"

He banged it yet again, and the bridge lurched. I looked at the guards. One raised his fist again, ready to strike again.

"Enough, ok? Fine. Do you want the Starlact? Here, take it."

I reached into my pocket.

"Logan, no!" Muggins yelled.

"What are you doing?" Ginny screamed.

I pulled my hand out of my pocket and flung it toward the edge, near one of the guard's feet. It flew through the air with the slightest twinkle, just enough to draw his eye. He scrambled to save it, but it went right in without a splash, disappearing into the abyss that was the Blackpool. He should have known better, but he looked down where it went in anyway, confused and desperate to catch it. When his eyes met the Blackpool, a liquid form of his reflection reached up and pulled him right in by the heavy plate armor on his shoulders.

It's one thing to know what could happen. It's entirely different to *see* it happen. There was no buildup, no struggle. It happened quickly and unremarkably. There was no splash, no ripple. No nothing. He just disappeared right into the Blackpool. The other guard extended a hand to help him, but as he did, his own reflection reached up, grabbed him by the arm, and dragged him in, too. He put up a good fight, and for just a fleeting second, I thought he might actually break free. He never actually stood a chance, though; and soon, he was gone, too.

"Holy cow, did you see that?" I said. "It worked. I can't believe it worked! They're gone!"

"Please tell me," Muggins said slowly and deliberately, "that you did not just throw the Starlact, the only thing standing between us and Karma's total Camerian domination, irretrievably down into the putrid depths of the infernal Blackpool."

I swallowed hard. He sounded as angry as he ever had.

"Of course I didn't," I said, pulling the Starlact from my other pocket. "It was just my last Shmelding. I didn't think it would actually work, but I didn't know what else to do. Did you see his face, though? That was epic."

Muggins chuckled to himself and nodded approvingly.

"Very clever, young man. Very clever, indeed. Perhaps there is hope for you, yet. I daresay you've almost impressed me."

"Hey!" I shouted back.

"Great job, Logan," Ginny said.

Muggins made the clicking sound with his mouth, and the burbles happily trotted off the bridge.

"Now the real work begins for us," he said. "From here on out, don't count on anything being that easy ever again."

17

As we approached Karma's lair, Smidge emerged from my pocket to ride on the nape of the burble's neck. He stood vigilant, keeping a close watch for what may come.

"He has good instincts," Muggins said. "You've got something truly special there."

"His wings really grew," I said, as he stretched them. "They're not just little wing buds anymore. They're nearly full-grown."

"As happens," Muggins said. "He's moving through his own adolescence, much in the same way you are. When you grow, your bones hurt, and you get tired, right? And I bet you eat a lot."

"Yeah, that's right. But you don't have to judge me."

"I'm not judging you; I'm just trying to make a point. When Teaspoon Dragons grow, they go into short periods of hibernation, with fast bursts of growth. Like a butterfly in a way, but without the cocoon, and they develop quickly, as you can see."

"So, he's been *hibernating* in my pocket?"

"For lack of a better word, it is something akin to hibernation, yes."

"And *metamorphosing*."

"Wow!" Ginny said, teasing. "Give Logan a gold star for the big word!"

"Yes, in a manner of speaking," Muggins said. "I suppose that Smidge is, in fact, metamorphosing."

Smidge surveyed the meadow, crouching and chittering loudly. His tail twitched and his wings flicked with short, quick movements. Muggins put his telescope to his eye and stared into the distance.

"Oh dear. I was hoping to avoid this," he said.

"Avoid what?" Ginny asked.

"Another all-out war," he said. "I'm afraid they learned nothing from the Eight Days War. Adharma is there. He's with Karma. Kismet, too, and they've assembled legions of Vapor Wraiths. Kismet has rallied the Shadow Pack as well, and their numbers are great. They're lined up and ready to charge. The destruction they are about to unleash will be absolutely devastating."

I looked up to the clouds, hoping to see some good news for a change. Smoak and the Avians were coming. They were actually coming. All of them. They were hardly more than specks in the distance, but the beating of their wings was unmistakable. From the rocky cliffs high above the Camerian meadow, they took flight. Thousands of them.

"They're coming," I said. "It's working."

I glanced toward the Qud Palmon forest.

"Some Qud Palmon Guards are coming, too. The Chancellor sent them to intercept."

Muggins raised the telescope back to his eye.

"There are some Qud Palmon," he said. "But they aren't intercepting, Logan. They're joining."

"Joining?"

"That's right. Adharma has done his job well. Many are now sympathetic to Karma, and they'll be willing to fight their own brothers without remorse in furtherance of his ridiculous cause."

Muggins looked up at the Avians, approaching from what still remained a very great distance. All but one. One set of wings was much closer than the rest.

"At least Smoak and the Avians are coming," I said. "They'll be able to help."

"What do we do now?" Ginny asked.

Muggins pointed to the tallest turret where the swirling funnel of Light drained down.

"The Lighthold will be at the bottom of that turret."

The flapping of powerful wings approached from behind us. Gabriel landed gracefully, and tucked his beautiful white wings in neatly behind him.

"Gabriel," Muggins said. "I'm glad you came."

"My lieutenants have agreed to help," Gabriel said. "We're in. They understand their orders and will do everything they can to assist. We will work together, Avians and Angelics included, for the greater good, and in the name of the Light."

"Karma is assembling the Vapes and the Shadow Pack," Muggins said. "Their numbers are strong."

Gabriel nodded.

"Kismet and Adharma are with her now," Muggins continued. "They've planned a massive assault on all Camerians. They've infiltrated the Qud Palmon and weakened the resistance of other factions. Karma has never been closer to success than she is right now."

Gabriel looked to the sky. The flapping wings grew closer, an even mix of the Avians and the Angelics—Smoak's people and Gabriel's people defying odds to come together again.

"I never thought I would see the day," Muggins said with a smirk.

"Avians and Angelics working together against a common enemy?" Gabriel said, smirking back. "Neither did I. But they have their orders, and they will follow them dutifully. How can I help?"

"Karma is out there," Muggins said. "They're dividing into groups. They'll likely split up and attack each of the rival factions simultaneously. We need to get inside and find the Lighthold. It won't be easy. Are you in?"

Gabriel nodded.

"To the death."

"Hopefully, not," Muggins said. "Hopefully not."

Carefully, we crept our way toward the main gate.

"Archers to the fore!" Karma yelled as the Avians and Angelics approached.

Her voice was faint in the distance but carried well through the cold air.

"Pluck them from the skies one-by-one, and spare not a single one of them. Fire at will!"

The sound of the archers letting loose a flurry of arrows was overtaken by the thundering footsteps of the Qud Palmon charging across the meadow and the rabid barking of the shadow wolves. It was a riotous symphony of fast-moving destruction.

"It's started," Muggins said sadly. "I didn't think she would do it. But she's actually doing it."

~

THE VAPES and the Shadow Pack spread across the meadow, some toward the Qud Palmon forest in the east, others toward the rocky cliffs in the south where the Avians nest. A third detachment marched toward the Grand Council building.

Muggins raised his telescope.

"A handful of Wraiths stayed back. Look at them. Karma, Kismet and Adharma, standing there so smug. It seems they think they've already won."

Ginny looked up to the sky.

"The Avians are still pretty far," she said. "Will we have enough time to find the Lighthold?"

"I don't know," Muggins said. "I can only hope. Look, I feel terrible about pushing the two of you into this. I never should have done it."

This is not the pep talk I need right now.

"We'll work at this together," he continued. "I will give it my all. I will give everything I have to protect you and see you through this safely. Ok?"

"I place my fate in the hands of the Light," Gabriel said, turning toward me. "And I trust the Light to see me through this. You have my full and complete support and the support of all my people."

"Where are all your arrows?" I asked. "Your quiver is nearly empty. You only have five left."

"My quiver fills itself from the Light. Look around," he said. "There is precious little left."

"Oh."

"For my family," Muggins said. "For my people. Let us make this right. We only have one chance."

He glanced down to the ground and counted some rounded rocks nestled in the dirt, poking out to expose their top halves.

"Four, five, six," he said. "Yes, these will do just fine."

Muggins swept his arms upward to summon the rocks from the ground. They slowly rose from the dirt, but the rocks weren't just rocks. They were the tops of the heads of earth golems, bulky earthen creatures. The golems climbed out of the dirt and stood guard like husky, earthen zombies.

"Be quick," Muggins said. "Stay low, and don't draw attention to yourselves. The golems will buy us a little bit of time if anyone comes in behind us. Hopefully, it will be enough."

The golems closed ranks behind us as we climbed the jagged black steps to the entrance. In the meantime, the horrors of battle played out behind us.

"I hope there's nobody inside," I said. "Could they all be in the meadow?"

"Just keep moving," Muggins said. "Time is short."

Time.

At the mention of the word, I reached into my pocket to check. What difference did it make what time it was at this particular moment? But I pulled out Grimes and pressed the button to release his cover anyway.

"You are absolutely correct," he screamed as the lid swung open. "You do not have much time at all! Very little time, in fact. Almost no time at all, to be honest!"

"Shh," I whisper-yelled.

I snapped his lid shut and jammed him back into my pocket.

"Do you think they heard?" Ginny asked.

Muggins turned and looked through his telescope.

"They heard. And now they're coming. Move it."

Through the dark distance, I could barely make out their silhouettes. But I saw them well enough to know that half of the silhouettes had disappeared into a tiny puff of vapor.

I turned to Ginny.

"Are you ready for this?"

"I guess we'll find out," she said.

We raced up the steps and through an enormous archway that led to a vast open chamber. Long, dark hallways branched in every direction.

"It's a labyrinth," I said. "How in the world are we supposed to find the Lighthold? It could be anywhere."

"It could take hours," Ginny said.

"Hours that we don't have," Gabriel said.

Grimes agitated in my pocket. At this point, how much more trouble could he possibly cause? I pulled him out and flipped his cover open.

"To the right," he yelled.

"Honestly, why so loud, Grimes?" I asked.

Then he calmed down and spoke in a more regular tone.

"Sorry, mate. I just get excited, that's all. It's not easy being clamped up under that cover and stuffed in pockets all the time. It builds up. I can't control it. You should try it sometime. See how you fare."

"I see," I said.

"Really sorry about that, didn't mean to startle ya', and hope I didn't cause too much fuss now. I certainly didn't mean any harm by it."

Muggins cleared his throat at Grimes.

"Sorry," he whispered. "It'll be just down to the right, mate."

"Yeah, I've got it," I said. "To the right."

We paused at a four-way cross, and Smidge popped up and chittered. He climbed up on my shoulder, wings flitting nervously, and chittered even louder. Down the hall, a blackness emerged from nowhere—a nothingness in the shape of a wolf. Then there were three. Behind them, a vapor poured across the floor.

"Muggins?" I said with trepidation. "This is bad, isn't it?"

～

"This way," Muggins said, pointing to the left, away from the wolves.

"But Grimes said we have to go this way. To the Lighthold."

"I realize that, but there's no choice. We'll have to find another way."

Muggins swooshed his hands through the air, and a blast of air hit the shadow wolves. They tumbled backward, end-over-end, as the vapor broke its person-like shape and swirled like regular smoke.

"Now," he said.

We scrambled away as quickly as we could, ducking around every available corner to get away from them before stopping at another four-way cross.

"I think we lost them," Ginny said.

"That's fine," Gabriel said. "But where are we? And where do we go from here?"

I flipped Grimes' cover open.

He whispered something I couldn't understand.

"What?"

I held him closer as he repeated himself, but I still couldn't tell what he said. I held him right to my ear as he repeated himself a third time.

"Hey, Logan," he said. "I'm whispering now, mate. That's pretty good, yeah? You're welcome, by the way."

"Well, what did he say?" Muggins demanded.

"He said he's whispering now."

Muggins ran his hand, frustratedly, through the thin tufts of white hair on his head.

"Which way, Grimes?"

"Well, if *you're* not going to whisper," Grimes said, "Then neither am I!"

"To the right!" he yelled.

"Are you sure?"

"Yes. A hundred percent, mate, give or take a bit."

We forged a twisting route through a network of tunnels deep into the belly of Karma's lair. The passages were dark and jagged, with imperfect surfaces glistening as we moved. No matter where we were, everything looked the same, until we came to one spot in particular.

"Look at this," I said.

We stood at one end of the longest hall I'd ever seen. At the other end were two tall doors, with wrought iron pulls. The walls that stretched from one end to the other, however, were unique. Both sides poured down like an infinite waterfall of sand, softly lit by torchlight. The grains rushed against each other causing a soothing hissing sound, and pouring into—I don't know what. There were no piles on the ground, but it kept pouring, nonetheless.

The cascading sand flows were smooth initially, but then a sandy face poked through. Then another. As each face took shape, protruding through the sandy falls, it only held its form for a few seconds. Then it melded back in, only to be replaced by another, like bubbles in boiling water, rising and then disappearing. Each expression was tortured and pained in its own unique way. When their mouths opened to speak, sand poured out ahead of their voices, and fell downward to take the shape of another face just below.

"Go back," one said. "You'll not want to go that way. Not at all, I warn you."

"Turn around while you still can," said another with a raspy growl. "Or else you'll end up like us."

A sandy arm reached out from the wall, with sandy grains falling from its sandy shape. I jumped back from its reach. Then it pulled back into the wall's surface.

Muggins froze. His eyes were locked on one face in particular.

"Help me," the face said, before fading back to nothing.

"Fey'ona?" he said. "Fey'ona, Was that you? It can't be. Please come back."

He shook his head.

"It looked just like her. But it can't possibly be."

He stared for a moment more, watching in disbelief. More faces rose and faded away, but never the one he recognized.

"Run," one of the faces said.

"Leave now," shouted another.

"You should never have come here," warned a third. "Such danger."

You're nearly out of time," screamed a fourth. "Don't end up like us. Turn around now while you can."

Muggins was still shaken.

"Should we turn around?" I asked.

"That seems like a definite yes," Ginny added, taking a step backward. "Crystal clear. Were you not listening?"

I stepped back with her.

"No," Muggins said.

His eyes darted back and forth across the wall, checking every face as quickly as he could, desperately looking for the one.

"We should absolutely go this way," he continued.

"Didn't you hear them?" Ginny said.

"I did, and that's precisely their purpose. Please make no mistake, we have no friends here. Nobody is looking out for our interests. They said what they said for a very specific reason. To scare us away. To cast doubt in our minds, and to send us off the right track."

"Are you sure about that?" Gabriel asked.

"Absolutely. This is the way. We'll keep going."

"But—" I said.

"No buts. This is definitely it."

"Definitely what?" I asked.

∽

WE PRESSED FORWARD, further down the hallway. The deeper we went, the more desperate the warnings grew.

"Sadness and misery await you at the other end," said one.

"You'll be trapped here forever," said another. "Tortured like us for all of eternity."

"You're doing exactly what she wants," said a third. "Why are you doing what she wants? You're smarter than this. Run out of here while you still have legs to carry you."

"Carry on, then," screeched another. "Doesn't matter anyway. You'll be dead soon enough."

"I don't know, Muggins," I said. "Are you absolutely sure about this?"

"I second that," Ginny added.

"This doesn't feel right," Gabriel added.

"That's exactly why we need to keep going," Muggins said.

"Help me," said a voice as we finally reached the end. "For the love of all that is holy. Please help me."

Muggins froze and looked back over his shoulder again.

"Fey'ona?"

But there was no answer. Just new voices with new ominous warnings.

"Well, go on," Ginny said. "Open the doors, then."

I grabbed the iron ring and gave it a pull. The door was heavy and moved slowly. But it moved nonetheless.

"I got it," I said proudly.

"Oh, damn it," Muggins said. "Look away."

So, of course I did the exact opposite. I turned and looked to see what he was concerned about.

"A mirror maze?" I asked. "Like at the funhouse? That's so weird."

Then my eyes met my reflection and something—I don't know what—hit me in the stomach so hard I left my feet. I sailed through the air backward and landed on my back.

"Are you ok?" Ginny said, rushing over.

"Oh my god, that hurt so bad!" I said, gasping for air. "What in the world was that?"

I lifted up my shirt. My stomach was imprinted with the biggest, reddest, puffiest, most savage five-star I'd ever received. I could barely breathe it hurt so bad. It had already started to bruise.

"Damn it," Muggins said. "Now she's using the mirrors against you. I told you not to pick those berries! Do you see where it's gotten you now? Nowhere good, that's for sure."

"Karma did that? Oh, man, that hurt so bad!"

"She most definitely did."

"I can get us through," Ginny said. "Watch this."

Muggins groaned in disbelief.

"Miss Ginny, please don't do that. That's just a terrible idea, I have to say."

Ginny closed her eyes. She put her hands out and tried to venture into the maze.

"See?" she said. "It's easy."

Then she slammed face first into a mirror, and then another. She looked ridiculous.

"Ow," she said, slamming her nose into a third.

Upon colliding with a fourth, she was catapulted backward through the air and landed on the ground right next to me.

"Uhhhh," she said, holding her stomach. "I tried to sneak a peek. But it didn't work. I definitely don't recommend it."

"Muggins, what do we do?" I asked.

There was a noise behind us, footsteps perhaps. I climbed back to my feet to see what was coming, and Smidge flew up to my shoulder, chittering as angrily as ever. His tail flicked, and he took flight toward the mirrors.

In what sounded like a cute little Smidge-sneeze, his head snapped, and a white sonic ring left his mouth and traveled toward the mirrors. The ring smashed through the first layer, then the next, then each one that followed. I'd never heard so much glass break in my life.

"Well would you look at that," Muggins said. "He just might be a Caboodle after all."

"Caboodle?" I asked.

"Yes, of course. Are you familiar with the term *the whole kit and caboodle*?"

"Sure, my grandpa used to say that a lot. When he was talking about the whole thing, or all of something."

"Exactly. And Smidge here appears to be a Caboodle. It's the rarest type of Teaspoon Dragon. Remember when I told you they favor a single power?"

"Sure."

"Well, Smidge may not settle for just one. He may just keep them all. Forever. The whole kit and caboodle. Do you follow?"

"Get. Out!" Ginny said. "Are you serious? That's the coolest thing I've ever heard of."

Smidge purred his appreciation.

"Can you understand her?" I said.

I didn't expect him to respond, but it seemed like he could.

Just as I finished my sentence, three silhouettes rounded the corner, growling.

"I think we'll just be going this way," Muggins said, carefully stepping across the broken shards of glass.

"Just like dogs, the pack have tender pads on their feet. They won't follow us through here. Come on now."

18

We strode through the tunnel of shattered glass to enter a spacious inner chamber. At its center, a crystal the size of a bowling ball— and the shape of an icosahedron— sat atop a pedestal. Light poured down into its core.

"Holy cow, that's the Lighthold," I shouted.

"Now you're catching on quickly," Muggins said.

The sky was visible through the top of the turret. The Avians and Angelics circled high above, their numbers growing by the second. The slivers of dimly-lit sky peeking between their wings shrank as they clustered together more tightly. It was working. Their wings were forming a shield to block what little Light was still left to be taken.

"They're doing it." Ginny said.

"I only hope it's not too late," Muggins said. "If it's too far gone by now, there will be no good left, and Cameria will be lost forever."

"Just release it now," Ginny insisted.

"If only it were that easy," Muggins said.

"Why wait?" Gabriel asked, just as Karma entered through the doorway across the room.

"How dare you enter this sacred place, uninvited no less," she said sharply. "I have a good mind to slice you open and hang you by your necks out front. What do you think of that? Would that send a strong enough message to any like-minded intruders?"

"Gross," Ginny said, involuntarily.

Adharma sauntered in behind her, looking even more obnoxious than usual.

"So nice to see you all," he said. "Thank you all for coming. Together, no less. This makes everything so much easier."

Then came Kismet, flanked by two shadow wolves. A vapor grew from nowhere and spread across the floor.

"We're in serious trouble," I said.

"Muggins, what do we do?" Ginny asked.

"I'm working on it," he said, his eyes shifting around. "There are two ways out of here. One is back the way we came in, and we already know what's back there. And the other is the way *they* came in. But we have to go through them to get there."

Ginny pointed upward.

"And up the turret, too," she said. "That makes three."

"Well, yes," Muggins said. "But we can't very well fly, now, can we?"

She shrugged.

"It's still a way out," she said. "I'm just saying."

The shadow wolves bared their teeth, steadily creeping toward us; toward Ginny, to be precise. She was barely separated from us, but it was enough to drive a wedge. Smidge chittered louder than ever.

"Logan?" Ginny said. "I don't like this. I don't like what's happening. Can you do something? Why are they coming right at me?"

The wolf closest to me rose on its hind legs and bit at the air. I flinched, and so did Muggins, and that was all they needed. The gap between Ginny and us got bigger, and the shadowy beasts stepped in to fill the void. Ginny stood alone and pale faced as they backed her away from us, into a corner.

"Logan? Muggins?" Ginny pleaded. "Please help me."

I glanced toward Karma and Adharma. The vapor behind them grew thicker, and one began to emerge.

Vapes.

"Muggins, we have to help her," I said.

The Vape raised its hand and conjured the Spark of Aramore. With its palm awash in a soft blue glow, it glided toward Ginny. She was trapped.

Gabriel stepped forward.

"That is enough," he screamed, addressing Karma directly. "You've been allowed to run unchecked for far too long."

"And precisely what do you plan to do about it?" she asked.

"Whatever it takes. If I must make a sacrifice in the process, one justified in the name of the Light, then so be it."

"As you wish," she said. "I'll take great pleasure in this."

She raised her mirror toward Gabriel and flicked it at him, to catch his reflection.

But he stared directly into the mirror, undeterred.

"Impossible," she shouted.

She thrust the mirror harder at him.

"It's useless against me," he said. "I have dedicated my life to the purpose of the Light. I have lived as the purest of the pure. You have no punishment to give. I'm owed nothing from you."

"Is that so?" she asked.

"Do you not believe your own eyes?"

"Very well," Karma said. "Score one point for Gabriel. Now, Kismet, conjure more of them."

Kismet knelt near a shadow stretching across the floor, cast from some stray torch light. He wagged his fingers gently above it, as if to coax something out. Then he whistled. A wolf rose up, climbed out from the shadow on the floor, and shook itself off like a wet dog. Then he conjured another. And another.

"What the—they just crawl right out of the shadows?" I asked. "How is that even possible?

"It just is," Muggins said.

Kismet whistled once more and motioned toward Gabriel. The wolves galloped across the floor with their gaze fixed on him.

~

GABRIEL RAISED his bow and nocked an arrow. Four remained in his quiver. But they were dim, and hardly there at all. One arrow faded and disappeared completely, and then there were only three. Then two.

Gabriel let loose the nocked arrow. It struck the closest wolf, and the wolf collapsed back into a shadow on the floor before fading away completely. A second wolf leaped at Gabriel and knocked him to the ground. He lay on the floor, prone, as the wolf stood on his chest. Gabriel lodged his bow in its jaws to push it back, to avoid being bitten.

"Ginny," I yelled, realizing I'd lost sight of her. I spun around to look into the corner.

The Vape stood over her as she lay motionless on the ground. The Spark of Aramore cast a soft blue glow across her face.

"Hey," I shouted fiercely.

The Vape looked at me and squeezed out a wheezy hiss, the sound of pure and unrestrained evil.

It knelt beside her and slid a cold, slender finger over her lips and into her mouth. With its fingertip resting on her bottom teeth, it opened her mouth wider. Its other hand hovered over her face, the Spark of Aramore keeping her deep under its control. It pulled a metal tube from its belt and held it beside her face. Like a ghostly thin mist, Ginny's breath drew out from her chest, wafting past her lips and through the air into the tube's opening. It was only a matter of seconds before it stopped.

"No!" I screamed loud enough to strip my throat raw.

Gabriel struggled under the weight of the wolf. He rocked back and forth, uselessly trying to flap his wings, but they were pinned beneath him. He grabbed his last arrow and stabbed the wolf in the ribs. The wolf collapsed into a vague shadow.

Gabriel sprang to his feet, and used the same arrow he stabbed the wolf with to shoot the Vape. The Vape disintegrated into a vapor, and dropped the tube to the ground. The tube clanged against the obsidian floor and made a terrible noise. Gabriel reached to his quiver for another arrow, but his quiver was empty.

"I thought you could never run out," I said.

"It's like I told you. No Light, no arrows."

Karma clapped a slow clap.

"Well played," she said. "This has all been very entertaining. It truly has, and I thank you for that. I really do. But are you quite finished now?"

Gabriel stared back. He accepted his fate quietly, and without regret.

"Very well, then," she said. "Kismet, go."

Kismet whistled and sicked the remaining wolves on Gabriel.

"Look away, Logan," Muggins said as they pounced.

I was too slow. I glimpsed his beautiful white wings being streaked in red. The wolves were just too much for him to overcome.

"There's too many," I said, as more Vapes continued to emerge.

"I can't allow this," Muggins shouted. "Not again."

He looked up the turret, pondering what Ginny had suggested. He stared intently into the palm of his tiny hand. With the other hand, he twirled a finger in a circular motion. A funnel cloud grew from thin air, a tiny little hand-held tornado. As he twirled his finger faster, the funnel grew taller. Muggins pushed his hands forward, sending the swirling mass of air meandering across the floor toward the misty vapor and the oncoming Wraiths. The funnel grew louder and more forcefull as it crept across the chamber, gaining more strength and sweeping across the floor.

Its height rose up the turret and toward the sky, and the base traveled closer to the Vapes. It sucked up the Vapes, and the wispy white vapor itself, sending them all up the turret and out through the top.

We rushed to Gabriel's side.

"Gabriel!" I shouted.

"We're too late," Muggins said.

"But—," I said, fighting back a tear.

"Gabriel was a hero for the ages," Muggins said. "He sacrificed himself for us, for the Light and for the greater good. Karma will take us next if we aren't careful. We can't allow Gabriel's sacrifice to be for nothing."

THE PACK TURNED their attention to Muggins, and were closing in. He reached desperately into his bottomless bag and pulled out his telescope.

"Not that," he said, tossing it away. "Oh, dear. Where is it?"

He reached back in, only to pull out an old hat, crumpled and out of style.

"Not that either. Goodness, where has it gone?"

"Quit messing around," I yelled. "Do something, Muggins!"

He tossed the hat aside and reached back in as they grew closer.

"Oh dear," he said, fumbling around. "Where could it be? Ah, yes, that's it."

He pulled out a small glass bottle of black liquid. He snapped it open and poured its contents on the floor. It was just a line of black on the floor, a symbolic barrier at best. Karma huffed at the sight of it.

"Ink? Is that supposed to stop us? Please."

Two shadow wolves crept closer to Muggins. As one got closer, it bent down to sniff at the blackness. Its eyes met its reflection, and a black, liquid wolf head rose up from the liquid and grabbed the wolf by the throat. The wolf yelped and tried to pull away, but it was quickly dragged down into the blackness. The other wolf rushed over to sniff where the first had disappeared, only to meet a similar fate.

Muggins strutted confidently and retrieved his telescope from the floor. He twirled his hand in a circular motion like he was wiping a window. Rumbling shook the floor as the rigid obsidian walls bent to his will. He swirled faster, and a hole in the wall opened up where none had been before. Not just the chamber wall where we stood but every wall behind it. All the way through Karma's labyrinthian lair and all the way to the outside. He raised his telescope to his eye, and aimed it though the series of holes.

"I was desperately hoping to avoid this," Muggins said. "Our allies are out there. The battle is well underway, and casualties are high. Some of the Qud Palmon still fight alongside the Vapes and the Pack. They'll know the strategies and the weaknesses of the other guardsmen. But that knife cuts both ways, and they'll have to deal with the same disadvantage themselves."

He sighed.

"The losses are tremendous," he said, shaking his head. "Our once-lush meadow is now but a tragic battlefield, littered with the bodies of the fallen. History will not view this favorably."

Karma moved closer Muggins.

"What do you know of history, you disruptive little fool? You are going to pay dearly for your interference. And it will be long and slow, if I have my way."

"I've already paid dearly," Muggins said. "But it doesn't have to be this way. Have you forgotten where you come from? Have you forgotten all that I did for you?"

"Silence," she shouted back.

"We need to unlock the Lighthold," I whispered.

I pulled the Starlact from my pocket, mostly to confirm that I still had it.

"In good time, Logan," Muggins said quietly. "We still have some challenges to overcome."

Smidge chittered, and before I could even consider why, another wolf shed its shadowy form, right by my side. It snapped at my arm, but only caught my sleeve. I struggled to break free from its grip, and in my panic, I dropped the Starlact. The wolf let go, and before I realized what happened, it snatched the Starlact up in its jaws and trotted back to Karma's side.

Smidge chittered as fierce as ever. He leaped from my shoulder to take flight, and darted through the air, quick and sharp, like a bat in the night. With a snap of his head, he blew out an icy kryoplume, and froze the wolf solid. Smidge swooped back around for another pass. He chittered, and let out a fiery blast, leaving the wolf's head defrosted while its body was still cast in ice. The hair at the tips of its ears smoldered and water dripped from its chin.

Smidge chittered loud and fast at the wolf. It spat the Starlact to the floor, and Smidge swooped in, scooped it up in his paws, and returned to my shoulder. I pocketed the Starlact once again to keep it safe, and cringed at the thought of how close we had just come to complete and utter defeat.

"Great work, Smidge!" I said.

Smidge chittered proudly, and nuzzled my neck.

I looked down at Muggins, hoping he would be as impressed as I was. But Karma had already fixed her mirror on his gaze. His tiny little body jerked and writhed. His head snapped back, and his spine arched. Muggins tipped backward in what seemed like slow motion, powerless to do anything to break his own fall. As he crashed over backward, his head smashed to the floor.

"No," I screamed. "Stop it. Stop it right now!"

"Or what?" Karma said dismissively. "It's just you and me now. Nobody else can help you. Just wait until you see what I have in store for you."

I fumbled in my pocket, searching desperately for an answer. Something useful. Anything at all.

"What could *you* possibly do to the likes of me?" she asked, moving her mirror my direction.

"This," I said.

I pulled the small glowing bottle from my pocket as she looked on doubtfully. I uncorked the bottle and pointed its mouth at her, ready for something amazing. But the light just danced around inside the bottle.

Tink-tink-tink.

Like a firefly unaware of its bounds.

"What the—"

"You'll have to do better than that," she scoffed.

She raised her arm and thrust the mirror at me.

Then it happened. The little dancing light finally found its way out of the bottle. When it did, lightning shot out. Massive lightning. The kind you see on the cover of a magazine. A blinding, massive arc sprung straight from the opening directly toward her.

Holy crap, it worked.

It only lasted a second before it was done, then thunder rumbled through the chamber. When the smoke cleared, there was nothing more than a scorch mark streaking the floor, right where her feet had been a moment earlier. Karma had disappeared into a smoldering plume. I locked eyes with Kismet and Adharma, staring them down from across the room and reaching into my other pocket.

"You want some of this?" I shouted.

Did that seriously just come out of my mouth?

But my bluff, mercifully, worked. They looked at the scorch marks where Karma had stood mere seconds ago. Then they looked at each other, turned on a heel and sprinted back down the hall from where they had come. I felt ten feet tall in that moment. I felt like one of the haves. Thank goodness they believed it. The only thing left in my pocket was the Starlact. And then I realized—

Gabriel.

Muggins.

My sweet, sweet Ginny.

Muggins lay close by on the floor, sprawled out and still. I knelt by his side, looking back at Ginny. She lay there, prone and lifeless, as did Gabriel. I wondered if somehow this could all be my fault. I began to understand Muggins' profound guilt. How could so much have gone so terribly wrong? What would I do from here? Where would I go? It was overwhelming.

Muggins groaned a pathetic little groan. It was barely a sound at all. He tried to roll to his side, but he was frail.

"Oh, thank goodness," I said, as I helped him to sit up. "Are you alright?"

He rubbed the back of his head.

"I don't know for sure," he said. "But I suspect that I am probably not. Not even close. Regardless, our work is not finished yet. Where is Miss Ginny?"

I pointed sheepishly in her direction. She still hadn't moved.

"Help me up, please," he said, reaching out a hand. "We have to hurry."

He was stiff and sore, and limped a little. He leaned against my leg for support, and we walked to where Ginny lay.

"Is she—" I stuttered. I couldn't bring myself to say the last word.

"In a manner of speaking," Muggins said. "It pains me to say it, but yes, she is."

My shoulders fell as another tear streaked down my cheek. Why did I bring her here? This was all my fault.

"But she's also not," he continued.

He looked around, seeming confused. I was confused, too.

"Ah yes, there we have it."

Muggins limped over and retrieved the tube the Vape had dropped. He picked it up and limped back to Ginny's side.

"By the power and the grace of the Light, please let this work," he said.

He popped the cap and held the open end near Ginny's mouth.

Nothing happened.

"Come on now, dammit," he demanded. "Work, will you?"

I felt panic set in all over again.

"Is she gone for good?" I asked.

"I refuse to accept that," he scolded. "Not again. Not ever."

He wiggled the tube as if to shake its contents, trying to break something loose. The faintest foggy wisp drifted out of the opening. As if being sucked through a straw, Ginny's breath drifted lazily into her mouth and returned deep within her. At first, there was just a twitch at the corner of her eye, then a weak quiver of her lip.

"It's working!" I said. "Did you see that? It's working!"

Before I could say another word, Ginny's eyes shot open. Her arms stiffened. She gasped and gulped for air, as if breathing for the first time after being held underwater, near drowning.

"Oh my gosh, what just happened?" she shouted.

"You're ok," I shouted. "Oh, man, you're ok!"

She gasped again, panicking until her eyes met mine. I tried to help her up, but as I reached for her hand she pulled me in close. She hugged my neck so tight I could feel my pulse in my eyeballs. It was probably the best hug I'd ever had, a feeling I wouldn't ever forget. I still haven't forgotten it, not even to this day.

"Ahem," Muggins said, clearing his throat.

"Right. Sorry," I said. I turned back to Ginny. "Do you need a hand up?"

"Yes, please," she said with a nod, still sounding hoarse.

With Ginny back to her feet, I peered up the turret. The Avians and the Angelics were still hard at work, tirelessly circling above and shielding any more Light from being pulled down. Only the tiniest drips of Light made it through the gaps between their wings.

"What about Gabriel," I asked. "Can you help him, too?"

Muggins shook his head slowly.

"How do I say this? Well. Some things just can't be fixed, my dear boy. What Gabriel did was noble, and heroic and selfless; and I wish I could do more for him."

"But—"

"It's time," he said. "We need to open the Lighthold."

I pulled the Starlact from my pocket.

"What do I do with it?"

"It's like Jarvis told us," Muggins said. "We need the Starlact. We need a key to open it. So go on, and open it."

Ginny reached to swipe the Starlact from my hand.

"Here, I'll do it," she said.

"No!" Muggins and I screamed in unison.

"Miss Ginny, only a Keeper can handle such intense power."

"Yeah, didn't you hear about Too-Bad-Timothy?" I added. "You. must have by now. *Bzzzzzt.*"

I ran my thumb over the star-shaped device and studied the Lighthold. Through its intense glow, I could barely make out the thin outline embedded in its top facet. The indentation was star-shaped, and it was Starlact-sized.

Muggins nodded, but said nothing.

"So, I just set this in, and that's it, right?"

No response.

"I need your help, Muggins!"

"What you need is to believe in yourself, Logan."

I looked down at the Starlact resting in the palm of my hand. Shiny and mechanical, I hadn't taken the time to look at it closely before. It was like a fancy watch, designed to show its inner workings, gears and all.

"Go on," Ginny insisted. "Do it, then."

I placed the Starlact in the top of the Lighthold. It was a perfect fit, and it set in smoothly. As soon as it touched the Lighthold, its tiny gears started turning and a tab raised up like the head of a house key.

"Turn it," Ginny yelled. "Hurry up and turn it!"

I pinched the tab between my thumb and forefinger, and I twisted.

"It's not moving!" I shouted.

I turned with all my might.

"Turn harder," Ginny said.

"I can't! That's the best I can do!"

With both hands, I turned with every ounce of strength I had left.

"It's not working, Muggins. What do I do?"

But he wouldn't answer.

Ginny shoved in between, and she reached for the tab.

"Don't touch it!" I yelled.

But she did anyway. She put her hand right on it. I expected she would go the way of Too-Bad-Timothy; but much to my surprise, she did not. She turned it as easy as you might unlock your own front door. And in what I can only describe as a geometric impossibility, the Starlact sank down into the core of the crystalline Lighthold. Its facets folded and flipped, transforming its shape to open a hole in its top. And with that, the Light beamed up out of the Lighthold like a spotlight, shining back up the turret with outlandish intensity.

The Reflexor at the top of the turret worked in the way it had before. Except, instead of pulling the Light all together and focusing it down into the Lighthold, it did the precise opposite—it broadcast the Light broadly throughout Cameria, back to where it belonged. The Light was strong, and it was powerful, and it was beautiful.

Chips of the obsidian walls began to crumble and fall to the chamber below, shattering into smaller shards as they hit the floor. Smidge chittered a frantic warning into my ear and quickly ducked back into my jacket pocket.

"I think we need to get out of here," I said, turning to Ginny.

"Hundred percent," she said.

"Indeed," Muggins said. "Out the way we came, and let us be quick about it!"

We dashed through the chamber door and tip-toed through the broken mirror fragments from Karma's mirror maze.

"Don't look down," I said. "You never know. The mirror bits might still work even if they're broken."

Black shards fell from the ceiling and crashed into the mirror fragments below.

"It's working," I said. "You can see it! The Light is being restored, and everything is getting brighter."

"We need to get out of here before the whole thing comes down on top of us," Muggins said.

"I can't believe we just did that," Ginny exclaimed. "Did you see what we just did? I mean, did you see it?"

"Please save the celebrations for an appropriate time, Miss Ginny," Muggins warned.

We reached the end of the broken mirrors and passed through the wooden doors. We made it back into the long hallway where the sand had fallen from the walls, and Muggins stopped.

"Fey'ona!" he exclaimed.

She was standing right there. In real life, right in front of us, right in the middle of the hallway.

"I can't believe it," Muggins said. "After all this time, bless our souls, I can't believe I've actually found you."

The sand that had once flowed down the walls flowed no longer. Instead, the hall was filled with tiny people emerging from doorways where the sand had once been, and they all bore a remarkable resemblance to Muggins.

"Is that her?" I asked. "Is that your wife?"

"We've been trapped for so long," she said. "I thought we'd never be together again. But then I saw you come past us, and I saw you go in there," she said. "I was so worried for you."

"I would have done whatever I had to, for all my days," Muggins said. "There's nothing I wouldn't do, even if only to get an inch closer to finding you."

Muggins' people, the Elementalists, continued pouring out. They looked confused like they'd just awakened from a terrifying dream, not quite sure how they had arrived at this particular place, at this particular time.

"This was it. This is what he was talking about," Muggins said. "This was the Hall of Tortured Souls."

Fey'ona nodded back sadly.

"It was terrible," she said softly.

"Oh, Fey'ona. I am so incredibly sorry for what you've endured," he said. "And all because of me."

He fell to his knees, with his hands clasped like a beggar.

"All of you. All of you were here because of my mistakes; because of my poor judgment. It was entirely my fault that you suffered such punishment, plain and simple. I can only begin to imagine your terror. I know it will take time, perhaps more time than I have left in this life. But nonetheless, I beg you all for your forgiveness, and I will continue to do so until my final, dying breath, so help me."

He paused.

"Oh, what am I saying? Such nonsense, after all. How could you ever find it in your hearts to forgive such a worthless old fool as me? I understand that it could never be, but please just know how sorry I am. If nothing else, please just know that."

Fey'ona stepped closer and wrapped Muggins in a tender embrace.

"The Light does what it must," she said. "The Light does what it feels is just, and from adversity springs triumph and renewal. Just as it always does."

She looked over her shoulder at everyone behind her. They nodded their unified approval.

"You've made right of your wrongs, my dear Muggins. You've freed us all from that awful place. We are the Elementalists. We are family. And always will be, no matter what circumstances we are faced with."

She kissed him gently on his wrinkly little forehead.

"All is forgiven, my dear, sweet Muggins. Such a burden need not be hoisted on your shoulders any longer. We're happy to be together again. The Elementalists are back, and ready to do what they must. Ready to fulfill their destiny."

Muggins bowed his head and wept in somber relief. His shoulders shook as he sobbed.

"Thank you," he murmured through tears. "Thank you so much. Thank you all. I am so incredibly fortunate to have you back, and I am honored and humbled by your kindness. I don't deserve you."

It seeemed like he had more to say, but the ground shook under our feet again. Giant shards crashed to the floor, shattering on impact and scattering razor sharp shards in every direction. Muggins pushed his way through the crowd, pulling me and Ginny to the front.

"This way, everyone, there's no more time to waste. Logan, what is the fastest way out?"

I snapped open Grimes' lid, with one thumb on the button, and one finger in my ear.

"To the left, to the left," he screamed. "Left, left, left."

19

I'd never run so hard in my life. When we all emerged, it was bright outside, and we could see by the full light of day. I had never considered how much I would miss something as simple as daylight. But when it's not there when it should be, you take notice. That was, perhaps, the last day I ever took the simple things in life for granted.

From the safety of the wide-open meadow, I looked up at the tallest turret at the corner of her lair. It once seemed menacing and impenetrable. But despite its darkness, the Light beamed out of it, sparkling and dancing and spreading across Cameria, as far as the eye could see, kissing everything it touched with life anew. Tender green shoots rose from the soil at my feet. The trees broke free of their dead, black husks to reveal fresh bark. Leaves sprouted from branches, and buds broke through. New tendrils of growth sprouted everywhere, and everything was given new life by the return of the Light.

At first, there was just a single, loud crack. Then came more. Cracks rippled through the obsidian walls. Shiny, black boulders crashed down into the central chamber below as it steadily imploded, as streaks of Light burst out through the gaps.

"Light. Cutting through such darkness," Muggins said. "What a beautiful metaphor."

"We actually did it," Ginny said.

"We sure did," I said. "I can't believe it."

It wasn't all good news, though. As Karma's lair continued to crumble, I looked to the mountains where the Avians nest, and then toward the giant trees of the Qud Palmon Forest. Feathers drifted quietly across the meadow, carried on a soft and silent breeze. Remains of the fallen Avians, too many to count, littered the ground as far as they eye could see. Some of Smoak's bravest and fiercest fighters, and his most devoted lieutenants. No one was spared. Not the Avians, not the Qud Palmon, not even the Angelics.

Muggins sighed deeply.

"In matters of war," he said. "There are no winners. One side may lose less than the other. But all involved are losers just the same, and a terrible cost is extracted in the meantime."

He paused to reflect on the scene.

"It's quite a contrast, isn't it?" Muggins asked.

"What do you mean?" Ginny said.

"The beauty of the Light, washing over such destruction. Too late to make any difference at all, but trying nonetheless."

I stood in somber silence, wondering if any of this had really been necessary. I was convinced that it hadn't been.

"Hey Muggins," I said.

"Yes?"

"Not to change the subject, but about what happened in there. Does this mean Ginny is a Keeper, too?"

"She is certainly descended of one. There's no denying that, and her powers are tremendous. She would appear to be a little different from you, however."

"How so?"

"It took me up until just moments ago to realize it. But do you remember what Jarvis told us? You need the Starlact, you need a key?"

"Yes, of course," I said.

Ginny nodded her agreement.

"The Starlact *was* the key," she added.

Muggins grumbled.

"I'm afraid not, Miss Ginny. The Starlact and the key are two different things. We needed a Starlact, *and* we needed a key."

"Ohhhhh," I said.

"Exactly," Muggins said. "Miss Ginny, you *are* the key. A unique type of Keeper, very special indeed. I should have realized it much sooner."

"But she wasn't anointed by the Council," I said. "How can she be a Keeper without being anointed?"

Muggins chuckled.

"It's like I've told you all along, young man. You've always had it within you, Logan. Council approval or not, it doesn't matter. She did, too. I realize that now. I knew another was close, I had sensed it. But I had no idea just how close she was."

"Then why did I have to go through all that business with the Council?"

"It's part of their process, Logan. Formality. It's their rules. But it's not yours and it's not hers."

"There you go again," I said, "saying weird things."

"It was always within you. You had a gift. You never needed anyone to tell you that you have it, and you don't need their blessing to exercise it. It's always been there. It was just up to you to use it. So don't ever rely on others to tell you that you're worthy, or that you're good, or that you're capable. Deep down, just know that you are, and that's what really matters."

"I guess," I said.

"Look. Does anyone need to tell a stone that it is heavy? Does a bird need anyone to tell it that it can fly? Of course not. And much in the same way, you don't need anyone to tell you that you have great-ness deep within you. You just need to believe in it."

"Yeah, that makes sense, I guess," I said, scratching my head. "Mostly."

"It's like this. Sometimes grownups like to indulge in ceremony for the sake of ceremony," he said. "The Council didn't make you great. They only acknowledged it in their own time and on their own terms. But both of you were great already."

"Thanks, Muggins" I said. "I think I understand now."

"I understand, too," Ginny said, with a sly grin. "And you didn't even have to ask me to say so."

Muggins nodded and smiled, happy that we were all tuned to the same wavelength for once. As I looked down, more green shoots sprouted from the damp soil around my feet. Green shoots of hope. Green shoots of promise and potential. Green shoots of a brighter future.

Despite all that happened, I felt a glimmering sense of happiness again. It really was the dawn of a new day in Cameria.

20

The journey home was long, I'm not going to lie, and I couldn't wait to be there. I longed for the comfort of my own bedroom, my own bed and my own stuff. I longed to be in a place where I knew how things worked, I understood what people cared about, and I could find the things I needed. A place where Ginny and I could just sit under the willow tree and laugh for hours, telling stories and drinking lemonade. We would get there in due time, of course. But I could hear my mom shouting my name as I stepped back into my grandpa's yard through the portal.

"Logan," she screamed desperately.

The police had already gone by then, but she never gave up looking.

"I'm right here," I said, standing in front of the tree. "I'm sorry if I scared you."

"Honey, honey, I was so worried about you," she said, rushing over. "Where have you been? What have you been doing all this time? Didn't you hear us calling out for you?"

A long conversation followed. Very long. It took a lot of explaining, and it didn't start off very well. At first, she gave me the stiff arm, just like she did with Grandpa. Not that I can blame her, but at first, she was annoyed that I would try and make up such a ridiculous story. Karma? Burbles? Blackpool? Lightning in a bottle or some Grand Council? Mystical Mirrors? Ginny helped me to set things straight with her, though, and after some major convincing, I finally got her to reconsider. I'd never had to work so hard at anything in my life.

The breakthrough came when Smidge wriggled around in my pocket after I mentioned Karma's name. Mom saw the movement in my jacket, and then saw Smidge pop onto my shoulder. After she saw Smidge, and I explained where I found him, things got a lot easier. At first, she couldn't see Muggins. But eventually, she did. I told her about Muggins and Grandpa and Karma and everything else. She was so angry at first, which I couldn't understand. Maybe she was angry at herself. But anger became confusion, confusion became wonder, and wonder became many, many more questions.

First, I had to explain the massive pile of money on my bedroom floor. And why I couldn't set Smidge free like she wanted me to. Then I had to explain the cuts on my arm, and how shadow wolves come to be. Eventually, I told her about the tree, the lighting, and seeing right through the burn mark. That was the most challenging part, but she got there. She eventually saw right through, the same way Ginny and I could. She saw the good version of Cameria, the beautiful lush version, restored in all its splendor.

"Sweetheart," she said, wiping a tear from her eye. "I'm so sorry I didn't believe you."

I shrugged.

"I'm sorry I didn't *believe*. How could I have been so wrong about Grandpa all this time? And about you, and so many other things? Honey, I am so sorry."

"Me too," I said. "You must have been worried."

"You have no idea," she said, wrapping me up in another hug.

Things mostly got back to normal after that. Bryce was friendly for a day or two, but then he went back to being ordinary Bryce. He hid my outfit in the freezer, and after Smidge saw what happened, he torched Bryce's new basketball shoes, shorted his gaming console and lit his favorite magazines on fire. I didn't even know Bryce had a magazine collection under his bed, but he was pretty upset about it for some reason. After that, Bryce thought twice before he messed with me. Chet Masterson laid into me pretty good as well, but after Smidge froze his feet to the cafeteria floor for an entire lunch hour, Chet left me alone too.

I still missed my grandpa. All his stories, lessons and wacky ideas about things. I wasn't sure if that feeling would ever go away. I suspected it wouldn't, but I also figured that was a good thing, because we shared such a strong bond to begin with. Not everybody gets that in their life, and I'm glad that I did. Although I still missed him dearly, I grew more comfortable with the idea that grief is the price we pay for a life full of love, as they say.

Back at school, I came to an important realization. I'd wanted to be a have for so long, and so badly, but I had always viewed myself as a have-not. Chet, with his muscles and popularity, was impressive. But I had my family. I had Smidge, Muggins and Ginny. I was a Keeper of the Light. I saw and did some amazing things; and let's not forget, I ultimately saved Cameria. I helped defeat Karma and release the Light. Not that anybody at school would understand what any of that means, but that's not what's important. It didn't matter what they knew. I had a lot, regardless of whether anybody else acknowledged it. I had a lot to be thankful for, and that was plenty for me. Given the chance, I wouldn't change a thing.

It really didn't matter what anyone else thought. I *was* a have and I always had been. It just took some time for me to realize it on my own.

I became much better friends with Teddy and James, too. Once I got comfortable being myself around *myself*, then it got a lot easier for me to be myself around them, and others too.

And Ginny. My sweet, sweet Ginny Mason. We spent an awful lot of time under that willow tree, and every moment became more memorable than the last. Every now and then, we ventured back to the tree to check on things. With Karma out of the picture, things got back to normal in Cameria too. The Angelics held a funeral for Gabriel, and virtually all of Cameria joined in honoring him.

Of course, Adharma lost his seat with the Council, but he still remained a threat. With Adharma in hiding, his people installed a new leader. But they all feared he would return one day, seeking some level of vengeance.

Muggins, on the other hand, got his seat back at the pentagonal table, and the Elementalists used their newfound freedom to make tremendous contributions to Camerian society. The One Day War had exacted a terrible toll. Far worse than the Eight Days War or any other tragedy Cameria had ever borne witness to. The damage would be lasting, but efforts were underway to repair and support the new normal in Cameria.

And everyone understood the importance of protecting it, even at great cost.

EPILOGUE

"**W**hat do you want to do this weekend?" Ginny asked, sipping her lemonade.

"Maybe we can get a ride to IncrediBurger," I said. "To grab lunch and watch a movie."

She was sitting cross-legged under the willow, and Smidge was napping on her leg.

"Ok, sounds good to me," she said. "I'll ask my mom if she can take us."

"Ahem," came the now-familiar interruption, as Muggins appeared from nowhere and cleared his throat.

"Hey, Muggins," we both said in harmony.

"Hello, Logan. And hello to you, Miss Ginny. I'm afraid I come with some troubling news," he said.

"Did your whole faction disappear again?" I joked. "Sorry—too soon?"

"No," he said flatly. "It's about Karma."

"Karma? But she's gone. You saw it just like I did."

"I'm afraid it's not that simple," he said. "I saw the lightning leap from the bottle, yes indeed. There was a bright flash, and then she wasn't there. With that, I don't disagree. In fact, I do fully agree."

"Then what's the problem?" Ginny asked.

"Well, it has to do with how she ceased to be there."

"Are you saying I did something wrong?"

"No, I'm not saying you did anything wrong. I'm just saying you didn't do what you think you did."

"Can you just spit it out," Ginny insisted. "What are you trying to say, Muggins?"

"What I'm trying to say is that, as we continued to clear the rubble from Karma's crumbled lair, we discovered another portal where the main chamber was. I thought it was strange at the time that she would disappear after being struck by lightning the way she was. There should have been something left behind. A skeleton perhaps, or part of her robe. Something. Anything. But not nothing at all."

"And?" Ginny asked.

"We believe she escaped through the portal. Badly injured, perhaps, but escaped nonetheless."

"That's bonkers," I said.

"It was no mistake that she raised that lair where she did," Muggins continued. "It was built on top of another portal, just like the one in your grandpa's backyard. She must have discovered it and kept it to herself. Nobody else in Cameria knew about it, as far as we can tell. When you let the lightning out of the bottle, I think she was badly hurt by it, but she wasn't destroyed."

"Are you sure?" I asked. "That can't be right."

"I'm quite certain. I've been through it," he said. "And it's a very different world from Cameria. Your work is not yet done, young man. Not even close. And neither is yours, Miss Ginny. Come on, I'll take you there now."

"Wait. More than one portal?" Ginny said.

"More than one? Oh, good heavens, yes, you already know about two. The portal from Gideon's yard to Cameria and the portal at Smerconish's. Aisle 21, as you know it. This is, of course, now a third you know about. But there are more than that. Much in the same way that you entered Cameria, there are other doorways leading to other places. Cameria sits in the middle of it all, and now the Grand

Council is tasked with governing and overseeing the peace within Cameria, and all those other places. It's a system that has become far more complicated than you may have ever realized."

"That's why I saw the Listener at the coffee shop? He's like a spy that helps keep the peace here?"

"Yes, that's right."

"Are there others?"

"There are others, yes. Lots of them. In places you might never suspect, but they're definitely there."

"Is it anybody I know?"

Muggins paused, considering the question carefully.

"That's not important, Logan. But I'll tell you what is. The Council has asked me to pay you a visit, and to invite you back. They'd like to talk to you about a few things. Are you in?"

"Heck yes, I'm in."

"And you, Miss Ginny?"

"Hundred percent," she said with a nod.

"Very good, then. Please follow me. We've got some important work to do, and very little time to do it."

AFTERWORD

Thank you so much! Really!!

Thank you for taking the time to read *The Keepers of the Light*.

I hope you enjoyed it, and I would greatly appreciate if you could leave a review on Amazon, Goodreads, tell a friend or recommend to a book club.

I work independently, with no publisher. That means that the more reviews, star rankings and recommendations this book gets, the more likely it is to be discovered by others. So if you enjoyed it, please help spread the word so others can enjoy it too. And thank you once again!

ALSO BY TREVOR A. DUTCHER

Michael McGillicuddy and the Most Amazing Race

From Goodreads and Amazon Reviewers:

5 stars - *"Loved this story and the world it is set in. Great characters, both heroes and villains. And lots of action. I do hope there is more to come."*

5 stars - *"Wonderful story, great characters."*

5 stars - *"This imaginative story keeps you involved from the beginning. The characters are engaging and some are mesmerizing...Well played!"*

5 stars - *"Fun fun fun romp! I loved it! Good work, great read, and I am definitely looking forward to the sequel!"*

5 stars - *"I enjoyed this book, found the puzzles fascinating, liked the characters immensely. Looking forward to the next installment of the adventure!"*

www.ingramcontent.com/pod-product-compliance
Lightning Source LLC
Chambersburg PA
CBHW071256250626
47159CB00004B/1207